"I've been thi  **e moment. "Ab** **circumstance**

"Yes, so have I. And I wondered—"

"I was making a list." They kept talking over each other.

"So have I. You do not have a great deal of time. It might be difficult to find someone, um, congenial."

"Yes."

"And perhaps it would not be fair to marry someone when you are in love with Lucinda, not without telling them."

"It is not the sort of thing one could discuss, is it? It would hardly be gentlemanly."

"But you told me." Izzy met his gaze squarely, her green eyes bright as they always were when she was in earnest.

"Because you are my friend."

"Yes."

He took a deep breath. "Izzy, could you—"

"Leo, might you—"

"Marry me?" he asked before they both tangled themselves in a complete knot.

"Yes," she said. Then added, "Oh my goodness, do you really think we should?"

Author Note

I have always enjoyed friends-to-lovers romances and marriage-of-convenience stories, and I found myself wondering what would happen if I combined both—this is the result.

It was very interesting trying to untangle Leo's emotions as he marries his old friend while believing himself in love with someone else, and it was certainly emotional being in Isobel's shoes as she tries to hide her feelings for her old friend turned husband.

I do hope you enjoy discovering how they reach their happy-ever-after as much as I did.

LOUISE ALLEN

———

Becoming the Earl's Convenient Wife

ISBN-13: 978-1-335-59576-8

Becoming the Earl's Convenient Wife

Recycling programs for this product may not exist in your area.

For questions and comments about the quality of this book, please contact us at CustomerService@Harlequin.com.

Harlequin Enterprises ULC
22 Adelaide St. West, 41st Floor
Toronto, Ontario M5H 4E3, Canada
www.Harlequin.com

Printed in U.S.A.

Louise Allen has been immersing herself in history for as long as she can remember, finding that landscapes and places evoke powerful images of the past. Venice, Burgundy and the Greek islands are favorites. Louise lives on the Norfolk coast and spends her spare time gardening, researching family history or traveling. Please visit Louise's website, www.louiseallenregency.com, her blog, www.janeaustenslondon.com, or find her on Twitter @louiseregency and on Facebook.

Books by Louise Allen

Harlequin Historical

Visit the Author Profile page
at Harlequin.com for more titles.

To all the wonderful NHS staff who
got me through 2022 and safely into 2023.

Chapter One

*The village of Little Bitterns, Kent
—6th October, 1816*

Autumn was here, gaudy with yellow and red foliage, the scarlet of hedgerow berries, the scent of wood smoke and the harsh tannin smell of fallen oak leaves. The sun was shining, the wind had shifted to the south—it was a beautiful day. Unfortunately.

Isobel Martyn sidestepped a muddy patch on the path, climbed a stile and continued under the eaves of Tyler's Wood. It was a shame to waste a lovely morning feeling so miserable. Her mood was one for persistent rain or, better, a violent thunderstorm, because that felt closer to the mounting frustration that threatened to consume her.

She could hardly blame Cousin Edward for the centuries-old legislation that meant that titles and entailed lands and property went to the nearest male heir, which meant that he had been Lord Martyn ever since the death of the fourth Baron, her father, a year ago.

But, however fair she was, she could definitely blame him for being a smug, self-satisfied bore with the most appalling taste in wives. Dear Cousin Amelia was utterly infuriating.

There was someone in the clearing in front of her, a man sitting on a fallen tree trunk. Isobel slowed her brisk walk and trod more quietly on the damp turf.

Leo. Her heart did that strange little flutter that the sight of him always seemed to produce, then she saw his dark head was bowed, his shoulders slumped, and she forgot her own troubles as she stepped deliberately on a small dry branch. It snapped and Leo sat up straight, then turned to see who it was.

'Izzy.' His smile was wide and welcoming as he got to his feet and she wondered if she was the only person who could have told that it was not genuine. 'Lovely day, isn't it? Taking the air?'

'As you can see.' She acknowledged the question with a sharp gesture of her hand and crossed the clearing to his side. 'Now, tell me what is wrong, Leo.'

'Wrong? Why, nothing,' he said as they sat down.

He really was very good at dissembling, she thought, studying the handsome face, the wide, disingenuous brown eyes under strong dark brows.

'You forget that I have known you since I was an infant and you were four,' Isobel said tartly. 'What is it? The estate? The girls?'

Leo had recently inherited not only his uncle's title of Earl of Halford, but also his debt-ridden estates and his two fifteen-year-old twin daughters by his second wife.

He gave a slight shake of his head and his lips tightened. She read a flash of pain, not worry, and her heart sank.

'You have proposed to Lucinda, haven't you?' Isobel asked bluntly. 'Oh, *Leo.*'

'I know. I should have waited. She refused me, of course.' There was no sign of the bowed head or slumped shoulders now: Leo Havelock had too much pride for that.

'Foolish of her,' Isobel said lightly as she tried to ignore the conflicting, and thoroughly ignoble, emotions she was feeling. She had been in love with Leo since the morning eight years ago when her sixteen-year-old self had experienced an eye-opening revelation about her childhood friend. At the time she had been watching him playing cricket, of all things.

But Leo, of course, was not romantically interested in tall, brown-haired, self-contained, sensible girls, however much he might value her friendship. He had set his heart on their neighbour Lucinda Paxton, who was everything Isobel was not—petite, blonde, pretty and bursting with interesting emotions, all of which she freely expressed at the slightest provocation.

Lucinda was the belle of the neighbourhood and had been ever since she had begun to attend the dancing parties and picnics that were intended to prepare young ladies and gentlemen for their come-outs into society. They had all learned to dance there and to make polite small talk, but Lucinda had also honed her skills as a devastating flirt.

Virtually every gentleman in the district over the age of fourteen was smitten with Miss Paxton's charms, although the other young ladies and their mamas were not. Even the most hard-headed and sensible of the young men of Bishop's Carsington, the nearest market town, fell under her spell. And Leo, to Isobel's horror, was as captivated as his friends.

She had thought he had more sense, more discernment, but it appeared there was some magic in wide blue eyes, combined with an ability to make any man feel as though he was a cross between Sir Lancelot, Adonis and Isaac Newton, that threw a spell of enchantment to disable their critical abilities.

But at least she had the sense, and the pride, not to speak slightingly of Lucinda to Leo. That, she was all too aware, was the easiest way to lose his friendship, because he appeared to have fallen utterly, deeply and helplessly in love with the enchanting, spoilt and self-centred Miss Paxton.

Lucinda was younger than Isobel and, at only just eighteen, ready for her very first London Season. Isobel had experienced two London Seasons, but her calm good sense and perfectly ordinary looks had failed to attract a suitor capable of displacing Leo in her heart. Now she was four and twenty and, as Cousin Amelia took relish in pointing out, teetering on the edge of the shelf.

She took a steadying breath and tried to feel sorry that Leo had been refused and was, no doubt, deeply hurt.

'Did she say why she would not marry you?' she asked, sliding her hand under his elbow and giving his arm a comforting squeeze. It was important not to think about the muscles under her fingers.

'She laughed and said I must be teasing her,' he said. 'Surely I knew she was about to have her first London Season, one where she would meet many titled gentlemen?'

'You *are* a titled gentleman,' Isobel said, indignant at the slight.

'*Wealthy* titled gentlemen, not debt-ridden earls. There are even a few unmarried marquesses or their heirs out there, apparently, even if available dukes are a trifle thin on the ground,' Leo said with a stab at bitter humour. 'I am her dear, dear friend, of course I am, but she was good enough to tell me that she had already turned down three of her other dear, dear friends this month.'

'Leo, if all Lucinda cares about is wealth and title, are you sure she is the right wife for you?' It was the nearest she dare get to actually criticising his beloved.

'If she loved me it would not matter to her, so at least I know where I am now,' he said with flat good sense. The almost convincing smile was back now. 'When my uncle was dying she was… No, there is no point in looking back now. I misread her sympathies for more than they were.'

'I am so sorry,' Isobel said and rested her head on his shoulder. And she was, she realised. She wanted him to be happy, even if she could not imagine any man being happy with Lucinda for long. She could never have Leo for herself, after all, and it was totally selfish to wish away other women. One day he would find one who was worthy of him. One who would make him happy.

'I know you are, Izzy, bless you.' He put an arm around her shoulders and gave her a hug, and she bit her lip hard so as not to let a sob escape. What would it be like to be held by Leo, not in friendship, but in passion?

'But what about you?' he asked, clearly unwilling to talk any more about his problems. 'How are you coping with life with your cousins? When we last spoke about it you were finding them very trying.'

'That is putting it much more moderately than I would have,' Isobel said, sitting up straight and putting a few inches between them and the temptation to hug back. 'I am on the point of scouring the advertisement columns of the news sheets to look for posts as a lady's companion.'

Leo shifted around on the tree trunk to stare at her. 'But paid companions are generally nothing more or less than superior servants, at the beck and call of cantankerous old ladies.'

'Well, what am I now?' she demanded. 'I am the spinster cousin living by my relatives' charity under the roof that used to be my own home. I should be thankful for a respectable, secure place to live, I am told, and I am ungrateful if I do not wish to pander to every little wish and whim of my dear cousin. Besides,' she added bitterly, 'a paid companion is just that—paid, which is more than I am.'

'Surely your father left you well provided for?'

'Cousin Edward, who has the oversight of my inheritance, assures me that it would be insufficient for me to maintain any level of gentility if I lived independently.'

'Oh, yes? And when was that?' Leo was sharply focused on her now, his lean features showing the intelligence that had somehow failed to penetrate past Lucinda's loveliness to the shallow woman beneath.

'It was after the last lecture on my general ingratitude and lack of enthusiasm for my new role in life. I told them that I would take myself off to lodgings and be independent, but apparently I could not afford a proper maid, let alone more than a single room in some dreary lodging house.'

'I would be inclined to set a lawyer on them to establish just what is in trust and how your money is being invested. Do you receive an allowance?'

'Pin money. Cousin Edward says it would be foolish to squander my limited resources and, besides, I have my board and lodging.'

'Don't do anything rash, Izzy. They are right in that you are under a most respectable roof, living in a community where you are known and valued—even if your cousins fail to appreciate you—and life is perilous out there for an unprotected lady.'

They sat in silence for a while, so still that birds began to flutter down and poke about in the leaf litter on the floor of the clearing. Isobel counted a robin, two chaffinches and a blackbird before she said abruptly, 'What will you do now? Try again to persuade Lucinda? Go up to London and join in the Season and hope she realises you are more to be valued than any number of wealthy marquesses when she can compare your virtues with theirs?'

'No,' he said with a small huff of laughter. 'Things are bad enough without frittering money away on the cost of that.'

'How are the girls?' Isobel asked, turning the subject. It had seemed to her that the twins and Leo were taking their time adjusting to being a family.

'In serious need of a firm governess,' he said with a sigh. 'Miss Pettigrew is a dear soul, but they run circles around her, both literally and mentally.'

'They are just fifteen, a difficult age, as I recall,' Isobel said.

'They need a mother.'

Which Lucinda most certainly would not have been.

They were pretty girls and did not need someone in charge of them who was likely to resent their youth and looks.

'And the debts?' There was one thing to be said for their long friendship—Leo had felt able to confide the worst of the problems he faced with his inheritance. She doubted he had told anyone else beside his lawyers just how bad things were.

'The most pressing accounts are paid off. Now I need to decide between the roof on the Hall, a superior governess for the girls or the tenants' poor housing,' he said. 'I have resolved to sell off the library.'

'Oh, no! But it is such a fine collection.'

Leo shrugged. 'I can hardly sit under a leaking roof admiring my library as the leather bindings turn green with damp, can I? Or, even if I could, I can't ignore the tenants who would be in a far worse case.' He stood up and held out one hand. 'Were you walking into the village, or just enjoying the sunshine?'

'Just walking. And fuming.' Isobel put her hand in his and let herself be pulled to her feet. 'I had best go home now, or Cousin Amelia will be caustic about me frittering my time when I could be doing something useful, like hemming sheets.'

She took a deep breath as they both turned and began to walk towards the path she had used to enter the glade. 'And I really must stop feeling sorry for myself and make a proper effort to find a suitable position. London, perhaps, or Bath, although that is very dowdy these days, they say.'

'Yes, all the most fashionable set take themselves off to the seaside in the summer and Bath is miserably foggy in the winter.'

'I shall find a dashing widow who has set up home opposite the Pavilion and go to Brighton then,' Isobel said, making a joke of it. Leo had enough to worry about without her being miserable all over him.

'At least you will not be short of male company if that is your new employer,' he said with a grin. 'Shall I walk you home?'

'No, I am perfectly all right,' she said as they emerged from the wood. 'You go back to the Hall and write to book dealers.'

Leo watched the tall, slender figure make its way across the meadow towards the just visible roof of Long Mead, her family home.

If he had to expose his broken dreams to anyone, he supposed there was nobody better than Isobel with her calm good sense and welcome lack of dramatics. He had male friends aplenty, but he could not have confided something so personal in any of them, he realised. And

Izzy understood that what he needed from her was not an outpouring of emotion, exclamations of distress and lamentations, just solid, caring friendship.

In contrast to Lucinda's vibrancy and lively chatter, talking to Isobel was like taking a long draught of cool water after drinking too much champagne.

He wished there was more he could do in return, but all he could offer was an ear for her to pour out her own troubles. Not that she ever did really do more than mention how difficult life was after the death of her father. Her mother had died when she was only seventeen, so for six years she had been mistress of Long Mead. It must be galling to be displaced by someone as insensitive as the new Lady Martyn.

The last glimpse of Izzy's simple straw bonnet vanished and Leo turned back to the wood, trying to ignore the sick feeling in his gut. It was his own fault, he knew it. He should have taken the time to woo Lucinda properly so she began to see him as a serious suitor, not the youth who had come to live on the neighbouring estate when his parents died more than ten years ago in an outbreak of the influenza.

He had needed support so very badly when it had become clear his uncle was dying and leaving him not only the title and estates, but the burden of debt and responsibility. Izzy had been wonderful, of course, but somehow Lucinda's wide-eyed admiration over his new role had given him strength to face it, which Izzy's practical, undemonstrative advice and sympathy had not.

Leo reached the glade again and walked on through it. There was no time to be sitting on that log wallow-

ing in disappointment. No time for self-pity. Yes, he
should have waited, but he had been afraid that Lucinda
would forget him when she entered the hectic world of
the London Season, would have her head turned by men
she would find infinitely more intriguing and glamorous than he was.

And richer. She had tossed in that comment about his
dire financial position in a way that would have been
cruel from anyone else and he realised that she'd had
no idea how bad things were when he had inherited.
But it was foolish to feel hurt—Lucinda was young
and heedless and, he had to keep reminding himself,
did not love him. She had certainly not taken his declaration seriously.

He had been a fool. A romantic fool, he told himself.
He should have known better. It was hardly as though
the extent of his problems had come as a shock to him.
He'd had years of watching his uncle sink further and
further into depression following the death of his wife.
Further and further into the poisoned talons of gam-
bling and alcohol.

He had refused all Leo's offers of help, spurned his
suggestions for retrenchment or improvement. Leo, and
everyone in the neighbourhood, had watched helplessly
as the earldom and its once great estates sank into ruin.

He stooped to look at a vivid scarlet toadstool beside the path, then saw it was riddled with wormholes.
A fitting parallel to his situation. What had he thought
he was doing? Even if Lucinda had thrown herself into
his arms and declared her undying love for him, her
parents would have turned his offer down out of hand.

And quite right, too. He wouldn't approve the match if he were her father. Mr Paxton was a shrewd guardian, even if his wife filled her daughter's head with dreams of ermine, jewels and a leading place in the *ton*.

It had been that sleepless night, tossing and turning, watching his responsibilities and liabilities pile up into an unmovable mountain that had finally tipped him over the edge, sending him to make one last throw of the dice in a gamble for happiness.

Lucinda had always behaved as though she thought he was wonderful, strong and capable, and he had been too blinded by her loveliness and her ability to make him feel he was the only man who mattered to her to realise that this was simply her nature. She was young, indulged and a natural flirt. He could not blame her, only himself.

Now he could stop dreaming, stop fantasising and settle down to the hard grind of digging the estates, his cousins and himself out of this quagmire.

'Havelocks do not give up,' his father had been fond of saying. 'We came over with the Conqueror as nothing more than foot soldiers and look where seven hundred years has taken us.'

This might take another seven hundred, Leo thought as he came out of the far side of the wood and into his own park, sending a herd of fallow deer scattering in panic.

The woods were encroaching on the open grassland and the small copses that were scattered across it were overgrown. He could sell timber. He dug a notebook from his pocket and jotted a reminder to speak to Harding, the estate manager he had inherited from his uncle. The man was depressed and pessimistic. Leo could hardly blame him, but he had to either galvanise him into a change of attitude or sack him. A woodland management programme with quick outcomes might be just the thing to set him right.

Feeling better, he quickened his pace. The house looked lovely in the autumn sunlight, its grey stone mellow, its turrets romantic. At this distance you couldn't see the crumbling corners, the slipped tiles or the peeling paintwork. One day, Leo resolved, it would be perfect again. One day.

Then the sunlight caught the panes in the windows of what was the Countess's suite and the dark ache inside came back. Why did people talk about a broken heart? This felt like a punch in the guts.

A man was walking across the lawn where the ha-ha made a barrier to the parkland. Leo waved and called, 'Harding!' The man stopped and waited until Leo reached the spot and vaulted up to join him on the grass. 'I've had some thoughts about the timber.'

They talked as they walked back to the house. Harding stood up straighter, his furrowed brow clearing a little as he nodded agreement to the points his employer was making.

That was it, Leo thought. *One foot in front of the other, one small scheme at a time. I will get there somehow.*

It couldn't be worse than being one of the Conqueror's foot soldiers, fodder for English arrows and axes, seasick and facing a foreign shore with just a dream of founding a dynasty to keep you going.

But it was going to be a lonely journey without Lucinda at his side.

'*There* you are.'

And there you *are, unfortunately,* Isobel thought, untying her bonnet ribbons as she stood at the foot of the stairs.

'Yes. It is a lovely day. You should try a walk, Cousin Amelia, I am sure it would do you good.'

'To what end, might I ask? Tramping about in the damp like some village woman? I may go out in the carriage later. I hear the Vicar's wife is holding a meeting of local ladies to decide whether to form a sewing circle to make garments for the deserving poor.'

The undeserving, by which Isobel suspected Amelia meant anyone who did not grovel sufficiently to the new lady of the manor, could presumably spend the winter shivering in their rags.

'That is a very charitable thought, Cousin.'

'Yes, naturally it is not something that I myself would wish to be involved in, but I thought it would be a suitable occupation for you.' Lady Martyn swept on past towards her sitting room door. 'You must have a great deal of time on your hands, Isobel, if you can spare hours to go walking. Oh, and do not forget to arrange some foliage in the vases. I believe I mentioned that at breakfast.'

And I decided at breakfast to start scouring the advertisements for a companion's post. Perhaps I really can find a dashing retired courtesan in Brighton who needs me. That would be amusing.

Amelia turned suddenly and walked back to peer into her face. 'I am most certainly not going out in an open carriage. It must be positively raw out there. Look at your eyes and nose: quite pink. Anyone would think you have been crying.'

Chapter Two

Cousin Edward took a wide range of news sheets which he read assiduously, eager to appear well informed and up to date on all the issues of the day.

Not that he had a settled opinion on any of them, Isobel reflected, spreading marmalade on her toast the next morning. Edward's views always chimed with those of the most important gentleman in the company at the time.

I am becoming acid and catty, she thought, surprising him with a smile as she handed him the preserves pot. *I really will become a sour old spinster if I'm not careful and that is thoroughly unattractive.*

'I am calling on Lady Flowers this afternoon,' Amelia announced. 'She invited me after we met at the Vicarage yesterday. This morning I intend to go into Bishop's Carsington. I need more embroidery silks for the chair seats I am stitching. Unless you require the carriage, that is, Edward?'

'No, my dear. You take it,' he said from behind the

pages of *The Times*. 'Tush, tush, this is a bad business with the French. The King appears most unpopular. You would think they would settle down and be grateful that we have rid them of the Corsican monster.'

'Really, dear?' his wife said vaguely.

'Do you need me to accompany you today, Cousin Amelia?' Isobel said.

'No. I do, however, require you to see to it that Mrs Watts reviews the linen cupboard. The sheets on our bed that were changed yesterday are positively threadbare. I cannot think what she is about. Most neglectful.'

As Isobel had heard at length the housekeeper's views on people who tore through perfectly good linen sheets as a result of becoming tangled when rising in the middle of the night to use the chamber pot, she was able to nod earnestly and assure Amelia that she would look into the matter and deal with Mrs Watts appropriately.

That would take five minutes, leaving her free to scour the papers Edward had finished with the day before.

When Lady Martyn had finally been driven off to the nearest town and Edward had retreated to his study, Isobel rescued the previous day's news sheets from the housemaid and settled down to make a list.

She wanted a widow, if possible, because households with husbands held the risk of amorous gentlemen who thought that governesses and companions were fair game. There was always the danger of unmarried sons at home with their mama, of course, so finding a widow was not foolproof.

An address in a town promised more entertainment than one in the depths of the country, but she did not like the idea of the smoky industrial towns of the Midlands or the north such as Manchester or Birmingham. Somewhere like Winchester might be pleasant, perhaps.

An hour later she had a list of eight possibilities. All gave accommodation addresses, which was a concern, because there was no way of checking that the advertisers were the respectable ladies they said they were, but she would write to all of them and see how the answers struck her before considering what further checks she could carry out. She was not so naive as to be ignorant of the perils that lay in wait for unprotected young women.

There was no time to compose her letters now, for Amelia would be back at any moment. She would write them once her cousin had gone out that afternoon and walk up to the Spread Eagle, the village's inn and receiving office, to post them. She must remember to have a word with Mr Philpott who dealt with the mail and tell him she wanted any replies held for her to collect. Amelia was not above demanding to know what every piece of mail she received was about, and who it was from, under the guise of the need to protect an unmarried lady in her care.

It was sheer nosiness, of course, and Isobel usually retaliated by reading out loud the contents of her friends' letters slowly and at length. That would not answer in this situation.

* * *

Three days later Isobel excused herself after breakfast on the grounds of visiting the receiving office to take the parcel of new sewing silks that Amelia had decided, once she had examined them at home, she did not like and wanted returned to the shop.

'And enquire of Mr Yarrow, the grocer, if he has any new blends of tea in stock. Oh, and call at the Vicarage and ask if I left my parasol there the other day.'

'Yes, Amelia. How much tea should I buy?'

'Just obtain a sample, of course. How can I tell until I have tried it?'

'Yes, Amelia.' Isobel escaped through the front door with her bonnet in her hands and her gloves unbuttoned before her cousin could add anything else to the list.

The housemaid who answered the door at the Vicarage said that they had found the parasol and were unsure which lady had left it. She handed it over and Isobel made her way to the grocer's where she was presented with three samples of tea. Finally, she crossed the road to the Spread Eagle.

'Four for you, Miss Martyn,' Miss Philpott, the postmaster's eldest daughter said, fetching them from the pigeonhole behind the counter, handing them across and taking the parcel of silks in return. 'There's fourpence to pay, please, miss. Oh, good morning, Your Lordship.'

Isobel dropped the letters and Leo picked them up, smiled at Miss Yarrow, which made her blush, and took his own post.

'We'd have sent it up, Your Lordship. The boy was

going in just a moment and there are quite a number of items for the Hall.'

'It doesn't matter, I was passing.' He took the leather bag she hoisted on to the counter. 'Put any charges on the account.'

Isobel gathered up her post. Four letters, so half of her enquiries had produced some result.

'May I walk you home, Miss Martyn?' Leo slung the bag over one shoulder and offered his arm.

Isobel took it and walked away from the inn and out of the hearing of the few passers-by. 'I want to look at these before I get home,' she said, holding up the letters.

'In that case, shall we sit under the market cross?' Leo made his way to the small structure in the middle of the crossroads that provided shelter for a few stalls on Fridays. 'I'm sure my bills will look better in the fresh air as well.'

Isobel rather doubted it, but nodded agreement. Even Amelia couldn't fault her for sitting with their neighbour the Earl in plain view of the entire village.

She broke the seals on all four, then spread them out to read.

Beside her she could hear Leo muttering under his breath as he sorted through the contents of the bag. 'Invoice, invoice, overdue invoice... Letter from Charles Standon. I'll be damned—he's getting married. Quote for the roof repairs...'

Isobel scanned the first reply. Birmingham—one of the industrial towns she was resolved to avoid. The second was from Bath, which was more promising. Her duties would involve the care of six lapdogs and an elderly parrot. Hmm, perhaps not. The third required four character references, two to be from ministers of the church, and assurances that the applicant came from a God-fearing and sober household.

Depressed now, Isobel read the fourth which proved to be from a mother in Norwich who had three small boys and a husband who was a pillar of the local business community. She had an active social life and required a diligent young person to assist in all areas of domestic affairs.

She sighed and Leo put down his post and looked across. 'Not good news?'

Isobel handed him the four letters and sat back to hear his verdict.

'I have to say that even your Cousin Amelia sounds preferable to these.'

'I know. But I sent off eight enquiries, so there are potentially four more replies to come and, if those are no good, I will just have to keep trying.' She tried to sound bright and optimistic. 'Are all your letters depressing, too?'

'Mostly, although my friend Standon has found himself a bride, so that was a wedding invitation, and the quotation for the roof is not quite as dire as I had feared.' He rummaged in the bottom of the bag. 'Two for the girls, one for the housekeeper and this' He held up an impressive document written on thick parchment, sealed in black and addressed in a fine hand. 'I wonder who that is from. It looks worryingly legal.'

'Well, go on, open it. Honestly, people who stare at letters and wonder who they are from are utterly maddening.' She gave him a nudge in the ribs. 'Almost as bad as people who spend an age opening a present when you are itching to see what it is.'

'This looks like trouble to me,' Leo said grimly as he broke the seal. 'Lawyer trouble.' He read it through in silence, turned the page and then caught his breath. 'I do not believe it.'

'What?'

But Leo was reading it again from the beginning. 'I still don't believe it. Miracles like this do not happen.'

'What?' She was going to hit him with Cousin Amelia's parasol in a minute.

'My Great-Aunt Honoria has died. She was my grandfather's unmarried elder sister. And she has left me everything.' He scanned through the letter again and prodded one sentence with his forefinger. 'She said, "In the hope that he may prove to be a more diligent, upright and sober person than either of my late nephews."'

'But that is wonderful. Even if it isn't a huge amount of money it will pay for the roof, perhaps.'

'Oh, it is a great deal. They have spelled it out. See here.' Leo pointed to a paragraph. 'And all the property and contents as well.'

Isobel read it and felt a little dizzy. 'Oh, my word. That will solve everything—pay off the debts, repair the estate, give the girls a dowry. Oh, Leo, I am so glad for you.'

'Yes, but, look.' His finger jabbed at another paragraph as he handed her the letter.

'Oh, a stipulation. "Provided that the said Leo Augustus Gerald Havelock, Fourth Earl of Halford, is legally joined in matrimony by the date of my death or within four months following it." But… What happens if you aren't? Oh, it all goes to the Society for the Suppression of Vice!'

'The timing is not brilliant, is it?' he said, his voice colourless.

'But now, if you go back to Lucinda and her parents, point out that you will be—' She broke off at the sight of his face.

'Over my dead body,' Leo said tersely. 'Lucinda does not love me and does not want to marry me. She made that quite clear and I will be damned if I try to bribe her into changing her mind.'

'No. No, of course not.' Whatever had she been thinking? 'What will you do now?'

'Go up to London and find myself a wife. Somehow. And the Season has not even begun.' He stood up and stuffed everything back into the leather satchel. 'I must go, Izzy. There is a devil of a lot to be done.'

She watched him stride off across the village green and felt heartsick. It was wonderful that those crushing money worries could be put behind him, wonderful that Penelope and Prudence would have dowries and fine come-outs and the tenants would be secure and comfortable. But Leo had only just been rebuffed by the woman he loved and now… Now he had to go and cold-bloodedly seek out a lady to marry. One he could not love.

That would be an honest arrangement, better than knowing that Lucinda had only married him for his money, she supposed. Yes, that would be ghastly, loving someone while knowing that they had only agreed to marry you for wealth and status. This way he could find someone he liked, someone compatible, at least.

Isobel folded her letters into small squares and pushed them down to the bottom of her reticule, then got up and began to walk slowly back towards the lane that led to Long Mead. How could she help him?

Who would suit Leo? She would have to be a lady of some status to match with an earl, a gentleman's daughter at least. She would have to like the countryside and be willing to put up with the state Havelock Hall was in now and have the imagination and willingness to set it to rights.

She would have to be prepared to take on two adolescent girls who needed love and attention and she would have to be reasonably intelligent and have a sense of humour. Most of all, she would have to like Leo, not simply as a man with a title to bestow on her, but as a person, because he deserved to be happy.

And what were the chances of him finding this ideal person and being able to marry her, all within a few months? The clock was already ticking, because his great-aunt must have died several days ago.

But Leo was determined and a good judge of character—except when it came to Lucinda Paxton— so he would find a suitable bride. She could only hope, selfishly, that she had managed to escape from Little Bitterns by then, because loving Leo was hard enough now, but seeing him bring a bride home and watching their marriage play out would be torture.

If only she could think of someone for him. Someone she liked and could trust…

Leo got as far as the lodge and gates into the park before the shock caught up with him.

'Morning, my lord. You quite well, my lord? You're proper pale, you are.'

Hell, it was old Simmonds, the gatekeeper, hobbling toward him, concern on his face.

'Yes, quite, thank you, Simmonds. I have just had surprising news, that's all. Good news. Nothing to worry about at all.'

He found a smile for the old man and strode on up the drive until it turned and he could sink down on a stone bench that had been set there with a view up to the house.

Money. He would have money. Enough to solve all his problems, secure his own future and, more importantly, that of the twins and the tenants. He should be glad. Happy. More than happy, ecstatic, and he was, of course. But the relief was smothered by the realisation that, if he had asked Lucinda to marry him tomorrow instead of last week, then she would have said *yes*. Not because she loved him, but because he was an earl with a fortune.

He wondered when he would have realised that she did not care for him. Or perhaps, given time, she would have come to love him as he loved her. He shook his head, making a rabbit that had ventured out of the undergrowth bound back into hiding. No, that was daydreaming. Fantasising. And he had no time for either now. It was his duty to find a bride and be married within just a few short weeks. He had three and a half months for a courtship and the wedding.

Right, he told himself firmly. *Pull yourself together and decide what you are looking for in a wife.*

A lady, of course, one who had been raised to understand the duties and obligations of a landowner's wife, one who could control a household. She must be intelligent, active and imaginative because there was a great deal to be done and someone who could not see beyond the current state of things would not be able to cope. She must be sympathetic and sensible, because there were the twins who needed, if not a mother, at least an older sister to guide them.

A sense of humour would be good, he thought, getting to his feet. Health, she would need that. And there had to be liking and trust, otherwise it would be a chilly and difficult matter to adjust to each other.

Surely, somewhere in London, there must be a lady who matched that description? He wanted someone like Izzy, he realised as he summarised it. Now where would he find—? Leo stopped dead in his tracks.

Izzy?

He turned and began to stride down towards the lodge, then to run. If he could catch her before she got inside the house... Somehow it was important to do this now, immediately, before he lost his nerve. She would laugh at him, of course, but he could persuade her, surely? It wasn't as though she was happy with her life as things were now. Wasn't marriage to him, a friend, better than being a drudge for some stranger?

* * *

He was halfway across the village green when he saw her walking rapidly past the market cross, coming towards him. She was pink and seemed agitated. What was wrong? 'Izzy,' he called.

'Leo.' When they met face to face she ran her tongue over her lower lip and glanced away as though she could not meet his gaze. 'I thought—it's ridiculous, of course, but—'

'I've been thinking,' he said at the same moment. 'About my ideal wife under the circumstances.'

'Yes, so have I. And I wondered—'

'I was making a list.' They kept talking over each other.

'So have I. You do not have a great deal of time. It might be difficult to find someone, um, congenial.'

'Yes.'

'And perhaps it would not be fair to marry someone when you are in love with Lucinda, not without telling them.'

'It is not the sort of thing one could discuss, is it? It would hardly be gentlemanly.'

'But you told me.' She met his gaze squarely, her green eyes bright as they always were when she was in earnest.

'Because you are my friend.'

'Yes.'

Leo took a deep breath. 'Izzy, could you—?'

'Leo, might you—?'

'Marry me?' he managed to say before they both tangled themselves in a complete knot.

'Yes,' she said. Then, 'Oh, my goodness, do you really think we should? What if Lucinda changes her mind?'

'Because I will have money?' He shook his head. 'She does not love me. I must accept her decision like a gentleman and put it behind me. People are in this position all the time and do not die of broken hearts. Besides, I could not face marrying someone who accepted me only for my wealth. You and I are friends, Izzy, we can make a success of this far better than two people who hardly know each other.' He kept the smile on his face, the positive note in his voice. If he repeated this enough, he would come to believe it in time.

'Yes, of course.' Izzy nodded firmly. She was trying to convince herself, too, he realised.

'But only if you really want to. I did think that perhaps I might be a slightly better prospect than looking after an elderly parrot or having to read sermons all day.'

'That is very true and at least you do not moult feathers everywhere or depress me with thoughts of hellfire,' she said in the very serious voice he had learned covered inner amusement.

Leo found his lips were twitching. 'This really is not the way a proposal should happen, is it?' At least, unlike his last attempt at one, he was smiling now. But then, Izzy usually did make him smile.

'No, and I certainly should not have said anything,' she said, suddenly serious. 'It was most unladylike of me. But this is not romance, this is a…a business agreement for our mutual benefit. A contract. When, and how, do we do this?'

'As soon as possible and by special licence in London, I should think. We could elope tomorrow? That will cut through all the nonsensical objections I am sure your cousins will see fit to raise and I think that the sooner the knot is tied, the better. But if you would rather be married here, of course, that is a different matter.'

'Oh, no. If Papa was alive, then of course I would want to marry in the village. But if he were, then we probably would not be doing this, would we? And the haste will cause talk however we do it and I would rather not be around to hear that, frankly.'

'All the old biddies will be counting the months up to nine, I suppose,' he said with distaste. 'Yes, we can well do without any spiteful gossip. If you have a maid who will come with you, then I could take you to an hotel while I deal with obtaining the licence and talk to Great-Aunt Honoria's lawyers, then we will get married as soon as we can find a clergyman.'

'Elope? Oh, I like that idea and I am certain Nancy will come with me. Cousin Amelia is always threatening to dismiss her for being too pert. But what about the twins? And where shall we live? Do we come back here immediately?'

'No, there is too much I must deal with in London. I will open up Halford House. I have only been there once or twice overnight and I have no idea what state it is in overall—fairly dreadful, I imagine—but Miss Pettigrew can bring them up to town once we are settled.'

'Can it really be this simple?' Izzy cast a rapid look around and began to stroll casually across the green. 'Best if we do not seem to be talking about something serious,' she said as he fell in beside her. 'Yes, I suppose it can be straightforward if we have no care for the conventions. Perhaps we should put it about that the wedding was very quiet because of the death of your great-aunt. What time shall we set out? I have no idea how an elopement is organised. Do you have to produce a rope ladder at some unearthly hour in the morning?'

'Certainly not,' Leo said, thinking hard. 'We shall set a trend for civilised elopements. After breakfast would be the best time, I think. Then we will be setting out in daylight and with food inside us. If you and Nancy can pack your trunks I will call at, say, half past nine?'

Isobel bit her lip, frowned a little and then smiled and held out her hand. 'We should shake on it.'

'A merger of two enterprises,' Leo said, taking the slim fingers in his. They gripped tightly for a moment, then Isobel laughed.

'Oh, no, look at the audience we have attracted.'

Leo let go of her hand and looked around. An interested goose boy and his flock watched them from the far side of the pond; two passing cottagers' wives, baskets over their arms, had slowed to a dawdle in their attempt to see as much as possible without seeming to and all the passengers on top of the morning stage coach just pulling up at the Spread Eagle were quite unashamedly staring.

'Let them stare,' Leo said and kissed her hand. 'Until tomorrow at half past nine.'

Chapter Three

Isobel stared after the tall figure as he walked away, the familiar warmth that she experienced every time she allowed herself to stare at Leo's broad shoulders, narrow hips and long, muscular legs stealing over her. Young ladies should not look at men and feel like that, she knew, but really, what did the matrons who lectured girls think went on in their heads? That they were completely unobservant, incurious and unimaginative?

What have I done? A sudden flutter of panic hit her as she turned and picked her way past the offerings the geese had left to reach the street. *Have I rescued us both—or made the most terrible mistake?*

She loved Leo and Leo loved Lucinda and those were the plain facts of the matter. And now she had to live with him and conceal her feelings and pretend not to care about his.

'Good morning, Mrs Hooper, Mrs Cookman.' The two curious housewives primmed their lips and then chorused a greeting in return. How long would it take that choice bit of gossip to reach her cousins? She must be prepared with some casual explanation for what she was doing having her hand kissed by an earl in the middle of the village green.

'Good morning, Miss Martyn.'

Oh, bl— Bother. Isobel fixed a smile on her lips and turned to see Lucinda Paxton on the steps of the village shop, her maid behind her. 'Good morning, Miss Paxton. What a pretty bonnet. Is it new?'

'Oh, this old thing.' Lucinda tossed her head, making the best of the beautiful golden ringlets that escaped around the hat. 'Was that Leo Havelock kissing your hand? What on earth were you doing?'

'Shaking hands on a small business transaction,' Isobel said. 'You know Leo—he was simply joking.'

'Oh. And how is dear Leo? Is he *utterly* cast down?'

Lucinda was so very clearly hoping that Isobel would ask why on earth Lord Halford would be despondent that she could have shaken her. She must have known he would be distressed by her rejection and yet she wanted to gossip about it.

'Cast down? Why, no, not at all. He seemed in the best of spirits to me. Positively energised, in fact. I did not like to pry, but it was almost as though he had been freed of some worry. Do excuse me, I have so much to do today.'

She turned and caught a glimpse of her own reflection, fractured in the numerous small panes of the shop window: unfashionably tall, lacking in curves, straight brown hair, perfectly pleasant, calm face. And there was Lucinda, younger, infinitely prettier and so much more animated. The other woman was hardly out and yet she knew instinctively how to flirt, how to attract men, what made them feel special.

Lucinda was already bouncing down the steps, clearly looking around her for someone more interesting than dull Miss Martyn who was, when all was said and done, almost a spinster. Someone to be pitied.

I will never be able to compete with that, Isobel thought, making her way slowly homewards, *so I shall simply have to make this marriage work as a relationship of friendship and shared comfort.*

It sounded worthy and just a little dull.

'Nancy.'

'Yes, miss?' The housemaid straightened from where she had been flicking a feather duster along the skirting boards in Isobel's bedchamber.

'Would you like to be a lady's maid? A countess's lady's maid?'

'Wouldn't I! That'd be… But who'd want me? I'm just a housemaid whose pa is a pig man. You've got to be trained, like, for lady's maiding. And I don't speak proper.'

'Even the most superior lady's maid had to start somewhere.' Isobel took off her bonnet and began to unfasten the buttons on her spencer. 'Two of the most important things in that position are loyalty and discretion—the ability to keep your lady's secrets.'

'I can do that, Miss Isobel. Never been one for tittle-tattle, me. But who is this countess who needs a maid? You don't know any, do you?'

'I will be a countess, Nancy. I am going to elope with Lord Halford tomorrow morning. We will be married as soon as possible.' She had said it now, so it had to be true. It was tempting to pinch herself.

'Cor, miss!' Nancy plumped down on the end of the bed, mouth open, then sprang up again. 'Oh, sorry, miss. *Eloping?*'

'Yes. And, if you want, you can come with us and be my abigail. But we've got to pack everything today without anyone realising, because there will be such a fuss when they find out.'

'Well, yes, I warrant there will be, miss. Lady Martyn won't half be in a taking. Ooh, her nose'll properly be out of joint, you a countess, miss, and His Lordship only a baron when all's said and done.'

'That is why I want to keep it a secret.' Probably now was not the time for a lecture on being respectful about one's employers. 'Can you ask Paul and Tom to bring my trunks down from the attic?'

'Aye.' Nancy frowned in thought. 'I'd best tell them I'm going to sort out your whole wardrobe and lay up some of the summer things in store. And I'll tell them to be quiet about it so as not to disturb His Lordship. I'll do that now and then, while we're waiting, we can sort out what you'll need for tomorrow.'

'And don't forget you'll need to pack your own things, Nancy.'

'Yes, miss. Where are we going, miss, if it's not a secret? Scotland?'

'London, Nancy. An hotel first and then His Lordship's town house once I am married.'

'Ooh, that's prime, miss. I can't wait. All those shops!' She opened the door, rushed back for her feather duster, straightened her cap and vanished along the landing, leaving Isobel to collapse into the armchair and try to think sensibly about the appropriate outfit to elope in.

Fortunately Cousin Amelia had been out for most of the afternoon and missed the moment when Paul, the younger footman, had dropped a trunk on his colleague's toes, but by half past eight the next morning Isobel was feeling as tense as any young lady planning to climb down a ladder at midnight and head for Gretna Green with her lover.

She had toyed with the thought of telling her cousins just what she was planning over dinner the night before, but Amelia had been so annoying that she realised that she couldn't do it, not without precipitating the most unholy argument. Instead, she had bitten her tongue and listened politely to a diatribe on the shortcomings of the curate and the choir and the quality of the tea samples Isobel had obtained for her.

At breakfast Amelia announced that she had a headache when Isobel asked her to pass the butter and snapped at her when she suggested that a gentle drive might help. 'I shall go into Bishop's Carsington and consult Mr Whyborne, the apothecary. He is certain to have just the remedy. The last time I spoke to him he expressed concern that my highly sensitive disposition lays me open to headaches. Edward, you will not require the carriage this morning.'

Lord Martyn obediently agreed that he would not.

'At what time would you wish it sent around?' Isobel was seized with the sudden nightmare vision of Amelia and Leo meeting on the threshold.

'Immediately after breakfast before the pain becomes any worse.' Amelia bravely managed another boiled egg and slice of toast.

As it was, the dust raised by the Martyns' carriage had scarcely settled when a much shabbier travelling coach drew up.

Nancy, who had thrown herself whole-heartedly into the drama of the situation, was immediately bustling about, chivvying Paul and Tom to bring the luggage down immediately.

'Shh!' Isobel urged with an anxious glance at the closed study door. 'We must not disturb Lord Martyn.'

'Are you going away, miss?' Tom asked as he backed down the front step, holding one end of the largest trunk.

'Yes, a visit to…to friends in, er, Leicestershire.'

Leo, who was supervising the loading, shot her an amused look, then set Nancy all of a flutter by enquiring politely if she was Miss Martyn's maid.

'Yes, me…er…my lord.'

'Up you get, then.' Leo handed her into the coach, making her burst into nervous giggles as he thrust the smaller valises on to the seat beside her. 'Is that everything?'

'It is,' Isobel said as he helped her in, too. 'Are you travelling inside?'

'No, I shall ride.' He tipped both footmen and low-

ered his voice as they went back down the garden path.
'We'll make the first stop at Boughton-under-Blean,
a distance of about fifteen miles if that is acceptable
for you?'

'Yes, perfectly,' Isobel said as the steps were put up,
the groom shut the door and the coach swayed as he
climbed up behind. She hadn't realised that she wouldn't
be able to talk to Leo on the journey, but, of course,
they could hardly discuss anything of any consequence
with Nancy sitting there.

And, as she had realised during a largely sleepless
night, there was a great deal they needed to talk about.
Like beds and the sharing of one. That was rather a
significant part of marriage and, for some reason, it
simply hadn't occurred to her to discuss it with him.
Not that one could do such a thing in the middle of the
village green.

It was one thing to be in love with a man and to desire him. It was quite another to commit to intimacy
with him, especially as he was her dear friend and there
had never been a single moment of that sort of aware-
ness between them. She had been far too wary of making the slightest betraying gesture and Leo, of course,
had eyes only for Lucinda.

Yes, he was in love with someone else, but she had
heard that men did not need to be in love to quite happily engage in…whatever went on in the bedchamber.
She had a fairly good idea of the basic process, ludi-
crous as it sounded, because one couldn't be brought
up in the country and not be aware of how the animal

and plant kingdom procreated. But that was theoretical and impersonal.

Perhaps Leo wouldn't want to, not with her. She bit her lip. But he was a man and he needed an heir, so of course he would want to…to do it. Soon.

'Are you all right, miss? Shall I open the window a bit? It's quite warm in here.'

Isobel put her hand to her hot cheek and nodded. 'Yes, please. It is stuffy, isn't it?'

How on earth was she going to look at Leo now without becoming one big blush? They should have talked about this right at the beginning, but that had only been yesterday morning, less than twenty-four hours ago. They had both been too focused on their scheme to save his estates and rescue her from the home that had become a prison to think about anything beyond a wedding and the legacy.

But this was Leo and she could talk to him about anything, couldn't she?

'Pardon my asking, miss, but did you leave a note for Her Ladyship? Only you told Tom you were going to stay with a friend in Leicestershire.'

'Goodness, so I did. It was the first county that came into my head, for some reason. That will certainly confuse everyone, because I do not think we know anyone in that area.'

'It's a good thing, then, miss. They'll be off chasing you on the wrong road, won't they?'

'Not really, Nancy. If we were heading for Leicestershire, or the Scottish Borders for that matter, we would have to take the road to London first.'

But she was not too concerned because she did not imagine for a moment that Cousin Edward would bestir himself to give chase. She had tried to compose a letter the night before, but had given up. She had no intention of telling anyone the facts of Leo's inheritance—that was up to him, and it was difficult to explain the urgency of the matter without doing so.

Then there was the plain truth that she hated the thought of the fuss Amelia would make over the wedding and flinched at the thought of Lucinda, who was thoughtless enough to comment on the fact that her rejected suitor had made do with very ordinary Miss Martyn. Everyone would say Leo had proposed out of pique at being refused by the beauty.

Really, when she thought of all the stories that the gossips could spin around her elopement—that she was with child, that she had taken advantage of the lovelorn Earl, that he was setting her up in London as his mistress—the further they were away from Little Bitterns, the better.

Of course, when the announcement of their marriage appeared, then everyone would know she was not a fallen woman, but it still wouldn't stop them counting the months to see whether she was with child, or pitying Leo for having been ensnared in a moment of weakness.

She looked out of the window and caught a glimpse of him cantering just ahead of the coach, riding on a loose rein, quite relaxed. Then he turned up his collar and hunched his shoulders and she realised it had begun to spit with rain.

* * *

Elopements should not be undertaken in this weather, Leo thought, tipping his hat down over his eyes. And anyone planning one should have a good night's sleep beforehand and not have to make do with a couple of hours snatched from planning, packing, explaining to two over-excited young ladies that they were going to London soon, pacifying the governess who had to organise their journey, writing notes for his steward and letters to his lawyers and attempting to persuade a slightly mutinous collection of footmen and maids that they really wanted to go to London and make a neglected mansion habitable.

He could order them, of course, but they would probably simply hand in their notice and find superior positions in houses where the roof didn't leak and the owner was not on the verge of repelling the bailiffs.

'And I suppose you want me to be off to London, too, my lord,' his housekeeper inquired, clearly braced for a fight.

'Thank you, Mrs Druett,' he had said, cutting the ground from under her feet. 'I knew I could rely on you. And on Cook, I am sure. I can manage for a day or so eating at my clubs as I usually do, but if you can arrange to leave a skeleton staff here and bring everyone else up to town by the end of the week, that would be ideal.'

'But why, my lord?' she asked. 'You usually just use a room or two or stay in an hotel. There's enough to be worrying about here without opening up that great place.'

'I am getting married, Mrs Druett,' he said, startling her into an exclamation. 'And we can't have the new Countess having to live in an hotel, now can we?'

Now the first rush of collecting Izzy was over he felt weary; the rain, although merely drizzle, was irritating and all the doubts he had been able to ignore in the flurry of preparations came sneaking back.

They should have taken more time to discuss this. It had seemed the answer to all their problems, mutually beneficial, in fact, but five minutes' urgent discussion in the middle of the village green was hardly a substitute for a careful examination of all the pros and cons.

He hunched his shoulders to stop the water trickling down his neck and tried to do that now. As far as he was concerned, he couldn't see any problems. If he could not marry the woman he loved and had to marry somebody, then who better than Izzy? She was intelligent, calm, practical, raised to be the mistress of an aristocratic household. He knew her and she knew him—there would be no unpleasant surprises.

But was it all positive for her? There would be gossip; there would most certainly be years of work ahead while they restored the estates to what they should be and she would have the responsibility for two unhappy young women who had lost their father, had found themselves with apparently no marriage prospects because they had no dowries and who had been allowed to neglect their schooling and their social education, too.

It had to be better than her life with her cousins, surely? There would be no worries about money, at least. And she would enjoy having a family, raising children.

At which point Leo sat up straight in the saddle and swore. They had not discussed children. Or the getting of them, which was rather more to the point at that moment. A lady accepting an offer of marriage would assume that a physical relationship would naturally follow, even if she was innocently unaware of what that involved. But this was not an ordinary betrothal and Isobel had been his friend—never anything *but* his friend—for years.

The wedding night was going to be hideously embarrassing for both of them. In fact, he went quite cold just thinking about it. The idea of initiating an innocent virgin bride was bad enough, even if she was in love with him, but... *Izzy?*

And with the maid in the carriage there was no way they could discuss it until they arrived in London and then it would be too late. In fact, it was too late now. They would have to marry because she would be ruined if they did not.

Very soon, in the midst of seeing lawyers about the will, finding a man of law to look after Isobel's interests and agree to a suitable settlement, extracting a special licence from Doctors' Commons and getting the house in order, he would have to find the time and the privacy for a very frank talk.

Should he suggest that they do not consummate the marriage for a while? Or would it be best to get it over with as soon as possible? Sooner or later they would have to get into bed together, because it was his duty to father an heir, just as it was his duty to restore the estates and care for the tenants.

* * *

The first stop to change horses gave Leo the opportunity to find a caped greatcoat in his luggage and put on a hat with a wider brim.

Isobel, emerging from the inn, found him rummaging in his trunk. 'Why not ride inside with us? Surely you aren't concerned about my reputation if you do?'

'It has almost stopped raining,' he said, fastening the coat.

'As you like,' she said with a shrug. 'Leo, we really need to talk about some things. Not that we can with Nancy there, of course.'

'Yes, I was thinking that,' he agreed and saw the colour staining her cheekbones. Had she been worrying about the same thing that he had? He put out his hand and touched the warm pink of her blush with the backs of his bare fingers. 'Don't fret, Izzy. We'll work them out, all the little problems.'

'I was thinking about something rather more than a little problem,' she admitted, the colour deepening.

Her skin was warm against his chilled fingers and Leo realised he was still touching her cheek. So soft… He dropped his hand.

'There's the question of settlements, of course,' he said. That should distract them both. 'I will ask my great-aunt's lawyers to recommend someone to advise you. You should have an independent advisor to look after your interests and then there's the matter of the money held in trust for you. Someone must deal with transferring the control of that from your cousin Edward.'

'Yes, of course. Thank you.' She was back to being

calm, practical Isobel again and he had probably imagined that blush like sun-warmed rose petals.

He handed her back into the carriage, mounted and
they set off again with possibly six hours' travelling
ahead of them. At least he was *doing* something, Leo
thought, and realised that he hadn't thought about Lucinda's rejection all day. Clearly keeping very busy and
finding things to worry about was the bandage to put
on a broken heart, even if it was no cure.

Chapter Four

By the time the carriage finally came to a halt in Albemarle Street outside Gordon's Hotel Isobel was thinking of nothing but taking off her boots, which were pinching, washing her face and hands, which felt grimy, and lying on a comfortable sofa with a good cup of tea.

No. A stiff glass of brandy.

She was beyond worrying about scandal, bedchambers or lawyers, let alone ladylike behaviour.

'Stay here for a moment,' Leo said, opening the door. 'I had best make certain they have suitable accommodation for you. There was no point in writing in advance to reserve a suite; we would have got here along with the letter.' He closed the door again and went inside.

Five minutes later he emerged with a tail-coated individual who bowed her out of the carriage and up the steps. 'Madam, we are honoured. I quite understand the need for discretion.'

Which is more than I do, Isobel thought, confused.

What on earth had Leo told this man who was clearly the manager?

'Do allow me to show you to your suite. Your luggage will be brought up immediately.' He snapped his fingers at a maid. 'Speak to Madam's woman, ensure she has everything she requires.'

He ushered her through a pair of fine double doors into a sitting room and lowered his voice. 'His Lordship has explained that because he is in mourning the strictest secrecy is being kept around his marriage. But please allow me to say that we are delighted that the future Countess of Halford is patronising our establishment.'

Leo appeared a few minutes later, followed by footmen bearing her trunks and valises. She took his arm and pulled him to the other end of the room. 'What on earth did you tell that man?' she whispered.

'A lot of mysterious nonsense,' he admitted with a grin. 'The more I lowered my voice and the more I hinted, the more excited he became. I believe I have left him with the impression of a wedding ceremony attended by all the available royal dukes, for one thing.'

'You dreadful person,' she said, managing to suppress her smile. 'I must warn Nancy to be discreet and I had better practise looking mysterious, too. The poor man is going to be so disappointed.'

'Nonsense, it will do him no harm to be able to mention that the Countess of Halford condescends to stay in his establishment.'

There was a slight flaw with that argument. Isobel thought about being tactful, then decided that frankness might be more useful. 'Will he not know that you have no money?'

'Oh, yes. But I murmured about settling the affairs

of Great-Aunt as her heir and, of course, he will know that she was very wealthy indeed.'

'You have an answer for everything.'

'I doubt it,' he said with a grimace. 'I have no idea what questions I will be asked before I can get a special licence, for one thing. Will you be all right here now? Just order up whatever you need. I have no idea when I will be back tomorrow.'

No, I will not be all right, she wanted to say. *I want to talk to you about bedchambers and I have never stayed in an hotel before and my clothes must be completely out of the mode and I have exactly one pound and four shillings in my purse and Nancy has no idea how to be a lady's maid, let alone a countess's maid, and we somehow have to keep up appearances here and—*

And I am panicking.

Isobel took a deep breath, found a smile and said, 'Of course we will be perfectly all right. I only hope that you do not find the town house in too dreadful a state.'

'From the occasional night I have spent there I expect the worst, from finding that the caretaker has installed lodgers in every room to spiders the size of soup bowls and an opium den in the basement. Goodbye, Izzy, and don't worry.' He touched the back of his fingers to her cheek as he had in the inn yard, then turned and was gone.

'Well, miss, what do we do now?' Nancy stood amid the luggage. 'How long are we staying?'

'A few days at least, so we need to unpack and make ourselves at home.'

Nancy cast a dubious look at the large mirrors, ormolu

tables and lavish dark green curtains in loops and swags. 'It ain't—isn't—very homely, if you ask me, miss.'

'No, it isn't, but we have to pretend that we are perfectly accustomed to all this luxury and that it is the least we expect. We have to keep up Lord Halford's reputation, you see.'

'Don't they know he's the Earl with no money? So is it all a game, miss? Can he pay the bill?'

'No, this is quite real and, yes, we can pay the reckoning! Lord Halford has inherited a fortune unexpectedly, so do not worry about your wages.'

'No, miss, thank you.'

'Is there somewhere for you to sleep?'

'Yes, miss. There's a bed in the dressing room.'

'Then ring for hot water for my bath. Then we can start unpacking and order dinner.'

Isobel made a start on her valise and dressing case while Nancy unstrapped the trunk and began transferring clothes to the drawers and presses. She paused at the window with its view into Albemarle Street. 'There's a circulating library almost opposite. I'll be able to borrow a guide book with a map so we can go and visit the sites tomorrow. I've never been to London before.'

'It's an adventure, miss, that's what it is,' Nancy said, peering over the top of an armful of under-linen.

'It is certainly that,' Isobel agreed as a knock at the door heralded the arrival of footmen with cans of hot water. Two days ago she was miserably trapped in her old home, plotting an escape that had seemed likely to be almost as unpleasant as staying where she was. Now she was engaged to be married and living in the luxury of a London hotel, facing scandal if she lost her nerve and went back to Little Bitterns, and with a completely unknowable future if she stayed.

If I stay, I can make my own future, she told herself, stepping out of the walking dress Nancy had just unhooked. *If I go back, then other people will make it for me. I know which I prefer.*

'Look, miss, there's some oil to put in the bath.' Nancy sniffed at the bottle. 'Lovely, that is. Can I climb in when you've finished, miss?'

'We can ring for fresh for you,' Isobel said, wishing that she'd thought of that. She must get used to having her own maid to be responsible for.

'Heavens, no, miss. You bathe every day, I'll be bound. I'm used to getting the bathwater once the three other maids have been in and once a week, that is. Turn around, miss, and I'll undo your laces.'

She must keep a notebook and start making lists of things to do, Isobel decided, sinking into the warm, rose-scented water. She knew about household management in theory, but the housekeeper at Long Mead had always dealt with the day-to-day staff management. Now she would have the welfare of a large establishment as her concern. And a husband.

Husband.

That was an uncompromisingly solid word.

Tomorrow, she told herself. *I'll worry about all that tomorrow.*

* * *

Leo arrived the next morning as Isobel was eating her breakfast at a table set in the window embrasure of the sitting room. Nancy had located a servants' hall for those travelling with their employers and reported that she had enjoyed a substantial meal at six in the company of 'some right snooty ones'.

'Have you been comfortable? No problems?' Leo asked. 'And may I join you?'

'Of course. Nancy, ring for a waiter. Is there no one to cook you breakfast?'

'There is not,' Leo said, tossing hat, gloves and cane on to the sofa and taking a seat opposite her. 'There is a caretaker who is recovering from the shock I gave him by arriving unannounced, the spiders are as I predicted, but otherwise the place is empty. Just rather dustier than on my last visit—' He broke off as a waiter entered.

'Ah, coffee, eggs, bacon—just bring more of everything, if you please. And the house is about as welcoming as a mausoleum, I'm afraid,' he added as the man went out.

'Never mind, we will soon have it habitable,' Isobel said. Then, seized with a sudden qualm, 'Just how large is it?'

'Four reception rooms, six bedchambers with dressing rooms, kitchen and so forth in the basement and servants' rooms in the attic. There is a mews as well, with rooms over the stables for the grooms. I have left them ordering in straw and hay and feed and being very tight-lipped about the accommodation for both themselves and the horses.'

'That is certainly a large establishment,' Isobel said, trying not to panic. 'Ah, here is your food—it sounds as though you are going to need it. What do you plan to do today?' She poured coffee into the cup the waiter set down and waited while Leo helped himself lavishly from the platters.

'Go to Doctors' Commons first. That is where they deal with ecclesiastical legal matters and apparently it is the correct place to go to enquire about a licence. Then to Great-Aunt's lawyers to inform them of my impending nuptials and find out about the funeral. Then I must find a lawyer for you and locate a domestic agency to hire staff. My housekeeper and cook are bringing up maids and footmen from the Hall by the end of the week, but I must have the place fit to live in before then.'

That would hardly leave him time for a conversation with her about what happened after they married. Isobel told herself to stop thinking about it.

'I had planned to borrow a guidebook and map and go out to see the sights,' she said, pouring more coffee. 'But I think instead I had better go to the house and begin making plans, don't you?'

'It is no place for a lady just now,' Leo said, looking dubious.

'When are the girls arriving?'

'In a week, along with Mrs Druett and the staff.'

'Then there is no time for me to be over-nice about a little dust. We have to have the kitchen fit to use, at least one reception room and some bedchambers in a respectable condition, as well as rooms for all the staff. Give me one of your cards, the address and the name of the caretaker and Nancy and I will go this morning and make a start. Nancy, how are you with spiders?'

'I don't mind them, miss. My nan showed me how to catch them. You don't want to squash them, you know. That makes it rain, so the old folks say.'

'Very well, then we will go to the house as soon as we have changed into something that can cope with dust.'

When they had all finished and he had scribbled details on the back of one of his cards, she walked with Leo to the door. 'Good luck with all those lawyers.'

'And beware of the spiders.' He hesitated and glanced towards the dressing room door, just closing behind Nancy. 'Izzy, on the way here we mentioned that there was a lot we have not spoken of which perhaps we should have done before we agreed on this plan.'

'Yes.' She fixed her gaze on the plain gold stickpin in his neckcloth.

'We can't discuss it now, but I do not want you to worry. We have no need to rush into anything once we are married, anything at all, if you understand what I mean.'

'Yes,' she admitted, still committing details of the pin to memory. 'I do know what you mean. Although it isn't legal, is it, unless we…?'

Leo shrugged. 'Who is to know? We are hardly medieval royalty with half the court in the bedchamber to witness proceedings on the wedding night.'

'That's true.' *Thank heavens.* 'Goodbye, then.'

Again, that touch on her cheek. 'I'm a lucky man, Izzy.' Then he was gone.

Lucky? To be spurned by the lady he loved, having to settle for marriage to an old friend just to provide for his cousins, his tenants and his responsibilities? Lucky, at least, that his great-aunt decided not to leave everything to an organisation bent on policing people's private lives and their amusements, even if those were immoral and unconventional sometimes.

Isobel rubbed her cheek, but that only made the tingling worse.

The caretaker at Halford House in Mount Street was an elderly man who Isobel guessed must once have been a footman. He was slow and rather bent with rheumatism and she suspected his eyesight was not what it had been. The first note that she made in her new memorandum book was to ask Leo to give him a retirement home and a pension, because he would certainly not find himself any way of making an income when he was no longer needed here.

'I'll have a look at the kitchen, miss,' Nancy declared. 'If that's not clean, we'll be in no state for anything else.'

'And I will make a quick survey of the rooms,' Isobel decided. 'Then I will find the nearest domestic agency and hire some local charwomen to attack the worst of it.'

If she tried to introduce the Hall's servants to that mess they would just turn their noses up, she was certain. Things might be in a shabby state at the Hall now, but at least it was clean and they had decent accommodation. Nancy, bless her, had no airs and graces and no objection to hard work either, even if she was now a lady's maid.

At a stationer's close to the hotel, Isobel had bought a London directory as well as the notebook and that listed several agencies, some in close proximity to the house, which was located between Grosvenor and Berkeley Squares. Presumably it was good for business to be handy for the smart houses of Mayfair.

When Nancy came up the back stairs, her hair tied up in a dish towel with another wrapped around her waist, she found Isobel dubiously surveying the bedchamber that Leo appeared to have set up camp in. At least there was clean linen on the bed, a washstand in the dressing room and storage space for his clothes. She suspected that he had taken a broom to it himself. 'We need three charwomen down there, miss.'

'And another four above stairs if we're to make any impact on this in a week,' Isobel said. 'If you can carry on here, I will go to the nearest agency and then come back and look at the linen cupboard.'

Ah, the glamour and luxury of a countess's life, she thought as, directory in hand, she hailed a hackney cab.

But she was determined that she was not going to begin married life in something that would provide a perfect setting for one of Horace Walpole's Gothic tales of horror.

Leo called at the house on his way to the hotel, fully expecting to find it deserted except for Finkle, the caretaker. Izzy would surely have taken one appalled look and fled to find some hardy charwomen.

But the windows were open in several rooms and, when he let himself in, he was greeted by an apparition wrapped in an apron that looked as though it had begun life as sheet. The female had smudges all over her face, hair was straggling from beneath a turban and her sleeves were rolled up to the elbow. On close examination it proved to be his betrothed.

'Leo! No, don't come near me, I am shedding dust like a sugar shaker.'

'Izzy? Thank heavens—I thought you were the ghost of the first housekeeper.'

'Not quite, but Nancy and I are on the point of expiring, so we may haunt the place yet.' She led him in to what had once been an elegant drawing room, where they found Nancy. Equally grubby, she was sprawled on a sofa, her feet propped on a footstool that looked as though it had been nibbled by mice.

'Stay where you are, Nancy.' Leo waved the maid back to her seat when she jumped up. 'There is far too much work here for the two of you, nor is it fitting for either of you.'

'We have a small army of charwomen coming in tomorrow.' Isobel collapsed inelegantly into an armchair that had been covered by a dust sheet. 'And sufficient coal in the cellar to heat water for a few days. I have told Finkle to order more. At least we now know the extent of the problem and I have drawn up a list of priorities.'

'I'll go and tidy myself before we go back to the hotel, miss.' Nancy got up and left, tactfully closing the door behind her.

'When is the funeral?'

'Tomorrow. Why they did not tell me that when they wrote about the bequest, I have no idea.'

'Perhaps they assumed you would have seen the announcement in the Deaths column of the newspapers. Where is it to be? Will you be able to get there and back in the day?'

'Fortunately, yes. She lived in Richmond, so I can easily put in an appearance. I have to say I would not have done so if it wasn't for this bequest. Both my father and my uncle had a tremendous falling-out with their aunt and I cannot recall ever having met her. They were, she said, a disgrace to the family. According to the lawyers it was only the realisation that I was the sole remaining Havelock in the direct line that made her decide on the terms of the legacy.'

'So there are not going to be any close relatives present, furious that you have been left her fortune and cut them out?'

'Yes, which is quite a relief. I have been recommended a lawyer for you, a Mr Parkin of Parkin, Deane and Prosser. He will call at the hotel tomorrow afternoon and I have asked Great-Aunt's lawyers to act for me for the moment, which will simplify matters.'

'Goodness, I had better find something that will do for mourning, or the poor man will be shocked to the core at the sight of me.'

'I am certain you will manage,' Leo said vaguely, clearly assuming that fashionable mourning was something she could produce out of a trunk like magic. Perhaps a dark grey gown, a black shawl and her jet brooch would suffice, although she suspected that a future countess ought to have ordered an entire new outfit in the deepest black.

'And I haven't been to a domestic agency yet,' he added. 'But it appears that you have?'

'Indeed. There's a very efficient one quite close by. And the licence?'

'That was much easier than I expected. Apparently recently bereaved earls must be treated with kid gloves. I am to return tomorrow afternoon for it. All we need to do is to identify which church we prefer and then I will speak to the clergyman in charge.'

'This is all remarkably straightforward,' Isobel said dubiously. 'Almost too easy.'

'I expect something will go wrong and convince us that this is real life and not a dream,' Leo said and grinned at her.

She smiled back and for a second it was as though he was just her old friend again and not the man who would be her husband in a few days. But this *was* a dream, or a nightmare. This was the man she loved. The man who loved somebody else.

They needed to talk more about what happened when they were man and wife, but it hardly seemed right to raise it again when they had just been joking about things going wrong.

'What is the matter, Izzy?' Oh, but Leo knew her so well. She could only hope that his perception went no deeper than recognising unhappiness or tiredness. Leo reached across and took both her hands in his. His grasp was warm and she could feel the steady beat of his pulse. 'Tell me. You know you can say anything to me.'

Even, *I love you*? She could feel the words forming on her lips as she looked into his eyes, so warm and dear, so concerned for her.

Chapter Five

'I am weary, dirty and longing for a bath,' Isobel said with a smile and a comical grimace, her heart thudding with the closeness of her escape from making a declaration that would change everything, make everything one hundred times worse.

She had expected Leo to pull a face in return, tease her about cobwebs in her hair or smudges on her nose, but instead he sat back and looked at her long and hard between narrowed eyes until she began to shift uncomfortably on her chair.

'I am not surprised and, if you say that is all that is wrong… Come then, find your bonnet and gloves and I will call a hackney for you. I assume Nancy can come over tomorrow morning and set the charwomen to work before she comes back to chaperon you with Mr Parkin. I think you should spend the morning resting.'

Reluctantly, she put her hands in his again and allowed herself to be pulled to her feet. 'I must spend the morning making lists, you mean.'

'Izzy.' Leo was still serious and he kept hold of her hands in such a way that it felt pointed to try to remove them. 'Are you sure about this?'

'Why?' she asked, suddenly seized with panic. 'You haven't changed your mind, have you?'

'Only about whether I have been very selfish in embroiling you in this.' His dark eyes were steady on her face when she glanced up at him. She read doubt and something else that she did not recognise in them.

'Goodness, it is as much to my advantage as it is to yours,' she said with a laugh and managed to slip one of her hands from his without tugging. 'If it was not for you, I could be grooming smelly lapdogs in Bath next week. Even the big hairy spiders are better than that.'

'If you are certain,' he said, still dubious. 'I know it would risk creating a scandal, but I could set you up in a nice house somewhere and you could become a wealthy young widow with a new name.'

'No,' she said, pleased with the smile she managed to fix on her lips. 'I would much rather be a comfortably off countess, if you please.'

'Yes, it pleases me,' Leo said, sounding faintly surprised as he said it. He raised the hand he was holding to his lips and brushed the lightest of kisses across her knuckles. 'Now, fetch your hat and your maid and I will call you a cab.'

Leo had expected to sleep heavily after his long day, which was crowned by several hours of reading through the papers his great-aunt's lawyers had given him. Instead, he had tossed and turned all night, his dreams haunted by vague anxieties that, on waking, he could not pin down.

It was simply the effects of a night on a lumpy, poorly aired mattress, he told himself at six the next morning as he shaved in the lukewarm water that Finkle had supplied, then swore under his breath as he wrestled with his neckcloth.

At home, one of the footmen acted as a valet when needed. From now on, if he was to fill his place in society as he must, he needed a suitable wardrobe and a valet to look after it. More things to add to the mile-long list.

Richmond was only eight or nine miles, he thought. He would tell his coachman to stop in Kensington where there was sure to be somewhere to take breakfast, then drive on to cross the Thames at Kew Bridge. The service was at noon, so he would be back in the early evening.

Would Izzy be all right by herself all day? She was anxious about something, despite her denials. It might only be the worries that any young lady would have about marriage when she had no mother or sisters to talk to and he was all too aware that they ought to have had a discussion about just what each was expecting before they set out. It was rather late in the day for that now, but she had seemed reassured when he had said they could delay consummating the marriage.

At least she had Nancy with her. The maid might not be familiar with London, but she struck Leo as being intelligent, loyal and determined. And all Izzy would be doing was meeting her new lawyer, after all.

He picked up the London directory he had purchased the day before, called down to let Finkle know he was leaving and went out to find his carriage waiting for him at the kerbside. The journey would give him time to study the possible churches and chapels in the area.

He sat back and gazed with unseeing eyes at the streets coming to life as the carriage wove its way towards Park Lane and realised that he had not thought about Lucinda for hours. That surprised him, then he realised that to do so was disloyal to Izzy. Even so, as he thought with a pang of his lost love's beauty and vivacity, he had not thought his will was so strong.

If Lucinda had said, *Yes,* they would be making plans now for a wedding in Little Bitterns's parish church, he would be frantically attempting to get the Countess's suite of rooms into a fit state for his bride and Izzy would no doubt have noted the date of the wedding in her diary and perhaps bought a new bonnet for the occasion. She would have wished him well, like the good friend that she was.

He smiled at the thought of Izzy's friendship as the carriage passed through the Hyde Park turnpike gates and began to lurch along the notoriously bad stretch of the Knightsbridge Road. It seemed she had always been there, sensible and stoic, loyally taking his side in childish squabbles and misdeeds, occasionally extracting them both from some ill-judged adventure of his own devising, sometimes telling him off with sharp-tongued accuracy when he, like all youths, was being an idiot.

Izzy had always been… He searched for the word. *Comfortable,* that was it. But now, strangely, she was not comfortable at all, but unsettling when she looked at him with those clear green eyes. It was because they had to negotiate an entirely new relationship, he told himself, that was all. Things would soon settle down when they were married.

'You did say seven o'clock, miss,' Nancy said defensively when Isobel peered sleepily over the edge of the blankets.

'I know. There's a lot to do today.' She lay there, looking up at the ceiling and trying to isolate the various anxieties that stirred into life as she woke up. The fact she was marrying Leo, of course. Then there was the anxiety about whether she would make a good countess and her uncertainty about the best way to approach the twins. And, on top of that, serious second thoughts about the letter that she had sent the day before to her cousins informing them of where she was and why.

It had taken half a dozen attempts. The first had been far too wordy and apologetic. The second, curt to the point of rudeness. Finally, she had produced a short, very polite and somewhat formal letter that explained that she was marrying Leo and reminding them of his London address, should they wish to respond. It was too late to change anything now. The letter was doubtless already on its way in a sack on the Canterbury Mail coach.

'Oh, thank you.' Isobel wriggled up against the pillows and accepted the cup of hot chocolate that Nancy handed her. 'We have to go to Halford House and make certain the cleaning women know what they should be doing, then I must find somewhere to buy a wedding dress.'

'But there's no time, is there, miss? Not to get one made.'

'I have the address of a Madame Claire who is, so I am informed, the best modiste in London.'

'Who says, miss?' Nancy finished lifting out clean linen and shook the creases from Isobel's best walking dress.

'Miss Lucinda Paxton.' There was real irony in Lucinda being the guide to where to buy her wedding gown. 'Apparently her second cousin, the Marchioness of Wyndham, never uses anyone else. I intend to throw myself on her mercy and hope that the *cachet* of dressing the slightly scandalous new Countess of Halford will appeal to her.'

'Blimey, miss,' Nancy said. 'Well, we'd best turn you out as smart as possible, then.'

'My name is Isobel Martyn, I am here on the recommendation of the Marchioness of Wyndham and I wish to speak to Madame Claire.'

The elegantly attired shop assistant subjected Isobel to a scrutiny that made her firm her lips and stare back, then bobbed a slight curtsy. 'If you would care to take a seat, Miss Martyn, I will see if Madame is free.'

She vanished through the deep blue velvet curtains at the rear of the shop. Madame would be available, Isobel was certain, because she would not dare risk offending someone she believed to be a friend of the Marchioness. How things would progress from there was another matter. Fashionable modistes were rumoured to be as fussy about the clients they accepted as the Patronesses of Almack's were about who merited a ticket of admission.

'Doesn't look much like a dress shop to me, miss,' Nancy muttered from her post at Isobel's right shoulder.

All there was to be seen in the little panelled space was a display stand with several lengths of beautifully draped fabrics and several upholstered sofas.

'If you could come through, Miss Martyn.' The assistant was holding back the heavy drapery across the doorway.

Madame Claire proved to be small, thin, exquisitely dressed and as gracious as a duchess inviting someone to join her for tea. It took several seconds for Isobel to register the decidedly un-French accent and the intelligence in the black eyes.

'How may I assist you, Miss Martyn?'

'I am about to marry the Earl of Halford,' Isobel said.

Madame Claire blinked, once. 'My felicitations, Miss Martyn. Do, please, take a seat. You wish to order a trousseau, I assume.'

'Eventually, yes. Now I wish to purchase a gown for my wedding and that as soon as possible.'

Two blinks, slower this time. 'And when is the happy day?'

'Tomorrow or the day after. I am uncertain. Lord Martyn is attending his great-aunt's funeral today.'

'I see. There would appear to be some urgency in the matter.'

'In the matter of the gown, yes. Not for any other reason.' Isobel did not want to encourage any more rumours than the ones that would be flying around at any moment.

The skin around the dark eyes crinkled as Madame

Claire smiled her understanding. 'But of course. Do you have any particular style or colour in mind?'

'Whatever is available at such very short notice,' Isobel said. 'I do not imagine that you would produce anything that was unflattering or not in the mode.'

'Ladies wearing my gowns *lead* the mode, ma'am,' the modiste said flatly. 'Could you stand up, please, Miss Martyn?'

She prowled around Isobel, muttering to her assistant who made notes and handed her a tape measure from time to time. 'Hmm… Slim. Bust… Hmm… Colouring not extreme, complexion good, posture good…'

Isobel half expected to be asked to open her mouth to have her teeth inspected, but refrained from comment, even about her unspectacular bosom. If this minor humiliation meant she could be married in a manner befitting a countess, then it was worth it.

After what seemed to be half an hour, Madame stood back and nodded. 'I have a leaf-green silk formal day dress that I think can be altered to fit you by tomorrow morning. The lady for whom it was ordered is *enceinte* and failed to mention that when the initial measurements were taken. Delphine, fetch the gown for Miss Martyn.'

So that was what the veiled enquiry about the need for haste in her marriage was about: Madame did not want to trouble herself with a new client who was expecting a child and who would not be showing off her creations for months.

The gown was exquisite and the assistant brought a

cream satin straw bonnet trimmed with matching ribbons and flowers.

'I had intended now to use this gown as a display piece, which is why we have the bonnet,' Madame said as the assistant helped Isobel into the gown and began to mark and pin for alterations. 'I think it will be suitable. You have shoes and gloves?'

'Yes, cream kid, which will work well.' Isobel tied the bonnet under her chin and smiled at her reflection. 'I think these will be admirable, thank you, *madame*. I am staying at Gordon's Hotel.'

'It will be delivered this evening. I hope we may have the pleasure of your custom in the future, Miss Martyn.'

'You most certainly will.' It was difficult to be certain with the gown half pinned and the assistant dodging around her, but Madame Claire had chosen something that suited her better than anything she had ever worn before. The warm glow that thought produced was almost enough to distract her from the butterflies that kept fluttering around inside her whenever she thought of what followed the dress being taken off.

Leo arrived back in London at eight in the evening and called at Gordon's Hotel to find that Isobel was about to sit down to dinner.

'I hoped you would come,' she said. 'You will stay and eat, won't you? Nancy has discovered the staff dining room and is making the acquaintance of other ladies' maids, so I am eating in lonely state.'

He took a chair and, when the waiter had taken their order and left, answered her questions about the funeral.

'It was not as bad as I had feared,' he concluded. 'The weather was sunny, which always helps, and the mourners were mainly various professional men who had been in Great-Aunt's employ, along with some old retainers. She has left them well provided for in her will and everything appears to be quite straightforward.'

'How disappointing,' Isobel teased him. 'No legacy to half a dozen lapdogs which you have to look after, or mention of a previously unacknowledged lovechild who must be supported?'

'There was a parrot,' he confessed. 'But I thought you would not be sorry to avoid owning that. I gave that to her doctor who has apparently always coveted it.'

'Excellent—' Isobel broke off while the waiters brought their soup.

'I have sent an express down to the Hall and asked everyone to come up as soon as possible, as the house is proceeding so well. Did your meeting prove helpful?' Leo passed the bread rolls. 'One can never tell with lawyers.'

'Oh, excellent. Mr Parkin is quite young and not at all dusty. He used plain English and made what sounded like eminently sensible suggestions that will ensure that my interests are protected if you run away to sea or take up with an opera dancer.

'I also gave him a letter of introduction to Cousin Edward. He says he will go down to see him next week. He seemed very interested in my inheritance, so I suspect he is going to enjoy extracting a full accounting from Edward.'

'I somehow do not think we are going to receive a

delightful wedding present from Lord and Lady Martyn,' Leo said with a grimace. 'Speaking of which, there is a chapel close by in South Audley Street. I thought it would be more private than St George's, Hanover Square, but I can go and speak to the vicar there if you'd prefer the more fashionable church.'

'The South Audley Street church sounds ideal. Any place of worship in this area is going to be quite acceptable, isn't it?'

'Perfectly, I imagine. I will call on the priest in charge tomorrow and see if he can perform the ceremony the day after. I had thought of asking Charlie Standon to be my groomsman. He's Lord Welnott's second son and he is getting married next month, so he should be in sympathy with me. And he is no gossip.'

'That sounds admirable,' Isobel said politely and he realised that, while all he needed was a groomsman and would be quite happy asking two passers-by to be witnesses, a bride would have rather higher expectations.

'But what about your attendants? Do you have any friends in London?'

'No real friends, those are all in Kent and I suspect that my London acquaintances will have mothers who would be shocked that they were attending a marriage arranged in such haste. Nancy can come with me and be a witness.'

'If you are sure.'

'Perfectly. Tomorrow, then, you make the arrangements for the wedding and I will make certain that the house is ready to move into, even if there are only a few rooms fit to use.'

Isobel sounded calm and unbothered and Leo felt his shoulders begin to relax. The headache that had been nagging at the back of his skull for hours ebbed away. How relaxing it was to be with someone who made no demands, but who composedly adapted to whatever was required.

Lucinda's liveliness and rapid changes of mood might be captivating, but she could not be described as restful.

I must be getting old, Leo mocked himself. *Welcoming the prospect of a restful wife, indeed!*

Even as he thought it the image of Lucinda's face superimposed itself over Isobel's features. The vividness of it took his breath away—the pretty pink pout of her mouth, the wilful little chin, the sparkle in those blue eyes and the playful toss of her curls.

Leo swallowed too quickly as a wave of desire hit him.

'Are you all right?' The vision of the enchanting little face vanished and in its place Izzy was looking at him, a line between her brows as she frowned.

'Yes, perfectly. A tough piece of meat, that's all.'

'Leo…' Isobel shook her head and let the sentence trail away.

'Yes? Is something wrong?'

'Not really. It is just that we agreed to this so quickly and we took no time to discuss some matters that…that perhaps we ought to have done.'

The ebbing evidence of that flash of desire for another woman made him guess what she might be talking about. They were back to the wedding night and that was rather a tricky subject to discuss over the roast beef. Still, it had to be done. 'Yes?' Leo said encouragingly. 'We did touch on the matter I think you are referring to.'

'Children,' Isobel said and promptly took a long drink of water.

Leo waited until she emerged from behind the glass. 'Yes, of course. I mean, you do want some, don't you?'

'I think so. I hadn't thought about it. But you will want an heir, of course.'

'Yes, I would. I mean, I would welcome children anyway—boys or girls. But not unless you feel that way too, Izzy.'

She was fidgeting with the cutlery now. Izzy never fidgeted. 'It's just that we are such old friends. It all seems…rather strange.'

'What? Children?' He was sure he was missing something now.

'No,' she said sharply. 'The getting of them. The idea of going to bed with you and being intimate, if I really must spell it out.'

'Ah.' Leo pushed away his plate. 'When we spoke of this the other day I really did mean what I said. We do not have to rush anything. I imagine that living together will make things feel different.'

'Perhaps.' She was still rearranging the cutlery. 'I thought that men needed—um, expected… That if you don't…' Her voice trailed away.

It was so unlike Izzy to dither and stammer that Leo couldn't think of words for a moment, then groped his way to an answer. 'There's no need for haste. Celibacy never hurt anyone—look at all those monks.'

And suddenly the old Izzy was back, grinning at him mischievously. 'You mean there is nothing that will rust with disuse and fall off?'

'Exactly. We can creep up on it, you know. It is not as though I am going to stride into your bedchamber, twirling my moustaches, and leap on you demanding my marital rights.'

'At least that will give me time to become accustomed while you grow twirlable moustaches,' she remarked.

'Idiot,' he said, making the waiter, who had entered before the sound of his knock had died away, jump. 'Not you.'

'Yes, my lord. Sorry, my lord. Would you like dessert served now, ma'am?'

'I would, thank you.'

They sat in silence while he cleared the plates, went out and came back a few minutes later with a tray bearing a variety of little dishes and pots. 'The chef sent a selection, ma'am,' he said, bowing himself out.

'Are you feeling more comfortable now?' Leo asked when Isobel had chosen a lemon tartlet and was thoughtfully licking the cream off her spoon.

She nodded and a ripple of desire went through him at the sight of her pink tongue exploring the delicacy. Izzy might be feeling more relaxed, but he was not at all sure he was. Confused, certainly.

That was better, Isobel thought. It felt safe to be joking with Leo, teasing him.

She put down her spoon, considered another lemon tartlet, decided that was greedy, and then looked up to find Leo watching her. 'Would you like this?' She indicated the plate.

'No, not that,' he said, oddly serious. Then he smiled. 'I must get back.'

'Yes, of course. We both have a great deal to do tomorrow.'

Leo came to pull back her chair for her. Isobel stood up and found herself very close to him. Once again, there was that gold tiepin at just the right height to stare at. On impulse she tipped back her head and looked up into his face. It seemed they were both holding their breath.

Chapter Six

Too close, far too close. Too sudden. Isobel felt dizzy, put out her right hand, groping for the chair back, and Leo caught it in his.

'Careful, Izzy. You stood up too quickly.'

'Yes, that was it.' She still did not feel steady. When Leo released her hand she reached up and laid it against his chest, solid and reassuring. 'Or perhaps I have had one too many glasses of wine.'

'You should have warned me—I had no idea you over-imbibed at dinner,' he said, teasing, and, in that gesture she was becoming used to, he touched the fingers of his left hand to her cheek.

Now they were so close she could hear the brush of his leg against her skirts, feel the warmth of his breath on her temple.

'Foolishness. You know I hardly drink wine at all,' she said with a laugh that sounded forced to her own ears.

Leo's left hand slid round to cup the back of her head. 'Shall I kiss you goodnight, Izzy?' More teasing... But, no, his eyes were intent on her face, his mouth was un-smiling. The mouth that she had dreamed of, on hers. Had dreamed of for years.

'Why not?' she said, attempting lightness. It came out as a whisper, but an audible one.

We should practise...

Leo bent his head and his lips met hers. Soft and yet firm, warm, pressing gently.

What was she supposed to do? *Press too,* instinct told her, so she did, perhaps too hard. It felt clumsy, their noses bumped and she stepped away, hitting the back of her knees against the edge of the chair. Isobel sat down abruptly.

'Perhaps we should practise that,' Leo said, echoing her thought as he so often did. There was the hint of a smile in his voice, but she had her eyes tight shut, so she couldn't be certain. Possibly he was simply gritting his teeth. 'But I had better go now. Goodnight, Izzy.' She felt the air move as he stooped, dropped a kiss on her cheek and let himself out.

That was a disaster. Isobel opened her eyes cautiously, as though expecting to find an audience mocking her clumsy, ignorant kiss. Practice? She should not need to practise kissing Leo: she had thought about it, imagined it, several times a day for years. She had certainly dreamt about it enough. It hadn't been anything like that.

Of course, Leo had doubtless kissed dozens of women. He had probably kissed Lucinda, who had a reputation for taking flirtation just a little too far. Lucinda, she was certain, would know exactly how to kiss a man.

And now Leo knew that the woman he was going to marry was not even able to kiss him without banging noses in possibly the most unromantic manner possible.

I am not only an old maid, I am a gauche old maid, Isobel told herself, piling on the misery.

At least, she thought gloomily, Leo was never going to guess she was in love with him, not after that performance.

There was another lemon tartlet on the table. Isobel picked it up, took a bite, then another, then finished it. Now she had an excuse for feeling decidedly unsettled.

What was it going to be like when they went to bed together, if simple kissing was that awkward? She had heard that a well-bred lady was supposed to lie still, thinking of nothing while her husband took his pleasure. She certainly must not expect to gain any pleasure from it. And, from one whispered conversation she had overheard at an assembly room dance, it was usual for the act to be carried out in total darkness.

'They say she insists on dozens of candles in the bedchamber,' one lady was telling another. 'Can you imagine! It must be like broad daylight.' The other had shuddered visibly. 'She must have the instincts of a courtesan.'

At least in the dark one had an excuse for clumsiness. Now she was worrying about how many women Leo had lain with in the past and just how satisfactory he had found the experience.

Isobel stood up and went to jerk on the bell pull. She was working herself up into a state of nerves. What she wanted was some quiet contemplation and a cup of tea to take away the taste of Leo on her lips. That was the rational thing to do and, when the waiter came in answer to her ringing, she ordered the table to be cleared and tea brought.

Slowly, she regained some composure and reached a number of what she considered to be sensible conclusions. Firstly, Leo was not in love with her and therefore would not be disappointed if she was an inept lover. Secondly, she was an inexperienced virgin and would, presumably, be less awkward with time. Everyone had to start somewhere, after all.

Thirdly, he knew she was a virgin, so he was expecting inexperience. Fourthly, she had almost resigned herself to life as an old maid, dwindling into middle age as a paid companion: this had to be better than that. And finally—and she was not at all certain this was a soothing thought at all—Leo would doubtless take a mistress after a decent interval and would confine his bedroom activities with herself to the production of an heir.

And, no, she would not be jealous or resentful about a mistress, any more than she was resentful of the fact that her husband-to-be was in love with another woman.

Isobel poured a second cup of tea and reluctantly listened to the voice of common sense that was telling her in no uncertain terms that she would be very unhappy indeed if her husband took a mistress.

But you didn't agree to this in order to be happy, did you? that sensible inner voice demanded. *You did it because it was better than the alternative for you and because you wanted to help Leo and, most of all, because you want to be* with *Leo.*

'So I will not repine now,' she said out loud. 'I have made my bed and I am going to have to lie on it, however uncomfortable it is.'

'Sorry, miss, I didn't hear you ring.' Nancy came hurrying in from the dressing room which had another door out to the corridor.

'I didn't. I was talking to myself,' Isobel admitted. 'Did you have a proper dinner? I should have asked before if you are comfortable here.'

'It's not bad at all, miss, thank you. Are you ready to retire now, miss?'

Isobel realised that she was not at all sleepy, but she might as well fret in bed as sitting there and Nancy wouldn't go to her own rest until she was settled, so she agreed.

'His Lordship is arranging for the wedding the day after tomorrow,' she explained as Nancy unpinned her hair and picked up the brush. 'And he has sent for the staff from the Hall.'

'That's perfect then, miss. Time for any little adjustments to your gown and there ought to be at least some rooms fit to live in at the Mount Street house.'

Isobel suppressed a smile. Nancy had grown so much in confidence since they had run away. She might not know all the tricks of the lady's maid's trade yet, but she had common sense and wasn't afraid to ask for advice.

Now all she had to do was to learn how to be a wife. And a countess. And a sister, if not a mother, to two girls on the brink of young womanhood.

Easy, really, she thought with a wry smile as Nancy dropped her nightgown over her head. At least thinking about what she could do to make the twins feel at home would be a more constructive subject to worry about than what happened on the wedding night.

The curate in charge of the chapel in South Audley Street proved helpful. Yes, the next day at eleven o'clock would be possible. The bridegroom was in mourning? Yes, he quite understood the decision to have a quiet ceremony. The licence was perfectly in order. There was the small matter of the fee. Oh, and His Lordship was making a contribution to the poor box as well? Most generous. Yes, certainly he understood the need for discretion.

Leo hoped that the man did. He put his hat back on as he stood in the porch, watching the traffic on the street outside. It was a fashionable area with smart houses and equally smart shops. Almost opposite was the establishment of James Purdey, the gunsmith. Purdey had made gunstocks for the Manton brothers before setting up on his own account and his reputation was as good as theirs.

Leo realised that now he could afford to buy sporting guns from any of them. Afford to have his boots made by Hoby and his hats by Lock for that matter. He could refill the wine cellar, employ a librarian, subscribe to as many journals as he pleased. After years of scrimping and saving it came as a shock to find he could now indulge himself in the luxuries that men of his class took for granted. He could indulge the girls, too, but no doubt Izzy would enjoy doing that.

Circumstances had given him a ready-made family.

He thought about that as he resisted the temptation to go and browse in the gunsmith's shop and, instead, turned right and then left into Mount Street. It did not take him long to reach his own front door—another fact that he must get used to: ownership of a fine town house.

There was no sign of either Izzy or her maid, but Finkle, who appeared to have been dusted and scrubbed along with the house, greeted him with the information that the basement, half of the reception rooms, two bedchambers and the servants' rooms had now been thoroughly cleaned.

Leo admired Izzy's priorities in making sure the servants would be comfortably accommodated and that the kitchen was functioning. 'We will need another two bedchambers preparing,' he told Finkle.

'Aye, me Lord. That's what Miss Martyn told me. For the two young ladies and their governess, she said.'

He should have known better than to think Izzy had overlooked that. 'Is that a new suit of clothes, Finkle?'

'Aye, me Lord. Miss Martyn, she said I deserved to look as though I was an important member of a nobleman's staff.' He straightened rather stiffly. 'But I don't think I'm up to being a butler, me Lord. Not even with a new suit of clothes. I was a bit worried that was what she meant.'

'Well, I think you deserve a comfortable retirement, Finkle. How long have you worked here?'

The old man frowned in thought. 'Since I was a nipperling, me Lord. Boot boy, I was, to the grandfather of the last Earl. Sixty years that is, I reckon.'

Leo thought it was more like seventy. 'Then you

definitely deserve a rest. How about moving down to Kent? There is a nice little cottage in the park, close to the south lodge. Mrs Simmonds at the lodge would make sure you were well fed and it's just a step to the village and the inn.'

'That'd be grand, me Lord.' The frown was replaced by a beaming, gap-toothed, smile. 'Thank 'ee.'

'The place needs some repairs, but I'll have that put in hand for you straightaway. It will be ready in a few weeks, Finkle.'

That felt good, being able to do something positive for staff who had suffered from the erratic governance of his late cousin. And the sooner the other cottages on the estate were put in good repair too, the better.

He walked through the house, mentally drafting instructions to Harding, the estate manager, as he took in the improvement the cleaning women had wrought. He found them on the first floor tackling the remaining bedchambers and thanked them for their hard work, then went to look at the two rooms that had been completed.

The two largest bedchambers, both with good-sized dressing rooms, stood next to each other, separated by a small sitting room. He paced out the space, wondering whether it would be possible to fit in a proper bathing chamber and even one of the new-fangled flushing water closets. Luxuries, he supposed, but Izzy deserved them.

And she deserved a bridegroom who looked the part as well, he thought, giving his wardrobe a rapid inspection. Thankfully, for Finkle would hardly pass muster as a valet, he had enough clean linen and his best suit of clothes needed only a pass with a clothes brush. At least he could give his shoes to Finkle, provided the man remembered his childhood skills as boot boy.

And flowers, he realised as he went down the steps to walk to Albemarle Street to tell Izzy about the time of the wedding. She must have flowers and the house needed them, too. He hoped the hotel manager could take care of that, but the first thing he must do, the day after the wedding, was to find himself a valet. And a secretary. At least the staff from the Hall would be arriving today with Mrs Druett. He only hoped the housekeeper would not find being faced with her employer's wedding the very next day too much and she handed in her notice.

Madame Claire's assistants had hardly left when Leo arrived, looking as harassed as Isobel had ever seen him.

The kiss he planted on her cheek was so rapid and absent-minded that she had no opportunity to feel shy about it.

'I have a list,' he said, pulling a notebook from his breast pocket and flipping pages before she could say anything. 'The girls and the Hall staff will be arriving today, so I must get back as soon as possible. The wedding is at eleven o'clock tomorrow, just around the corner in South Audley Street, so I will send a carriage for you at a quarter to the hour. I will speak to the staff here about flowers and sending your luggage around to the house. They are finishing off all the bedchambers,

I have just been to check. I will return there now, but I will call at the staff agency first to see about a valet.' He gave her a rueful smile. 'What have I forgotten?'

'Food?' Isobel said. Bless the man. It was not only her life that was being turned upside down. 'Leave that to me. I will speak to the manager here and have their kitchen staff send around something for tomorrow after the wedding. We will hardly need much. And I'll ask them to ensure sufficient supplies to last the first three days while your cook finds her feet.'

'I should have thought of that.' Leo jammed the notebook back in his pocket and ran his fingers through his hair.

She could not resist. Isobel put out her hand and tidied the tumbled dark locks. 'That's better.' She clasped her hands together tightly to stop herself touching him again. 'You most definitely do need a valet.'

He caught her around the waist one-handed and pulled her into a hug, the kind of comradely embrace they had often shared over the years. She made herself relax into it, closed her eyes and drank in the old familiar scent: a spicy cologne, leather, coffee and something indefinable that was just Leo.

Her cheek was against the breast of his coat and she could feel his breathing, sense the thud of his heartbeat. She let her lips form a kiss against the superfine cloth and stayed quite still, expecting him to release her immediately. Instead, Leo hugged her closer.

'You are the most restful woman of my acquaintance,' he said, his breath stirring her hair.

Was that a compliment? Rather an ambiguous one,

perhaps. Presumably he was thinking of her manner in contrast to Lucinda's liveliness and vivid enthusiasms. Cats consenting to be stroked, comfy old armchairs and footstools were restful. Still, it seemed to please him, so perhaps boring was better than irritating.

Isobel straightened up and gave Leo a little push. 'Go on, hurry off. You don't want the girls to arrive and you not there.'

'Are you going to be a nagging wife?' he asked, putting on his hat at a rakish angle.

'Of course,' she said, suddenly full of confidence. This was going to work. She would make it work. She went up on tiptoe and pecked a kiss on his cheek. 'Off you go, dear. There, wasn't that wifely?'

'Hussy.' His smile was warm and he touched her cheek with one fingertip. 'I will see you tomorrow.'

At five o'clock that evening Leo stood in his drab but dust-free drawing room, wondered if he was dreaming and decided that what he needed was to be drunk. Four days from that impulsive decision on the green at Little Bitterns and here he was in London with the big house echoing with the sound of scurrying staff, the echoes of Mrs Druett's stream of orders—a day on the road had not subdued her usual energy, he noticed—and the disturbance that two over-excited fifteen-year-old twins always seemed to produce.

And he was going to be married in the morning to his dear friend and not to the woman he loved. He had been poor and racked with worries and responsibilities. Now he was wealthy. He should have no cares in the world, only a great deal of planning and hard work. He should be happy.

Leo probed at his feelings like a man exploring a sore tooth with the tip of his tongue. He had to learn how to be a good husband—that was what was worrying him. Everything else he could manage, even the twins, now that he had Izzy to help him.

Was it better or worse that she knew of his feelings for Lucinda? Better, he concluded after pacing several lengths of the room, because he was not deceiving her. They were being honest with each other and honesty, he suspected, was very important to Izzy.

'Why are you pacing up and down, Cousin Leo?'

He hadn't noticed the two girls come in. They stood just inside the door, regarding him solemnly. Although they were twins they were not identical. Penelope, the more lively one, was a brunette with striking green eyes, her sister was blonde with hazel eyes. In figure and height they were much the same, both grown out of their childish plumpness and not yet at the stage where one could judge to a certainty what their more mature looks would be.

'Because I am getting married in the morning and bridegrooms are supposed to pace about looking harassed,' he informed them.

They laughed, as he'd hoped. He was still feeling his way with them, not certain whether they needed a father figure or a big brother. They had grown up with him since they were five, but their father had been alive then and Leo had been so much older and often away, that they had never been close before.

'May we be bridesmaids?' Penny asked, coming into the room and perching on the arm of a chair.

'This all happened rather quickly,' he explained. 'There hasn't been time to have dresses made for you.'

'We have our new white party dresses,' Prue said. 'They would go with anything Miss Martyn will be wearing.'

He could hardly disturb Izzy now with a request to include the girls, so he would have to decide himself. 'Yes, that would be very suitable,' he said and was rewarded by beaming smiles. It would make them feel more part of this new family of his, he concluded, and Izzy wouldn't mind.

'You had best go and speak to Miss Pettigrew about your dresses,' he told them, then sank down into an armchair as they ran out, talking excitedly about their hair and ribbons. This was very much a make-do-and-mend wedding.

How much did the day mean to a woman? Rather a lot from what he could gather from hearing of months of preparation and large sums spent to perfect the smallest detail. He imagined what style and show Lucinda would expect from her wedding day: it would not be this. But Izzy was practical and sensible, he told himself. It would be all right. It had to be, or he was going to hurt someone who meant a lot to him.

Chapter Seven

'Your carriage awaits, Miss Martyn,' the footman announced.

Were there ever more fateful words? Isobel wondered as Nancy gathered up the flowers and cast a last critical look over her.

If she walked out of that door and down the stairs now, she would be entering an entirely new life. A different world. She would marry a man she loved and who loved another woman. She would be a countess. That last did not worry her, she realised now as she pulled on her gloves and picked up the cream silk reticule.

All of this she could cope with without a qualm, all except the actual marriage itself. Well, now was the moment where her world changed for ever.

For better or worse...

Certainly for richer, the thing that matters least to me.

'All ready, Nancy? Then let us be off.'

A stranger was waiting for her in the entrance hall-way of the hotel, tall silk hat in hand, red rose in his buttonhole. 'Miss Martyn? Charles Standon, at your service. Lady Penelope and Lady Prudence are waiting in the carriage. Leo hoped you would not object to them acting as bridesmaids.' He grinned, a disarming smile that showed a gap between his front teeth. 'Frankly, I don't think he could have stopped them with a regiment of cavalry.'

'I am delighted that they wanted to be part of the ceremony,' Isobel said. And she was; it had been a concern that the girls would resent her, see her as a rival for Leo's attention.

They certainly seemed delighted when she settled in the seat opposite them with Mr Standon beside her. Nancy squeezed in opposite, next to the twins.

'Thank you for offering to be bridesmaids. And what pretty dresses. We have met before, I think, but only fleetingly.'

'Yes, ma'am,' the blonde one said. 'I'm Prudence, but everyone calls me Prue.'

'And I'm Penelope, ma'am. Penny,' her sister added.

'And I am Isobel. We are about to be cousins, are we not?'

They arrived at the doors of the chapel a few minutes later in perfect harmony with each other after mutual admiration of dresses and bonnets and Mr Standon's gallant compliments to all three of them.

He handed them down from the carriage, led them through the front doors and left them there for last-minute tidying of hair and skirts while he slipped through the inner doors into the chapel.

'All ready?' Isobel asked. She removed her gloves and exchanged them for the flowers Nancy held. The maid reached up and arranged her fine veil over the brim of her bonnet, then held open the doors and let them through.

It was not a very large chapel, so the two figures at the altar steps were very clear to her: Charles Standon, hastily brushing a hand through his hair and, next to him, tall and very still, Leo.

How often had she dreamt of walking down the aisle of a church towards him? The details of the building were always blurred in those dreams, the faces in the pews one pink mass, but Leo always looked the same, just as he did now. Focused, serious, very dear and achingly desirable.

What did he see when he looked back at her? An old friend? A convenient bride? A sensible choice for a man in a difficult position who had put duty before desire and common sense before the hopeless fantasy that the woman he loved might change her mind and discover that she had feelings for him, too?

At least Leo could not see her face clearly through the veil and recognise the struggle to keep the slight smile on her lips and the tears from her eyes.

The walk down the nave between the rows of empty box pews did not take long. There were some more modern open pews at the front and she saw two women sitting in the one to the right and another to the left with a gentleman behind her.

As Isobel came level she recognised Mrs Druett, the housekeeper from Havelock Hall, and next to her, Miss Pettigrew, the governess. The other lady she did not know, but, from her age and the way she was looking at Charles Standon, she must be his fiancée. In the pew behind was Mr Parkin, her new lawyer, who turned his sandy-grey head to watch as she passed.

And then she was at the altar steps and Leo turned to stand beside her to face the curate as she handed her flowers to the twins. Her knees were shaking, vibrating the hem of her gown. She stiffened them until they ached and focused all her attention on the minister.

The veil hid her blushes as he recited the reasons for marriage—the procreation of children and the avoidance of fornication for those who did not have the gift of continency. She could welcome the mutual society, help and comfort, though. No one leapt to their feet when he asked if there was any just cause to stop the marriage.

Isobel realised that she had been holding her breath, which was ridiculous. What had she expected? That Lucinda would appear in full bridal regalia to claim Leo, or that her cousins would arrive, full of protests?

The thought distracted her for a few seconds and then she heard Leo say, 'I will.'

The curate turned to her. 'Wilt thou have this man…?'

Now he had all her attention. 'I will.'

'Who giveth this woman to be married to this man?'

Isobel opened her mouth to say, *I do*, when two voices behind her chorused, 'We do!'

There was a ripple of laughter from the pews. Mr Standon snorted and hastily turned it into a cough and, beside her, she sensed Leo suppressing his own amusement. Even the curate's rather thin lips quirked into a smile as he reached for her right hand to place it in Leo's.

It was cold. She hadn't expected that. Leo always seemed warm, as though he radiated an inner glow of comfort. Perhaps he was as nervous as she was.

'I take thee, Isobel Frances Scott Martyn...' he said, his voice clear.

Then it was her turn. 'I take...' Her voice failed her and she swallowed hard. 'I take thee, Leo Augustus Gerald Havelock, to my wedded husband.'

The curate and Mr Standon made rather a business of handing over the ring, with Leo tense at her side until it was passed to him and then she sensed him relax as he took her hand again.

'With this ring,' he said and his hand was warm now and his voice steady.

'Let us pray,' the curate pronounced and she knelt, Leo steadying her, as she tried to concentrate on the words.

Almost there, almost at the point of no return.

The curate took their right hands and held them together. 'Those whom God hath joined together let no man put asunder.' There was more, but the blood was roaring in her ears now and she bit her lip hard, terrified that she might faint.

'I pronounce that they be Man and Wife together.'

They stood, still hand-clasped, and with his left hand Leo lifted the veil back over her bonnet. 'Well, Lady Halford?'

'Very well, Lord Halford.' It seemed it was possible to breathe and talk and even to walk, as she discovered when they were led to the vestry to sign the register.

Isobel Frances Scott Havelock, she managed without a blot under Leo's familiar and surprisingly legible scrawl.

Charles Standon, the young woman from the front pew—who was introduced as Lady Marietta Collingwood—and the twins, both biting their lower lips in fierce concentration, signed as witnesses.

It was done and everyone was talking at once as they formed up into a short procession with Leo and Isobel at the head, then the twins, then Mr Standon and Lady Marietta followed by Mr Parkin and finally Nancy, Miss Pettigrew and Mrs Druett.

They spilled out on to the pavement in the pale October sunshine. Leo and his best man shook hands with the curate, Miss Pettigrew called the twins to her and Mrs Druett hastened off in the direction of the house.

'I thought we could walk back as it is so pleasant. It is only a few steps, after all,' Leo was saying as Lady Marietta waved to a group gathered outside a shop almost opposite them across the road.

'Look, Charles, it is my cousin Anthea and the Duke.'

An elegant young matron in the midst of the gentlemen waved back and then the whole party crossed the road, calling out greetings as they came.

'Standon, old chap! And Havelock. Haven't seen you in town for months,' the tall man with Lady Marietta's cousin on his arm declared as he reached them. 'And what's afoot here? It looks like a wedding to me.'

'It is, my lord,' Mr Standon said, shaking hands. 'Let me introduce you. This is the just married Countess of Halford. Lady Halford, the Duke and Duchess of Northleigh. And Major Sir Thomas Eddington, oh, and Miss

Eddington—sorry, I didn't see you there, Tommy takes up so much room—and Lord Fitzmore and Mr Shardlake. You all know Halford, of course.'

Isobel shook hands in something of a daze, desperately trying to commit names to memory. Beside her she could hear Leo explaining that they had been planning a wedding, but then his great-aunt died and they decided to go ahead at once rather than wait out the mourning process. It sounded a little improbable to her, but everyone seemed to accept it readily enough.

Then she heard him say, 'We are on our way back to the house for some refreshments. Would you care to join us? It is just round the corner.'

What was he thinking? Six unexpected guests—and such high-ranking ones at that—and the house barely clean? She looked around and found Nancy waiting unobtrusively by the chapel door and beckoned to her. 'Nancy, run and let Mrs Druett and Cook know we are expecting six additional guests.'

She only hoped they could cope. Presumably, Mrs Druett had enough experience, but to offer poor hospitality to a duke and duchess was not the way to begin Isobel's career in London high society. Being a man, Leo probably assumed that dainty cakes and interesting savoury nibbles were conjured out of thin air somewhere below stairs.

She couldn't even be certain they'd have enough milk or bread and butter. Somehow she hadn't imagined that her wedding day would be quite like this: there had been many things to feel apprehensive about, but domestic crises had not been among them.

'There you are.' Leo took her arm and began to lead their impromptu wedding party along the pavement.

'They are all friends of yours?' Isobel asked, low-voiced.

'Yes, although Shardlake is more of an acquaintance.' Something about her lack of response must have alerted him because he added, 'You don't mind, do you? I thought it made it more of a celebration to have a small party.'

'No, of course not, it is delightful to meet your friends. I was just worrying about refreshments, but I have sent Nancy on ahead to warn Mrs Druett and Cook.'

'Lord, I didn't think of that.' Leo sounded almost comically alarmed. 'You don't think Cook will hand in her resignation, do you?'

'I would not blame either of them,' Isobel said. 'We have brought them up here at very short notice to a house that, for all the frantic scrubbing, must fall well short of their standards and now expect Cook to cater for a wedding party at five minutes' notice.'

'Presumably this also falls short of the standards expected of husbands,' Leo said ruefully. 'I forgot for a moment that I wasn't a bachelor any longer.' At which point his brain must have caught up with his tongue. 'I mean to say—'

'You mean that you are not used to being married yet,' Isobel said, finding that she was amused rather than hurt. 'I expect it takes longer than half an hour to become accustomed.'

'Forgiving woman.' He gave her hand that was tucked

under his elbow a squeeze. 'Look, there go Alfred and Henry.'

Two tall figures emerged from the basement area gate and set off up the road at a run. 'The footmen? What a good thing you don't expect them to wear powdered wigs and elaborate livery.'

'Couldn't have afforded it, even if I liked that kind of thing. I expect Cook has sent them to Gunter's. I just hope they can find a hackney to bring it all back.'

It did mean that the front door was opened by Finkle, and not a footman, but he was looking fairly respectable and Leo guided their guests into the drawing room without letting them linger in the shabby hall.

Nancy slipped through the door and whispered, 'Cook says she is going to send food up for a buffet so there will be a few plates at a time. She says to tell His Lordship she's put more champagne on ice and Finkle will bring wine up from the cellar and should she make tea as well?'

'Tell her, best to put the kettle on and give her my thanks for coping so well.'

She turned back to find Leo was addressing their guests who were disposed about the room, quite at their ease on the ill-assorted furniture. 'Of course, the proper way to go about it would have been to get this house into order before bringing my bride to it, instead of expecting her to make it civilised herself, but with Great-Aunt dying it just seemed so much simpler to marry as soon as possible. I tell myself that, as Isobel did not turn tail the moment she saw the state this place was in, the marriage has every chance of success.'

Everyone laughed, Finkle came in staggering slightly under the weight of an ice bucket and Isobel made her way across the room to sit between the Duchess and Lady Marietta.

'I remember you now,' the Duchess said. 'You had a Season—when was it? Three years ago?'

'Two Seasons. The second was four years ago. Then Papa died, the title passed to my cousin and I could not expect him and his wife to sponsor me for any more.'

'But you have known Leo for a long time, I think?'

'Oh, for years. We virtually grew up together and we are old friends, Your Grace.'

The Duchess laughed. 'Sometimes it takes men years to recognise what is right under their noses, bless them. But please, do not call me *Your Grace*. Every time someone does I look around nervously for my mother-in-law, the Dowager. My name is Anthea.'

'And I am Isobel.'

'And we are friends already, we must be, because I was a guest at the wedding, so you must call me Marietta,' Charles Standon's fiancée said. 'Do you know many ladies in London?'

'There are a few acquaintances from when I had my Seasons, but none of them are close. Certainly not close enough to invite to such an unconventional affair as this,' Isobel admitted. The Duchess, who was only a few years older than she was, might seem the very opposite of stuffy, but she was concerned that such a prominent figure might consider her fast, or undesirably eccentric.

'Well, now you have us and Chloe Eddington, too. We

will introduce you to everyone we think you will enjoy meeting and you will soon find your feet.'

'You are very kind,' Isobel ventured as Leo began to pour champagne and two breathless and slightly dishevelled footmen entered with the first platters of food.

'Leo is a dear friend of ours,' Anthea said. 'He was wonderful when my younger brother got himself into a most unpleasant situation with a card sharp and some quite terrifying moneylenders and the poor boy didn't dare admit it to Papa. And then Leo found himself burdened with his uncle's title and debts and quite vanished from London. We did so feel for him because he had to cope with a situation that was none of his making.'

'It has been hard for him,' Isobel admitted.

'But Lady Honoria was very wealthy, I believe,' Marietta said in a whisper. 'So everything is all right now?'

'I hope so,' Isobel said. 'Leo deserves some good luck.'

'He has you. And you have one of the handsomest husbands in London,' Anthea added as Leo directed one of the footmen to bring the tray of glasses over to them.

'You think so?' Isobel blinked a little. She had grown up with Leo, was as used to his face as she was to her own in the mirror. He was simply *Leo*. Of course he had a pleasing countenance, she knew that, but it had never occurred to think of him as handsome, exactly, let alone very much so. She loved him and she was coming to understand that she desired him, too, in a way she had never allowed herself to think about properly before.

Both women looked at her with expressions of exaggerated surprise, then Marietta laughed. 'You are teasing, of course. But I should warn you that you must be on your guard against all manner of ladies with roving eyes.'

'Really, Marietta! You should not suggest that a newly married man might be led astray, especially one as principled as Leo,' the Duchess chided.

'Of course he would not, any more than our men would: they love us and we trust them. But it still does not mean that they don't often need protection from encroaching females they are too much the gentleman to repulse. Do you remember the dreadful Mrs de Vere?'

Isobel hardly heard the anecdote—she was too busy trying to keep the smile on her lips. Of course a man in love would not stray, or even be tempted. But one who was *not* in love with his wife might seek to salve his wounded heart in the arms of someone glamorous and experienced...

Then she caught Leo's eye and he smiled at her with the affectionate warmth he had always shown her and she felt ashamed of herself. Leo was a gentleman, her loyal friend, and he would do nothing to hurt her. And she must show him affection in return, even if it risked revealing the depth of her feelings. What did shyness and embarrassment matter?

She smiled back and something of her thoughts must have shown, because his own gaze deepened and she felt a disturbing flutter inside, low down. Physical desire? She realised that she was blushing and he had seen that, too, and perhaps understood it.

Then he must have realised that they were staring at each other and ignoring their guests because he turned abruptly and began giving the footmen orders about setting out the platters of food as a buffet.

And she was neglecting her guests, too. Isobel stood up. 'I must circulate. Do come and help yourselves to some refreshments, unless you would prefer the gentlemen to bring a selection to you.'

'Certainly not.' Anthea was on her feet. 'They never bring enough of the things I prefer. Men seem to believe we exist on the occasional tiny sweetmeat and perhaps a slice of smoked salmon and I can see cheese puffs, if I am not mistaken.'

Isobel went to Miss Eddington, who was standing quietly beside her brother, not that she had much option as he and Mr Shardlake were deep in a discussion of horse breeding.

'Shall we select something to eat before the men descend upon the buffet, Miss Eddington?' she asked and was rewarded by a soft giggle.

'Thank you, Lady Halford.'

'Oh, do call me Isobel. I have no idea how long it will be before I answer to that title.'

'I am Chloe. My goodness, what a delicious spread. You must have a wonderful cook if they can produce this at such short notice.' She picked up a plate and made a beeline for the patties.

'It is all thanks to two very fleet-footed footmen and the fact that Gunter's is just around the corner.' Isobel realised that she was ravenous. Breakfast had been a cup of tea and a corner of toast she had barely nibbled at, her stomach tight with nerves.

She saw the twins standing at the side, hands folded,

meekly attending to their governess who had obviously told them to allow the guests access to the buffet before they could make their choices. 'Prue, Penny, come and help yourselves. And, Miss Pettigrew, please join us.'

With laden plates they retreated to a group of chairs and sofas at the other end of the room and Isobel gestured to the footmen. 'Champagne for everyone. Yes, Miss Pettigrew, you, too, and I think the twins deserve to try it, if only one small glass.'

She raised her glass to her little circle of new-found friends and saw Leo watching her from across the room. He lifted his glass and held her eyes for a long moment, his gaze darkly intent and, as clearly as if she could read his mind, she knew he was thinking about their wedding night.

Chapter Eight

An hour later the volume of conversation in the room had risen, everyone had stopped eating, Alfred and Henry were still pouring wine and Isobel's thoughts were an unsettling mix of desire, nerves, anticipation and uncertainty, all fuelled by champagne.

The twins, who had sipped at their wine with wrinkled noses at the bubbles, were drinking lemonade and interrogating Chloe Eddington, whose pet Italian greyhound had just had a litter: Isobel foresaw a request for at least one puppy in the near future. The men had pulled up chairs into the ladies' circle and a series of conversations were in progress, cutting across each other and mingling with delightful informality.

Sorting through her feelings, Isobel found that, despite everything, she was happy. How much of that was due to the wine she was not certain, but the friendliness of her new acquaintances helped and so did seeing how at ease Leo looked. He was too much the gentleman to appear anything but pleased in any social situation, of course, but she knew him well enough to be certain that he was not fighting an inward sadness that this was not his wedding day to Lucinda. That look he had sent her…

The Duchess was just in the middle of telling her about the problems she had experienced trying to find just the right furniture for their redecorated drawing room when there was the sound of someone pounding on the knocker.

'I wonder who that can be,' Isobel said, turning on the sofa to look towards the door. It opened to reveal a somewhat flustered Alfred.

'Lord and Lady Martyn, my lady,' he announced, then had to skip to one side as Cousin Amelia sailed into the room, Edward right behind her. They stopped dead and stared about them.

Isobel stood up, but Leo was before her. He strode towards them, hand held out. 'Cousin Amelia, Cousin Edward, for I feel I can address you so now. Welcome,' he added heartily. 'Do come in. How fortunate, you are just in time for tea.'

Isobel nodded vigorously at Alfred, who signalled his comprehension and went out.

'Do come and sit over here, Cousins,' she said. 'The girls will not mind moving, will you?'

Penny and Prue, with one look at Cousin Amelia's set expression, jumped to their feet and moved to sit with Miss Pettigrew who, despite encouragement to join in the conversation, had found a quiet corner and was working on her tatting.

Isobel, with the vague feeling that this was rather like lion taming and that she would be all right provided she did not let her guard down, kissed her cousins on their cheeks and gestured to the sofa. 'Now, do you know everyone?' She did not wait for a reply, but hurried into the introductions. 'Your Grace, my I present my cousins, Lord and Lady Martyn? Amelia, Edward: the Duke and Duchess of Northleigh. Lord Fitzmore, Major Sir Thomas Eddington and Miss Eddington...'

There were enough people in the room for the business to take several minutes, at which point the tea tray was brought in. With any luck, she thought, pouring with an almost steady hand, her cousins would have had time to realise they could not make a scene, not in front of some of the cream of London society.

'How delightful that you were able to get away,' she said to Amelia. 'Where are you staying? Oh, Brown's? I hear that is most comfortable.' She had never heard of the hotel, but prattled on, ably assisted by her new friends who had clearly recognised a tricky situation and were exerting themselves to be amiable.

Behind her she could hear Leo finishing his introductions to Edward. 'And this is Mr Parkin, Isobel's man of law.'

She could not turn around to stare, but Edward seemed to be making odd gobbling sounds.

'Delighted to meet you, Lord Martyn,' the lawyer said smoothly. 'And doubly so because this will save me a journey into Kent. I trust I may call on you tomorrow? I am sure you will welcome the opportunity to relinquish the burden of acting as Lady Halford's trustee as soon as possible.'

'Yes, of course. Tiresome business, but one's duty,'

Edward said pompously. 'However, I fear you will have to come down to Little Bitterns as I do not travel with all the paperwork.'

'You did not anticipate this meeting, Lord Martyn?' Isobel wondered whether Mr Parkin ever prosecuted in court.

'We were taken aback by the suddenness of the affair,' Edward said. 'Most unsettling, don't you know?'

'Yes, it must be. When do you expect to return home, my lord?'

'Oh, a week or so. Lady Martyn will wish to make calls, go shopping.'

'Of course. I will make a note to do myself the honour of calling upon you in a fortnight, then. Good day, Lord Martyn, Lord Halford.' He came around to say goodbye to Isobel, who shook hands and thanked him warmly.

Beside her, Amelia stiffened. 'What a *pushing* sort of man,' she said.

'Just doing his duty, as dear Cousin Edward has,' Isobel said with a smile that hid inward concerns. She was beginning to wonder just why Edward was sounding quite so defensive. Surely he had no concerns about his stewardship? He was not the most efficient of men, she suspected. Perhaps his records were somewhat slapdash.

The lawyer's departure seemed to act as a signal for the rest of their guests, or perhaps most of them realised that it was now almost four in the afternoon and they had set out that day with no intention of attending a wedding breakfast.

'We will leave our cards,' the Duchess said as she

kissed Isobel's cheek. 'I'll write my At Home days on mine: you must call very soon.'

When the front door closed Isobel looked around to see an almost empty room. Miss Pettigrew had removed the twins, the footmen had whisked away the remains of the buffet and only her cousins remained, sitting stiffly side by side on the sofa.

Leo caught her eye, raising his eyebrows in silent question, but then she heard the Duke's voice from the hall. It seemed they had not all gone yet. 'I say, Halford, can I just have a word about—?' Leo closing the door cut off the rest of the question.

'Well, what on earth do you think you are about, Isobel?' Amelia demanded.

'Getting married. I am of age and I am free to do so.'

'Without a word to us!'

'I wanted no fuss and botheration.' Isobel hung on to her temper. They did, after all, have good reason to feel affronted. 'Leo and I acted impulsively.'

'Impulsively? You caught the man when he was in a vulnerable state—oh, yes, it is all over the village that Lucinda Paxton turned him down and very right, too. With her looks she can do much better than marry a penniless man, even if he has a title. Whatever possessed you?'

'Why, his title, of course,' Isabel shot back. 'I married him to become a countess and perhaps he married me for my money.'

'Why, you shameless hussy—' Edward began to say.

She had not heard the door behind them open, but the sudden waft of air on her nape made her look around to see Leo standing there. Edward closed his mouth with a snap.

'Lord Martyn, I must insist that you treat my wife, my *Countess*, with the respect due to her or leave our house,' Leo said, his voice chilly.

They all stared at him. Isobel had never heard him sound like that—an aristocrat standing upon his rank— and then she realised it was not pride and privilege speaking, but that he was protecting her, demonstrating to her cousin, a mere baron, that she was no longer his pensioner, his poor relation.

Amelia was white with anger, two red circles burning on her cheeks, but Edward was immediately conciliatory. 'Oh, quite, quite. It is just that it was such a shock for us. Such a potential scandal.'

'Then I suggest that when you return to the village that you lay any gossip to rest. I am certain that mentioning the names of some of our guests this afternoon will soon demonstrate that there is nothing underhand going on.

'And now I believe that Isobel must be very weary and in need of a rest. We look forward to calling upon you when we return to Little Bitterns. The restoration of the estates must be our next concern once all is settled here.'

He stood by the door and her cousins got to their feet and went, stiff-backed, to leave. She heard him say something, perhaps to a footman, then Leo came back into the room. As he shut the door, she just caught Amelia's penetrating whisper, 'But where are they getting the money?' and then the front door shut.

'My poor Izzy. That was not the quiet wedding we planned,' Leo said. He came and sat beside her and took her hand in his.

'It was very enjoyable, I thought, right up until my cousins arrived. Although at least that encounter is over now and not looming somewhere in the future.' Somehow Isobel found she was leaning against him. She stiffened for a moment then relaxed against him, her head on his shoulder. 'This is pleasant, being alone again, though.'

'I think so, too.' His arms came around her and he bent his head so their lips were only an inch apart. 'It occurs to me that I have not yet kissed my bride.'

'We did before. I wasn't very good at it,' she said, trying to sound teasing.

'Noses are there to be negotiated,' Leo said. 'If I do this, and you—yes, you do that—and then—' His lips met hers and began to move, gently exploring.

Breathe, Isobel, she told herself and tried to relax, although it was difficult when Leo seemed to be trying to slide his tongue between her lips.

Although that was surprisingly pleasant, she realised with a shock, opening a little to give him access. He tasted of champagne and something that made her blood fizz in her veins even more than the wine.

Leo raised his head and sat back, leaving her breathless. He still held her against him, but the embrace was no longer charged with that dangerous edge of excitement. It was dear Leo, her old friend, who held her now.

Leo leaned back in the sofa, his arms full of the warmth and soft, rose-scented sweetness of his wife.

Wife. Izzy.

They had just kissed and the effect shocked him. He had expected it to be pleasant, a trifle embarrassing, because, after all, this was Izzy. Instead, he was aroused and aching with physical need. And damnably confused.

He was in love with Lucinda and he should desire only her. No. He smiled wryly at his own stupidity as Izzy's curls tickled his chin. He was male, he had been without female…companionship for several months and now his arms were full of a woman who was responding to his kisses. Of course he felt desire.

So, this was not confusion, this was guilt. He felt he was betraying Lucinda. And that was ridiculous because she had refused him, did not want him and if every unsuccessful suitor spent the rest of his life in monk-like celibacy, then there would be far fewer human beings on earth.

Leo did his best to logically follow his train of thought while Izzy curled up more comfortably on the sofa beside him and appeared to go to sleep. Typically, she did not appear to have a care for the state of her very expensive skirts, crumpled under her.

He had made certain vows that morning, among them, *With my body, I thee worship,* so it seemed he had a duty to get on with worshipping and it was merely wallowing in his own disappointment over Lucinda to try to talk himself out of enjoying the process.

But how did Izzy see this? It was not as though she was unaware of his feelings for Lucinda. Would she assume he was merely doing his duty? Or worse, that he was imagining that it was another woman in bed with him? It would be so very easy to get this wrong, because the first time was bound to be a shock for any innocent young lady and any emotional clumsiness on his part could leave lasting scars.

He should take it slowly, he decided. Izzy needed to realise that he valued her, that, even if he was not romantically in love with her, he wanted to make love to her for herself, not because she was his wife or because he was a man who needed a physical release. Which he did, he thought ruefully as a soft breast pressed against his waistcoat. He must court her.

'Izzy.'

'Mmm? Yes?' She sat up. 'Oh, my goodness, look at my dress.'

'That is why I woke you. Nancy is not going to be best pleased trying to get the creases out of that fabric,' he observed as she stood up and tried to shake the worst out of the silk. 'Why not go and change into something more comfortable? Then we can order dinner and spend some time planning what we want to do for the next few days.'

Out of bed, he reminded himself.

They went upstairs together, into their shared sitting room and then parted, he to the left and his bedchamber, she to the right and hers.

'You need a valet,' Izzy said, turning back with her hand on the door. 'How are you going to get out of that coat?'

'I'll ring for a footman,' he said hastily before she

offered to help. Being undressed by his wife was an experience that must most definitely wait.

Leo watched the graceful figure as she went through the door and stood for several seconds after it had closed.

The state of her skirts—anyone would think she had been rolling around on the sofa with a lover.

He let himself into his own bedchamber and fought his way out of the tight-fitting coat without help. He needed some time alone while his body calmed down.

Isobel submitted to Nancy's tutting as the maid helped her out of the gown, then surveyed her wardrobe for something that might be both comfortable and suitable for the first evening alone with one's husband.

'You need to do some shopping, my lady,' Nancy said.

'I know. I suppose this gown will do for now.' It was a simple evening dress of fine cream wool that she usually changed into for dinner when there were no guests. It wasn't fashionable and it wasn't particularly pretty either, but then she wasn't setting out to seduce her husband.

Yet, a small voice whispered in her head. She did her best to ignore it. What did she know about seduction?

'The hot water for your bath is on its way, my lady. And then I will do your hair, my lady,' Nancy said.

Isobel suspected that she was saying 'my lady' at every opportunity. Whether that was to get used to it or whether she was revelling in the status that she now enjoyed as lady's maid to the titled mistress of the house, she wasn't certain.

The bath was relaxing, or would have been if she had let herself lie there and soak, but it was soothing to have all the pins removed from the carefully formal style that she had worn all day. Nancy brushed it all out, making a straight, sleek fall. It always looked its best when loose, its lack of curl making it resistant to attempts to style it, but a grown lady could not go about with her hair down.

Nancy began to plait and then left it over Isobel's shoulder, a burnished brown rope. She tied it with a dark yellow ribbon. 'There, my lady. That will be comfortable and the plait might make some waves if we leave it in tonight.'

Reflected in the mirror, Isobel saw the blush stain the maid's cheeks when she realised what she was saying. 'Er…not that it matters if it comes loose.'

'No, of course not. Thank you, Nancy. You go and relax and enjoy your dinner.'

They walked into the sitting room together and stopped to survey it by candlelight. 'That has got to go,' Isobel said, pointing.

'What's wrong?' Leo came out of his room dressed in what looked like more comfortable trousers and a less fashionable coat.

'Oh, Leo, I didn't hear you there. Are you very attached to this painting? It isn't by someone terribly famous, is it? Only this room is so dark and depressing and it really does not help the atmosphere.' Isobel waved one hand at the gloomy still life of a pile of dead game birds that hung between the windows.

Their bedchambers were one each side of the frontage of the house with the small sitting room with its two narrow windows in between, over the entrance hall. It was certainly not somewhere anyone might feel tempted to linger as it was now.

'I am not at all attached to that picture and it can go off to the auction rooms tomorrow,' he said.

'Then may I redecorate this room? I thought it would make a pleasant retreat for both of us away from the more formal reception rooms downstairs. I won't make it frilly and feminine, I promise.'

'You may do what you wish with the entire house,' Leo declared expansively.

'Then I will make plans and consult you,' Isobel said. 'I would not wish to spend more than you approve. And, of course, I would not dream of interfering with your library or bedchamber.'

She felt herself blush as she said it.

Leo turned and strode back into his room. 'I've forgotten my watch. I will be with you directly.'

When Leo emerged again Isobel was waiting for him in the little sitting room. The fire had been lit and there was a stack of paintings, their faces to the wall, in one corner.

'When I looked at them they were all depressing,' she said.

'We can amuse ourselves over the next few days surveying all the paintings and then we will summon Mr Christie, who I am sure will be glad to offer them at his auction house. Shall we stay up here this evening now they have gone and the fire is lit? There is a table that we can take dinner at.'

'I'm not certain I can eat very much,' Isobel confessed. Her stomach seemed to be full of very acrobatic butterflies.

'That was a very good buffet,' Leo agreed tactfully. 'I went down to the kitchen to thank everyone for their efforts and Cook says there is a considerable amount left over. I thought we could just have a light meal from that—there is plenty for the staff as well and it will save them work.'

'What a good idea.' Isobel rang for a maid, gave her orders for supper, then tried the sofa and both armchairs. 'These are surprisingly comfortable.' She chose an armchair and curled up in it, kicking off her slippers.

Leo took the one opposite. He was wearing a handsome brocade robe in shades of amber and brown over his shirt and loose trousers and he leaned back with a sigh. 'This is pleasant. Shall we make plans? Miss Pettigrew sent a message to say that she and the girls are taking their dinner in the breakfast room and will then retire to what she calls the schoolroom. That does not sound very enjoyable: I must make certain they have a comfortable retreat of their own.'

'I agree. But what plans had you in mind?'

'We need plans for everything,' Leo said expansively. 'For the house, for the Hall, for the girls, for our entertainment, for all the shopping I am certain you want to do. My head is buzzing with ideas.'

'That sounds like old times.' Isobel wriggled more comfortably into the corner of the chair, suddenly relaxed. This was the old familiar Leo, her friend. Full of schemes and ideas, eagerly wanting to drag her along with him, however hare-brained the exploit or expedition proved to be. 'I have lots of thoughts, too. You first.' On a sudden thought, she jumped up, went into her bedchamber and found a notebook and pencil.

'Lists,' she said as she came back. 'A grand plan.'

Chapter Nine

The clock on the mantel struck ten as Isobel stifled a yawn. The warmth of the fire, the glasses of wine, the relaxed, informal meal all made her eyelids droop. It had been a long, long day.

But she must stay awake. Very awake, she told herself guiltily. This was her wedding night. The yawn turned into a gulp.

'Time for bed,' Leo said. He got up from the hearth rug where he had been sprawled, his back propped up against her armchair, and held out his hands. 'You look ready to fall asleep,' he observed as she let herself be pulled to her feet.

'Oh, no,' Isobel protested. 'It is just a little warm,'

'Liar,' Leo said amiably, leading her towards her bedchamber door.

'I—'

'Goodnight, Izzy, and thank you.' He bent and kissed her, his hands on her waist drawing her close against the thick silk of his robe.

She kissed back tentatively, hoping she was doing

it properly, wanting to lean in, wrap her arms around him. Then what he had said struck her. 'Goodnight? Aren't you—? I mean, you are—'

'I am seeing you to bed and then I am retiring to my own room,' Leo said. He stepped back a little, but his hand left her waist to take hold of her heavy plait, running his palm down it. It seemed to her that he was controlling his breathing. 'It has been a long day and this is all very new to both of us, being together in this way. We have spoken of this—there is no need to rush into things, Izzy.'

'Yes, of course.' Why did the gentle tug on her hair feel as though something deep inside her was tugging, too, sending heat and a pulsing ache low down in her belly? 'Goodnight then, Leo.'

They stood there, her hand on his forearm, his still stroking her hair, then Leo released her and stepped back. He swirled the open robe around himself in an almost theatrical gesture. 'Sleep well, Izzy. Sweet dreams.' He reached past her, opened the door, and she stepped through.

The bedchamber was empty, but the fire was crackling in the grate and the shabby curtains were drawn tight against the darkness.

Isobel closed the door behind her, walked slowly to the bed and stood looking down at it. Her marriage bed. Her empty marriage bed. Was she relieved or disappointed? She simply did not know, nor why Leo was being so…considerate? Or was it that he could not face lying with a woman who was not Lucinda?

Whatever the reason, she had her pride and she was

not going to admit to anyone that she would be alone on her wedding night. She tugged the bell pull and Nancy came, bringing with her a ewer of hot water.

'I wish we'd thought to buy you a nicer nightgown,' she lamented, shaking out Isobel's plain and practical cotton gown. 'And a lovely robe.'

But she cheered up when Isobel's hair was released from its plait. 'There's a wave in it, look.'

It would fall out by morning, Isobel knew, but she kept a smile on her lips and let Nancy fuss about, dabbing scent behind her ears and plumping up the pillows.

When she finally let herself out with a demure, 'Sleep well, my lady', Isobel got into bed and tossed and turned on both sides, denting the pillows and doing her best to make it look as though two people had occupied it. Then she blew out the candles, settled down, pulled the covers up over her shoulders and prepared for a long, sleepless night.

'Good morning, my lady.'

The curtains came open with a rattle of brass rings, flooding the room with sunshine. Isobel sat up, rubbed her eyes and blinked at it. It took her a moment to remember where she was.

'What time is it, Nancy?'

'Half past nine, my lady. His Lordship said to let you sleep. Would you like your breakfast on a tray in bed, or will you get up?'

Half past nine? Isobel realised that she must have fallen asleep almost as soon as she had closed her eyes. And she could not recall any dreams.

'What is His Lordship doing?'

'Oh, he was up early. He went for a ride after only a cup of coffee, my lady, and he has just got back. I think he's in his bedchamber changing his clothes.'

'Then I will get up now and we will both take breakfast in the sitting room,' she said. 'There is a great deal to do today. Shopping for clothes is the most important.'

Leo was reading the newspaper when she came out of her room, but he tossed it aside and jumped to his feet. 'Good morning, Izzy.' The kiss on her cheek was, she thought with an inward sigh, perfectly brotherly. 'What would you like to do today?'

'Buy clothes and shoes and hats,' she said firmly. 'I feel a complete dowd. And you?'

'I have decided that I need a valet, a secretary and, like you, clothes.'

'A secretary?'

'There is so much that needs doing,' he explained as the footmen came in with breakfast. 'There's work to order on the house, correspondence between here and the Hall, social affairs—which reminds me, the first thing I must do is compose a notice announcing our marriage. We need someone to keep hold of all the details or we will be run ragged.'

'How does one find a secretary?' Isobel began to pour coffee. At least, after so many years she knew that Leo liked it without sugar and with just a drop of milk. It made her feel quite wifely.

'Thank you.' He took the cup, set it down and began to lift covers off platters. 'Excellent, beefsteak as well as sausages and bacon.' He grinned at Isobel's shudder and helped her to the bacon and egg that she indicated. 'A valet I can enquire for at the domestic agency, but I think I will see if the Duke has any recommendations for a secretary. A younger son of good family is what we need. Someone organised, intelligent and discreet.'

'I had better consider furnishing a room for him, in that case. It needs to be made comfortable so he can use it as a sitting room as well.' Isobel reached for her notes and added, *Secretary's room*. 'Will you be home for luncheon?' Yes, she was definitely sounding wifely. She would get used to it in a while, she supposed, but just at the moment it made her want to giggle.

Then she looked across the small round table at Leo buttering toast and felt the familiar jolt under her breastbone. A wife and not a wife. He showed no signs of having passed a restless night or of suffering from frustrated desire, however that would show itself. Perhaps tonight he would decide she was rested sufficiently and they could begin married life in reality. This felt rather like make-believe.

Even shopping felt unreal. When she had made her come-out, her late aunt Maude had supervised her wardrobe and her personal spending had been limited to buying handkerchiefs and scented soap with her pin money. Now, with ample funds and no one to please but herself, she was free among the best shops the capital could provide.

She began with Madame Claire, because the sooner she ordered her gowns, the better. She emerged from the fitting rooms, Nancy at her heels carrying a swatch of fabric samples to match shoes and bonnets to, when she realised that there were other clients in the outer shop.

Three young ladies turned as she entered the room. 'Oh, my goodness, Isobel Martyn. Why, I never imagined I would see *you* here.' It was, Isobel realised with a sinking sense of inevitability, Lucinda Paxton.

'Good morning, Miss Paxton. I am puzzled by your surprise, given that you recommended this establishment to me,' Isobel said with a determined smile. 'And it is Isobel Havelock now.'

'Oh, yes, I quite forgot. Poor Leo must have been in sad need of consolation to have married so quickly.'

'Yes, it was distressing to lose his great-aunt, even though she was a considerable age,' Isobel said earnestly. 'I hope I can be of some support to him during the mourning period, as I was saying to the Duchess of Northleigh at our wedding breakfast.'

It was very naughty of her to imply that the Duke and Duchess had been guests at the church, let alone name dropping in such a vulgar way, but it wiped the smug smile from Lucinda's pretty lips and that was deeply gratifying.

'That was not what I meant,' Lucinda snapped. Her friends looked at her in some surprise and she added sweetly, 'I had heard he has recently been disappointed in love.'

A number of unpleasantly violent thoughts passed through Isobel's mind, but she laughed instead of upending the contents of the nearest flower vase over Lucinda's pretty Villager bonnet. That would wipe the smirk off her lips and those ringlets would go stringy and drip…

'Oh, these men! They do flit from lady to lady like bees after nectar until they find the one that suits, don't they?' she said to Lucinda's two companions. 'Of course, in the process they have narrow escapes, such as discovering the lady they admire is nothing but an empty-headed female thinking only of wealth and title rather than character.'

At which point Madame Claire came through from the back of the shop, all her attention on Isobel. 'The first items in your order will be delivered next week, Lady Halford, and the rest as soon as may be. Naturally the Court dress will take a little longer, but the embroiderers will make a start immediately.' She opened the door for Isobel herself, saying as she did so, 'Miss Perkins, attend to these ladies, if you please.'

'Well done, my lady,' Nancy said as they paused on the pavement. 'That put her nose out of joint, the little cat.'

She really ought to snub her maid for making such an observation. Instead, she said, 'It was that or tip a flower arrangement over her. Of course, if it were not for the fact that I am so plain she would not be so aggravated. Hats next, I think. There are two addresses in Bond Street that were given me yesterday. We can easily walk from here.'

'Plain, my lady?' Nancy hurried in her wake. 'You aren't plain. Elegant, that's what you are, ma'am, with real class. And you will be when you are eighty, whereas Miss Blue Eyes there will be stout like her mama—and double chins don't go with pert little noses like that.'

'Nancy, really!' Isobel chided as she found a few coppers to give to the crossing sweeper who was clearing the way for them to cross Piccadilly. But she was smiling. What a cheering image. And was she really elegant? Certainly she did not find that fuss and frills suited her.

Even so, she felt slightly queasy in the aftermath of that encounter. It had been unpleasant because it was always upsetting to encounter spite, but it also reminded her about Leo's feelings. What would he have thought if he could have overheard Lucinda? That he had had a fortunate escape, perhaps.

With the milliner's—four hats ordered to be trimmed to match the fabric samples Nancy produced—behind them they found shoe shops and a delightful emporium selling underwear of the finest linen and silk, exquisitely embroidered. It also had nightgowns and wrappers and frivolous little slippers to match. Isobel decided that even if Leo did not want to share her bed, she could still enjoy wearing beautiful fabrics.

They explored further, finding shoes and dress lengths for Nancy, handkerchiefs, shawls, umbrellas and finally arriving in St James's Street at a chemist and perfumier's where Isobel indulged herself with Castile soap, oils for the bath and dusting powders.

Nancy followed behind her, heaping sponges and back brushes, hair brushes, pins and combs into the hands of the assistant.

'Oh, and choose soap for yourself, Nancy,' Isobel said, making the assistant's eyes gleam as he totted up the total. She showed him Leo's card. 'Have it all delivered to this address and the account sent to my husband.'

'I must have some cards printed,' she told Nancy as they left. 'That will be a task for Lord Halford's new secretary, when he finds someone suitable.'

Leo was at home when Isobel returned, footsore and very ready for her luncheon. He was going to spend the afternoon at home interviewing valets and writing to friends to see if they could recommend anyone for the post of secretary.

'Why not ask about a librarian and archivist at the same time?' Isobel said, buttering bread to go with the soup and cold meats laid out in the dining room.

'A good idea. I keep forgetting I can afford such luxuries,' he said with a grin. 'And what about you? More shopping?'

'I shall wait until what I have ordered is delivered and assess what is still needed then, as far as clothes are concerned. Things for the house I would like to choose with you. I thought I would call on the Duchess this afternoon—it is one of her At Home days. I could take the twins with me: they are old enough now to begin making calls. Are they in?'

'They are upstairs eating with Miss Pettigrew. I believe they had lessons this morning.'

'Perhaps they should have breakfast and luncheon with us and occasional dinners. I'm not sure it helps girls being pitched straight from the schoolroom into their first Season without social skills.'

She thought there was a faint frown on his face,

quickly gone. 'Unless you object, of course.' Surely Leo did not want to have endless meals tête-à-tête with her?

'Yes, of course. We are a family now,' he said readily. She must have imagined that look of what? Disappointment?

'And I must take them shopping for clothes as well. Oh, and Leo—beds.'

'Bed?' He dropped his knife.

'Beds. Mattresses, I mean,' she said as he bent to retrieve his cutlery from the floor. 'I think it would be best to replace them all, including on all the servants' beds. Goodness knows how old these ones are. And I realised this morning that I need calling cards, I cannot keep using yours.'

'Finding an efficient secretary must be a priority,' Leo said. 'My head is spinning. What is it, Izzy? You look as though another thought has struck you.'

'Oh, it is nothing. Just something else for our endless lists.' She had been within a breath of telling him that she had encountered Lucinda. Not about their acid exchange of barbs, of course, but she ought to warn him that Miss Paxton was in town.

Or should she? There was every chance that they would not encounter each other and the less Leo thought about Lucinda, the better, surely? No, she would say nothing, even if it felt a trifle cowardly.

Isobel informed Miss Pettigrew that she and the girls would be taking breakfast and luncheon with herself and Leo, other arrangements allowing, and then gave the governess the afternoon off. At first she had thought that dismissing Miss Pettigrew—with excellent references and assistance with finding another post, of course—would be best. Now she was beginning to think that retaining her and employing tutors for music, drawing and watercolour and languages might be better. The twins had experienced enough upheaval in their lives and Miss Pettigrew was a kindly and familiar presence.

'Have you paid morning calls before?' she asked when they had settled in the carriage.

They shook their heads. 'Well, only at the vicarage,' Penny said. 'I don't understand why they are called morning calls when we are going in the afternoon.'

'I think it is from the last century when dinner was in the mid-afternoon, so calls made before dinner were morning calls,' Isobel said. 'But I am not certain I am correct. Anyway, if the lady we call on is at home and receiving, the butler will announce us. If she is not, then I will leave my card. Or Leo's, with the corner turned down, because I haven't got my own yet.'

'And we stay just half an hour. I know that,' Prue announced.

'Now, you will be the youngest people there, so you do not speak until you are spoken to and, if other ladies come in while we are there, you stand up.' They nodded, looking a little daunted by all this information. 'And try to recall everyone's names and anything they say about their families. Then, if you meet them again you will make a good impression by greeting them properly and you can enquire politely about their grandson in the navy, or their daughter's recovery from the measles.'

They still seemed rather subdued. 'You will be making your come-outs in just a few years. The more people you know in London, and the more comfortable you are with meeting new people and learning how to behave, the more you will enjoy yourselves.'

'Did you enjoy your come-out, Isobel?' Prue asked.

'Not very much,' she admitted. 'But that was because I knew no one and I missed everyone at home.' *Especially Leo.* 'That is why I want to introduce you to society gently.'

It seemed they could see the sense in that and they began to look less apprehensive. 'I thought of adding some more lessons—music and sketching and painting. Dancing and Italian, perhaps. You learn piano and French with Miss Pettigrew, don't you? You could try the guitar or the harp.'

They were wide-eyed with excitement by the time the carriage reached the Duchess's front door and Isobel realised that they must have been bored and sad, and not naughty as Leo had thought when he said they were running rings around their governess.

'I will see what I can arrange, but say nothing to Miss Pettigrew until I have spoken to her. We do not want her feeling that she no longer has a place.'

The groom opened the carriage door and helped them down. 'Which of you is the elder?' Isobel asked.

'I am, by three minutes,' Prue said.

As a result, when the butler announced them, it was as, 'Lady Halford, Lady Prudence Havelock and Lady Penelope Havelock, Your Grace.'

The girls were exceptionally well behaved: polite,

quiet but not shy and very willing to hand teacups around the six ladies already seated with the Duchess.

'You did very well,' Isobel told them as they drove back. 'I am sure we will have many of those ladies call on us and several of them have daughters of your age. You will soon make friends. And the Duchess has promised to send me a list of tutors she can recommend.'

They thanked her when they arrived back at Mount Street and ran upstairs, promising to write a list in their diaries of everyone they had met.

Isobel found Leo in the drawing room. He got to his feet as she entered and came and kissed her, but on the cheek, to her disappointment.

'Did you have a good afternoon?'

He listened while she told him about it and agreed with her about the additional tuition for the twins. 'I am sure you are correct and they have merely been bored and not stretched enough.' The warmth of his smile made her toes curl. 'I knew you would be good for them.'

And for you? she longed to ask, and then thought, *Say something. Perhaps Leo finds this as awkward as you do.*

'Leo, tell me—'

Chapter Ten

At the last moment her nerve failed her. 'Tell me about your afternoon, Leo.'

'Good news. I have a valet,' he announced. 'Basil Bertram, aged twenty-seven. He was with Lord Teddington, but Teddington was killed in a riding accident last month. Bertram has excellent references and he can start tomorrow.'

'It feels as though our new life is beginning to knit together,' Isobel said. 'I never imagined it would be like this when I suggested—we suggested—that we marry.'

'What did you imagine?'

Leo moved from his armchair to sit beside her on the sofa and she turned to him, finding the teasing words came easily. 'Oh, that it would be like one of our childhood adventures. We would run away together to London, where the streets are paved with gold, as everyone knows. We would find the treasure at the end of the rainbow and everything would be all right.'

'We found the treasure, even if it was rather boringly

stored in the bank, and everything *will* be all right, won't it?' he asked, smiling down at her.

'Yes, but there are so many other people involved now—the twins, Miss Pettigrew, an ever-increasing household, all my new acquaintances...'

'And that is a bad thing? I suppose we did not do it correctly. We should have wrapped our possessions in red spotted handkerchiefs and walked to London accompanied by our faithful cat or dog and listened for the bells of the City ringing for us, as Dick Whittington did. But I suppose, even then, we would find ourselves in this situation eventually.'

'You are right and we did do it the best way, and soon everything will be under control and not feel so strange. It is just that I... I want to be a good wife, Leo, and there seems to be so much of everything to deal with.'

'I think that you are already a good wife,' Leo said. 'All I want is for you to be happy, Izzy.'

Then why will you not make me fully your wife? she wanted to say. *Go on, ask him, now.*

'Leo.' She looked up into his eyes. 'I   '

And he kissed her.

Isobel sank back into the cushions, taking him with her. This time their noses did not bump and their bodies seemed to move in unison. She opened her lips to him as his mouth sought hers, his weight shifted on her and she felt a thrill of sensation as his chest pressed against her breasts and his thigh settled at the junction of hers. It was all strange and uncomfortable and she could hardly breathe, but she did not want it to stop.

* * *

She was no longer shy with him, Leo realised, carried away with the soft warmth of Izzy's surrender, the cautious trust of her tongue learning to caress his. She wanted him, or, at least, she wanted his kisses, because he was not at all sure whether she was fully aware of what would follow when they went to bed together. She had no mother, no sisters, and he could not imagine any young woman wanting to settle down to an intimate talk about marriage with Lady Martyn.

He had been right not to go to her last night, to give her time to become accustomed, he decided through an increasing fog of desire. Although perhaps it still needed a little more time for her to become used to these liberties, he thought, as she stiffened under him and then sighed as his palm grazed across her breast.

It was going to take a strong will to be patient, Leo realised. His body was clamouring for more and his imagination was filling with visons of long pale limbs and soft brown curls. He must stop this soon, or his dear friend was going to lose her virginity on a lumpy, dusty old sofa.

But just one minute more…

The drawing room door opened with a creak, there was a sharp intake of breath and then it closed with a slam.

Leo sat up abruptly, Izzy's eyes opened wide.

'What was that?'

'Someone came in.' Of course, he should have thought. In any genteel household the staff would quietly enter the public rooms without knocking, on the assumption that nothing would occur in those places that required privacy. His study, the bedchambers or a lady's boudoir were a different matter, but this was the drawing room and they were exceedingly fortunate that it had not been a footman announcing a visitor.

Izzy scrambled into a sitting position, tugging at her skirts and bodice. Her cheeks were scarlet and she did not meet his eyes. 'What…what did they see?'

'My back,' Leo said firmly. 'That is all. And a man is perfectly entitled to kiss his wife in their own drawing room if he wants to.'

'Yes, of course.' Izzy was ramming hair pins back as though they had personally offended her. 'I'll just go and—and do something with my hair. Will I— Will you be at home for dinner?'

Did she not want him to be? Leo wondered. As though he would dream of dining out one night after their wedding. 'Yes, certainly I will.'

'I will ask the girls and Miss Pettigrew to join us in that case. It will be good for them to talk about their first morning call.'

And it will mean that we are not dining intimately, right next door to our bedchambers, Leo realised.

Yes, it was far too early to progress beyond kisses.

He opened the door for Izzy, who left with the definite air of a woman escaping, and went back to the armchair to brood on the last hectic five minutes. It did him no good, except to stir his mounting physical frustration, but one thing was clear: when he was with Izzy his fantasies were all of her, not another smaller, curvier, blonder woman. It was strange, shaming perhaps, to know one could love one lady and yet desire another quite so fiercely.

After a rather stilted dinner, with Penny and Prue on their best behaviour and Miss Pettigrew silent as a mouse, and then breakfast with them all assembled again, Leo was beginning to wonder whether Izzy was using the twins as a barrier between herself and him.

But perhaps not. When he asked her about her plans for the day she said that she wanted to shop for the house and that she would be very glad of his company.

'Mrs Druett has pointed out to me that the china we are eating from is the best the house has and, although it is very good quality, there are only six dinner plates, eight side plates and ten soup bowls left uncracked. If we are to do any entertaining then we ought to buy a good service for at least twelve.'

'Better make it twenty-four,' Leo said. 'Shall we go to Wedgwood and Byerley's showrooms in St James's Square?'

They left after breakfast armed with a list from Cook of plain kitchenware she required as well.

The showrooms were on the corner of the Square and Duke of York Street and, although Leo was prepared for the quality of the products on display, he was taken aback by the magnificence of the rooms—the main one pillared and lined with glass and mahogany cabinets. It was necessary to walk with care and pick one's way between round tables set with various patterns. There was even a large indoor fountain in the centre of the room.

One of the male assistants took Cook's list and, after Izzy had made her choice of the quality of kitchen wares, promised to fill the order himself and have it sent to Mount Street.

'There is too much choice,' she said, staring around the main showroom. They prowled between the tables, finding what they thought would be a favourite, then calling to each other because of something more appealing.

'This one,' Izzy said, catching his arm. 'Look. A lovely Classical pattern in gold. Quite simple, but very elegant.'

She was right, it was perfect. The assistant, barely hiding his delight at their large order, began noting quantities and producing different serving dishes and platters for their approval.

Finally, they completed the set and turned towards the door. Beside him he heard Izzy say something sharply under her breath and followed the direction of her gaze. Coming through the entrance was Lucinda Paxton.

For a moment he thought she was one of the sculptures come to life, so perfect was the match of her blue gown and spencer with their white trim to the famous Jasper wares of Mr Wedgwood.

Then she moved and turned her head, laughing as she spoke to someone just behind her, and he felt his head spin. She had never looked more perfect, more enchanting.

'Do take care.' Izzy's voice, cool and calm by his side. 'You almost knocked into that table.'

'How careless of me. I was taken by surprise to see Miss Paxton here, of all places.' Even as he said it, the careful formality sounded false.

'That is her aunt and uncle with her,' Izzy said. 'I suppose she is staying with them while she orders her wardrobe for her Season and it is they who are shopping here. Ah, now they have seen us.'

It was Lucinda who had recognised them across the cluttered room and her reaction puzzled him. Her eyes opened wide, she caught her full under-lip between her teeth and then she smiled dazzlingly at him.

Surprise he would have expected, followed by some embarrassment, given the way they had last parted, but not this apparent delight. It must be an attempt to cover up her awkwardness, he decided. She said something to her companions, who looked across as the two parties converged.

'Miss Paxton.' His hat was already in his hand, so he bowed slightly.

'Oh, Lord Halford. Imagine seeing you here! This is my aunt and uncle, Lord and Lady Amberleigh.'

She did not make any move to introduce Izzy and Leo thought she probably had no idea about the marriage.

'My lady. Amberleigh. My wife, Isobel, Countess of Halford.' As he said it he realised that, somehow, Lucinda already knew, because there was no sign of surprise in her expression.

He saw that it came as news to the Amberleighs,

though, but there was no hint that they had heard of his failed proposal to their niece, no awkwardness in their manner.

'We have just been buying a new dinner service for the town house,' Izzy was saying to Lady Amberleigh. 'So difficult, there is such a wide choice here.'

Now Lucinda was looking puzzled. She blurted out, 'But this is so expensive!'

'Lucinda,' her aunt said sharply.

Izzy, still perfectly composed, laughed lightly. 'It is, but quality is worth it, I always say. We are renovating the entire town house,' she added to Lady Amberleigh. 'What would you recommend as the best warehouse for fabrics? All the curtains and bed hangings need replacement.'

'I always go to Curtis and Browne in Longacre,' Lady Amberleigh said. 'Oh, and Jacques Frères for trimmings and passementerie. So stylish. And are you looking for carpets?'

Izzy produced her notebook and the two women began exchanging information. An assistant approached Lord Amberleigh and asked a question and, for a few moments, Leo and Lucinda were alone.

'How can you afford all this?' she asked. 'Papa says you have no money, only debts.'

'Circumstances change and your papa is not always right,' Leo said, lowering his voice in the hope that she would, too.

'Oh! So Isobel has money? I never realised. The sly creature.' She gave a brittle little laugh. 'No wonder—'

'No wonder what?' he demanded, suddenly furious with her. It was as though everything he had loved about her—her spontaneity, her laughter, her mercurial moods—had been distorted by some warped mirror into something cruel and harsh. He had known she did not love him, but this was like a blow in the guts.

'Of course you had to marry her,' she said, her voice softening into sympathy. 'If only I'd had a large enough dowry that would have meant we could…' She fixed blue eyes swimming with tears on his face. 'We could have married. Oh, Leo.'

He stared at her. That moment of harshness just now had been—what? Disappointment? She wished now that they could have wed?

The question was on the tip of his tongue as Izzy closed her notebook and came back to him, Lady Amberleigh at her side.

Leo shut his mouth with a snap.

Saved. Lord knew what he might have said, what fatal words might have emerged from the confusion of questions in his head.

'Lady Amberleigh has given me so many useful suggestions,' Izzy said. 'I do hope you will call. But not just yet,' she added to the older woman with a laugh. 'You must give us a week or so. We are still in a state of dust and muddle. Goodbye.' She swept the three of them with her smile, tucked her hand under Leo's elbow and gave him a surreptitious nudge towards the door.

'She knew about us,' he said as soon as they were out on the pavement in St James's Square. There was no need to explain who *she* was.

'I encountered her yesterday at Madame Claire's shop—the modiste, you know.'

'And you did not see fit to tell me?' Leo demanded.

'Oh, I am so sorry,' Izzy apologised with what was clearly false sweetness. 'I had no idea you would want to know.'

'That the—' He broke off, suddenly realising where this was going.

'That the young lady you love, but who does not love you, but who would have married you if she had known you were wealthy, was in town?' She raised her hand and a hackney cab that had been circling the Square drew up. 'This is convenient. The warehouse for mattresses next, I think.'

She gave the driver the address and stood there, looking at Leo, one eyebrow raised. 'The door?'

He wrenched it open, helped her in, then climbed up himself, not best pleased when the carriage started with a jerk, sending him down on to the seat with an undignified thump. 'Izzy, damn it!'

'Are we having our first married argument?' she inquired with maddening calm.

'You know da— I mean, perfectly well that we are. I beg your pardon for swearing just now.'

'And I beg yours for not realising you would wish to be told that Lucinda was in London. I suppose I thought it would cause you pain to be reminded of her, which was foolish, as it must be worse, coming across her unexpectedly like that.'

'It was not pain,' he protested. 'Just shock. And it

was awkward until I realised that she knew about us already.'

'She knew we were married because I had told her, but I doubt she knows yet about your legacy. I imagine she is now very confused by our extravagant shopping.'

Leo hesitated, then decided it was best not to try to keep things from Izzy. 'She thinks I married you for your money,' he said.

'*What? My* money? Oh, that really is amusing, Leo. I am sorry she will have to find out the truth, but I suppose it is inevitable. Lucinda must be fuming if she thinks that plain old maid Isobel Martyn was actually wealthy.'

'You are not plain,' he said. 'That's ridiculous.'

'That is very sweet of you to say so, Leo, but I do possess a looking glass. I think we should agree to make up our quarrel, don't you?'

'You are not *pretty*, that is true. It does not mean you are not attractive, do not have style.' That earned him a flicker of a smile. 'Kiss and make up?'

He took the deepening of the dimples on either side of her mouth as agreement. Leo shifted across to sit beside her, gathered her into his arms and kissed her with considerable thoroughness. He was not certain how that made her feel, but it soothed the jangling emotions inside him, replacing them with a strong desire to be alone with her in a bedchamber.

Leo's kisses were becoming addictive. Even being kissed in a musty old hackney carriage made her want to pull him closer, drag off his clothes, her clothes. Heaven…

And Hell, because try as she might to surrender to the feelings flooding through her, the pleasure of the taste and feel of him, she could not help wondering if this sudden passion was because he really wanted Lucinda and she, Isobel, was all that he could have.

Something of her thoughts must have reached him because Leo sat back, releasing her. 'Izzy?'

The old pet name was beginning to grate on her nerves. This was not her old childhood friend, this was her husband. But now was not the time to confront that particular issue.

'We are in public, in a hackney carriage,' she protested, smiling in the hope that he would not see this as a rejection, only a protest against the location.

'Yes, of course,' he said, straightening his neckcloth with an answering, rueful grin. 'But I reserve the right to kiss you in our own carriage—with the blinds down, of course.'

'Of course,' she agreed gravely. The thought of those wide, cushioned seats and the effect of the motion of the carriage was curiously arousing. Isobel waved her hand in front of her flushed face. 'How stuffy this is in here.'

'We have arrived,' Leo said, looking out of the window as the hackney slowed.

Isobel wondered whether the thought of shopping for mattresses was as inconveniently arousing for Leo as it was for her, but ten minutes inside the warehouse wrestling with choices on horse hair, goose feather, flock, down and all the other combinations of bottom mattresses, middle mattresses and top mattresses that the eager assistant presented them with, rapidly removed any inflammatory thoughts from her mind.

'I am exhausted,' she confessed afterwards. 'Shall we go home for luncheon and see whether the notes we sent to our acquaintances have produced any recommendations for your secretary, or for tutors for the girls?'

'I agree. I now feel I could write a paper for the Royal Society on horsehair and the merits of stoneware for kitchen utensils,' Leo agreed, leaning back in the opposite corner of the carriage.

Isobel looked across at him, feeling the love and desire welling up. He was so dear—and so handsome, too, now she had allowed herself to have such thoughts.

'It is a good feeling, isn't it, Izzy? To think of home, somewhere we are creating together.'

'Yes,' she agreed. 'I am starting to feel married, Leo. And because of that—' She took a deep breath. 'Because of that, could you call me Isobel? Izzy belongs to our childhood, not to our life now.'

The hackney carriage turned a corner and light flooded in through the window, illuminating Leo's face in sharp relief. The smile had gone entirely and he was expressionless. But just for a moment she thought she had seen hurt in his dark eyes.

Chapter Eleven

'Yes, of course, if that is what you wish,' Leo said, perfectly pleasantly. She must have imagined that flash of feeling. A trick of the light, perhaps. 'You must forgive me if I slip sometimes: I have been calling you Izzy for all of our lives and it may be a hard habit to break.'

'Yes, of course,' she agreed hastily, as they pulled up outside the Mount Street house. 'I quite understand. It isn't that I do not still want us to be friends, or for you never to use that name. That would be absurd.'

'It would, wouldn't it?' He jumped down from the carriage and handed her out, then paid the driver.

Even so, Isobel was left with the feeling that she had blundered somehow, in a way she could not quite put her finger on.

The bustle of the household gave her no chance to brood on it once they were inside. Prue wanted to ask if a pianoforte tuner could be sent for because Miss Pettigrew had pronounced the instrument quite unplayable.

Penny had discovered that the kitchen cat had kittens

and wanted to know if she would have one. Or two. Or Miss Eddington's puppies. Or both.

Mrs Druett said, rather ominously, that she would be glad of an opportunity to talk to Her Ladyship about the maids and that they had had to send for a chimney sweep because there was a blockage in the kitchen flue and Cook was not happy.

Isobel promised to talk to both ladies that afternoon and fled upstairs to take off her bonnet and pelisse. She came down to find Leo sorting through a considerable pile of mail.

'We need a butler as well,' he said, glancing up. 'I want to leave Clevedon down at the Hall because once we start work down there it needs an experienced man in place. But there are a number of invitations here and that means returning hospitality.' He finished sorting and passed her a stack. 'These are yours, Isobel.'

The name sounded strange from his lips and she realised it was possibly only the second time he had called her that, the first being when they took their vows.

'Thank you,' she said, not sure herself whether that was for the name or the post.

They went through the correspondence in silence for a while. Isobel sorted hers into invitations, answers to her queries about tutors and decorators, letters and notices from various shops soliciting her custom.

'Two recommendations for the same dancing master, three names of music teachers and also some suggestions about language masters. Oh, and the Duchess recommends the joiners and decorators who have done some work for them recently. Have you received any-thing useful?'

'Lord Fitzmore suggests the youngest son of the vicar at his country place. He says Giles Norcross has just graduated from Oxford, is intelligent and reliable and, because he is the youngest of three, he's got his own way to make in the world. I will write and see how he responds.

'And Sir Thomas is recommending his first foot-man Wilmore as butler, although I hadn't actually in-quired about that yet. Apparently, he's an ambitious young man, but Eddington's butler is only middle aged and nowhere near retirement, so he is expecting Wil-more to give his notice at any moment.'

'That is excellent news,' Isobel said. 'We certainly need the assistance.'

They ate luncheon with the twins and Miss Petti-grew again, then Isobel went to listen sympathetically to Cook's woes and less so to Mrs Druett's opinion that exposure to London life was bad for the maids and that she had caught one flirting with the baker and another threading coloured ribbon through the lace holes in her cap. Then she went to her desk in the little sitting room and dealt with her letters.

How crowded their life seemed now. Somehow it had never occurred to her when she had proposed to Leo that this would be the case, which was foolish. She had been blinded by love and the excitement of realis-ing that marriage was an answer to both their problems. Now there were the twins, the servants and, in addition to Miss Pettigrew there would be Leo's secretary, a gentleman, and therefore someone else to be included as part of the family.

There were also an increasing number of acquaintances, she thought, prodding the small pile of invitations with one fingertip.

She no longer had Leo to herself for much of the day and, when they were alone, there was the looming issue of the consummation of the marriage. Leo appeared to desire her. His kisses were intense and she was beginning to understand the changes she observed in his body and breathing when they did embrace. But that was only desire and men apparently felt that very easily.

At first her reservations about the business had been because of shyness, of the strangeness of doing something so intimate with her old friend. Now, with that encounter with Lucinda and the passion of Leo's kisses afterward, she was filled with a kind of shrinking at the idea he would make love to her, but that he would be imagining himself with Lucinda as he did so.

Something fell with a plop on to the desktop and Isobel stared at it blankly for a moment before she realised it was a tear. She scrubbed angrily at her eyes before any more dared emerge. She would not give way to self-pity. She had married Leo knowing he loved another woman, but she saw now that in doing so she had lost her dearest, oldest friend, the one person she could say anything to, confide anything to, trust implicitly.

I am lonely. The more people who are in our lives, the lonelier I have become.

Isobel watched the one tear drop spread and slowly

vanish and something inside her seemed to harden. What was done was done. She would do her best to be a good wife to Leo and a good countess. She would make a new life for herself and find new friends. She had far more to be thankful for than most other people, she told herself fiercely, and she had work she could immerse herself in. It was time to put aside daydreams and wishful thinking.

She would begin with the invitations and the world outside this house.

A week passed and Isobel shed no more tears. Every night she went up to bed before Leo. Every night she wore one of her pretty new nightgowns and every night she heard his footsteps cross the sitting room towards his own bedchamber door, so every night she rumpled the bedding again.

Giles Norcross, Leo's new secretary, arrived and proved to be a delightful young man, blond, snub-nosed and freckled. He had a shy manner, but a quiet sense of humour, and he threw himself into the work and professed himself delighted with the comfortable bed-sitting room that Isobel had created for him.

He joined them at meals and took exactly the right approach to Penny and Prue, treating them as though they were his own sisters, which effectively quashed any attempts at practising batting their eyelashes at him.

The new butler, Wilmore, had started work on the Monday and everyone held their breath to see how he would manage with Mrs Druett, who was old enough to be his mother.

'It's like watching two cats meeting in the backyard,' Prue whispered. 'They are stalking around each other with stiff legs, but being terribly polite.'

'If he cannot deal with it, then he has been promoted too soon,' Leo said firmly and, after two days, they appeared to relax.

Giles created diaries for both Leo and Isobel and produced them every morning along with the day's post so that they could make decisions on what invitations to accept.

'Do you have the feeling that we are being managed?' Leo asked her when Giles had left, burdened with diaries and notes.

'Yes, and isn't it wonderful?' She sat back on the sofa with a sigh of relief. 'He has even organised visits by the music tutor and the drawing master, so the girls are happily occupied.

'Next, I suppose, we must plan some dinner parties to begin returning hospitality. We have already attended two and Lady Archibald's reception is tonight. There is more social activity in town than I had expected at this time of year. When I had my Seasons we only came to town in February.'

'It is because Parliament is sitting, so all the Members are up. And most of the families with sons and daughters to launch in the Season are here ordering wardrobes and for all the little daytime dances and tea parties that help the young people to get to know each other and find their feet.

'It will be thin of company over Christmas and the New Year, but even then, families who live a long way from town stay up because of the miserable travelling conditions at that time of year.'

'What do you want to do?'

'If you are agreeable, I thought to stay until late December, travel down to the Hall for Christmas and New Year, then return here as soon as the weather permits. I must take my seat in the Lords and you must be presented at the next Drawing Room.'

'I must make a note to tell Madame Claire that I shall need my Court dress in December, in that case. I must learn to walk in the thing and to manage those plumes.'

To her horror, Isobel had discovered that the vast hoops of the middle of the last century were still part of Court dress which, with the rise in waistlines, meant that ladies were trapped in a vast bell reaching from under their armpits to the ground. Then their hair must be piled high and topped with a tiara and three ostrich plumes. One had to learn to walk, to curtsy very low and to move backwards out of the royal presence, all without being able to see three feet in front or to the side.

She pushed the anxiety to the back of her mind— it was months in the future—and thought about what Leo was suggesting. 'Yes, I agree, staying here for now makes sense. I can have the house virtually finished by then and Prue and Penny will benefit from all the little tea parties and daytime dances for young people. Lady Archibald has invited them to one next week— her granddaughter is much the same age. And we are attending her reception this evening.'

Leo grimaced. 'I had forgotten that.'

'I could send our regrets,' Isobel offered.

'No, it is sheer idleness on my part. We need to become part of the social scene and we will not do it if I prefer sitting by my own fireside with my feet on the fender, talking to my wife.'

It was true, they had spent several very pleasant evenings doing precisely that.

Just like old friends, Isobel thought with an inward sigh.

And just like friends, they had slept alone afterwards.

She looked across at Leo, who was frowning as he studied the diary in front of him. This could go on for ever, an empty marriage in name only, until, she supposed, Leo woke up and remembered that he needed an heir.

He glanced at her as she closed her own diary with some force, then shut his own. 'If you will excuse me, Isobel, I have an appointment with my tailor.'

She smiled vaguely in acknowledgement, then, as the door closed, stood up and began to pace. She was not going to be relegated to the role of brood mare and she was weary of letting Lucinda Paxton dominate her marriage. If Leo would not come to her, then she would try seducing him and, if that did not work, then she would quite brazenly go to his bed.

The thought brought heat to her cheeks, but she firmly ignored the internal voice that protested she knew nothing about seduction. That was true, but she had a strong suspicion that, if she slid naked between the sheets of Leo's bed, he was not going to need much more persuasion.

But there was work to be done before things reached

that stage. Isobel went upstairs and found Nancy putting away clean under-linen in the dressing room. 'A gown for this evening, my lady? Is it a dinner?'

'No, a reception. There are three that might do, I think.'

Nancy laid them out on the bed. There was an elegant amber gown with an elaborate bodice, but plain skirt, which was best suited for a dinner party. Then there was a moss-green one with heavy beading.

'That's elegant, my lady.'

Isobel picked it up and held it against her. Elegant, yes, but dignified and rather restrained with quite a high neckline. She put it down again. 'That one.'

That was a golden silk with a pale yellow gauze overskirt, tiny sleeves and a daringly low neckline. The bodice just happened to show off her modestly sized bosom to its best advantage.

'With the gold and amber ear drops, necklace and bracelets? Very striking, my lady.' Nancy tactfully did not remind her that she had dithered over it for almost an hour, worried that the cut was too revealing.

'That is what I thought. And my hair in that gold mesh net, quite simple.' And very easy to let down as well.

Leo was waiting in the hall for her when Isobel came downstairs that evening. He was always punctilious about that and always made some thoughtful remark about how well a new gown suited her, or how he liked her hair in a particular style.

Isobel was never really convinced that these compliments were more than politeness, kind comments to boost her confidence. Now, as she swept down, her

skirts gathered lightly in one hand, she saw an unmistakably genuine reaction. Leo's lips parted and he took
a step forward to the foot of the stairs where he stood
holding out his hand to her.

'You look magnificent,' he said. 'I almost— That is,
to say, that is a new gown, is it not?'

*I almost did not recognise you. Is that what he very
nearly said?* she thought, annoyance warring with
amusement.

'Thank you. All my gowns are new,' she said with
a smile and took his hand. At least Leo was not looking at his dear old friend Izzy now, she thought, seeing
how his eyes lingered on the curves the bodice showed
off and trying not to feel shy.

I am a new woman, she told herself firmly. *The
Countess of Halford. I am looking my best, I am full of
confidence and my husband is going to desire me before
this night is out, even if he does not love me.*

'Your cloak, my lady.' Nancy had followed her down
and swirled the heavy velvet around her shoulders.
'Your reticule.' She handed Isobel the little gold mesh
bag. 'Have a good evening, my lady. My lord.'

'That was a very old-fashioned look that Nancy just
gave me,' Leo said as they settled into the carriage. He
was smiling, though, she could see in the flickering
light from the torchères beside the front door.

'I noticed nothing,' Isobel said. She wondered if
Nancy realised what her intentions for the evening were,
that she knew that her mistress was still a virgin and that
she and Leo slept apart. How embarrassing. It was said
that the servants knew more about the secrets of a house

than its master and mistress ever did: she could only trust in Nancy's discretion and loyalty.

It was not far to Lord and Lady Archibald's house and they spent longer with the carriage jostling for position to let them down than they had on the journey.

After fifteen minutes they were able to step on to the red carpet that had been rolled across the pavement and walk up the steps, doing their best, in Isobel's case at least, to ignore the crowd of onlookers who had come to stare at the guests and make loud remarks about what they saw.

As they mounted the staircase having shed their cloaks, Isobel was pleased to find she recognised several people and was able to exchange greetings or bows. And it was not just the ladies who were paying her attention, she realised as they climbed slowly to the receiving line; quite a few gentlemen smiled, lifted quizzing glasses or looked slyly at her bosom. It was not something she was comfortable with, but she would endure it if it helped her plan.

Once they had been greeted by their host and hostess and passed into the reception rooms, Leo accepted a glass of champagne for each of them and took her elbow with his free hand as if to guide her in the direction of Sir Thomas Eddington. He and his sister were standing chatting to a group not far off.

'Oh, you go on, I will talk to Chloe later,' Isobel said. 'I have just seen someone else I know over there.' She freed her arm and gestured vaguely towards the far end of the room. As the space was actually two large reception rooms with the dividing doors open between them, it was quite some distance away.

Before Leo could protest, she walked off, sipping her champagne and stopping now and then to speak to acquaintances, but still making for the far end where there were several young men gathered. She stopped in front of one group, looked around and said clearly, 'Oh, bother!'

'Is something wrong, ma'am?' The gentleman who stepped forward was tall, blond, handsome in a somewhat foppish manner and, perhaps, thirty.

'Oh.' She smiled at him. 'No, nothing really. I thought I saw a friend of mine here and came to speak to her, but I must have been mistaken.'

'Your glass is empty.' He snapped his fingers at a footman, who hurried forward with a tray.

'Thank you.' Isobel gave the gentleman a lingering look from under her lashes, hoping she looked more like Lucinda, who frequently used the trick to good effect, and less as though she had something wrong with her eyes. Flirting was not something she had ever attempted with any success.

'I cannot see a respectable matron within five yards to present me,' her new acquaintance said. 'Shall we be wickedly informal? I am Geoffrey Bostock.'

'I do not know my *Peerage* and *Landed Gentry* from cover to cover,' Isobel said with a little laugh, copied from Lucinda's repertoire. 'Should I be saying *my lord*?'

'You should be saying Geoffrey, if I had my wish,' he said. 'But I am Viscount Gaydon. My father is the Earl of Kelvewood.'

'And I, my lord,' Isobel said, primming up her lips in a clearly false attempt at a reproof, 'am Lady Halford. Isobel,' she added.

'But why have we not encountered each other before?' Lord Gaydon asked. 'I cannot believe I could have overlooked you.'

'Actually, I believe we have met.' It was coming back to her now. 'We have danced together once, at least. But it was several years ago when I had my come-out. I do not think you had much time for tiresome debutantes in those days.'

'No,' he agreed. 'I prefer experience. Sophistication.' His voice had dropped a tone and his gaze flickered down to her bosom.

Excellent. It was working, she was flirting and, yes, when she glanced down the length of the room she saw that Leo had seen her and was watching with a frown on his face. He shifted position, lifted his head as though to see better and she was suddenly very aware of the breadth of his shoulders.

Oh, dear.

Yes, she wanted to make him notice her as other men did, but she did not want him flattening what he saw as rivals in the midst of a social event.

Chapter Twelve

Yes, it was definitely time to move on before Lord Gaydon started trying to manoeuvre her into some little side chamber. Men like he always knew a discreet place for some serious flirtation, she was certain, and Leo would be furious if she vanished from the room.

'Ah, there is my friend,' Isobel said, pretending to see someone in the crowd close to where a string quartet were vainly attempting to be heard over the roar of conversation. 'So lovely to talk with you.'

She swept off, saw a Miss Armitage who she had met a few days before during an afternoon call, stopped with her long enough to make her excuse to escape Lord Gaydon convincing and then strolled on.

'Lady Halford, good evening.' Mr de Vere Walton, who she had met during the same call as the one where she had encountered Miss Armitage, stepped away from the two gentlemen to whom he had been speaking and beamed at her.

And, yes, his gaze dropped to her cleavage. Really,

men were so predictable. Isobel smiled back and allowed herself to be introduced to his friends, whose names she promptly forgot because Mr de Vere Walton could not seem to stop talking.

Then he broke off abruptly. 'Lord Halford, good evening.'

'Good evening, de Vere Walton. I must thank you for entertaining my wife. Lady Halford, my godmother, the Marchioness of Grantly, is here and is asking to meet you. Gentlemen.' He nodded abruptly to the trio and led Isobel away.

'Is she really here?' she asked.

Leo looked at her quizzically. 'Why on earth would I have said she was if she was not?'

'Because I thought you seemed annoyed that I had gone off on my own and was looking for an excuse to separate me from Mr de Vere Walton,' she said bluntly.

'Why on earth should I be annoyed?' Leo asked, as though he had not been glaring at her when she was flirting with Lord Gaydon.

Or perhaps he had not been and it had been a trick of the light. Which meant her efforts to make him jealous had failed. Isobel said a very naughty word under her breath.

'It is the purpose of these entertainments to circulate, to see and be seen, is it not? Ah, here she is.'

What in blazes was Isobel up to? If he had not known better, he would have thought she had been flirting with Gaydon and de Vere Walton. Izzy never flirted, nor did she wear gowns cut so low that the entire upper swell of her breasts was exposed.

No, Izzy did not, but perhaps Isobel did, which was an alarming thought and a thoroughly disturbing one at that.

'Halford, excellent. So, this is the gel.' Cynthia, widow of the late Marquess of Grantly, raised her eyeglass and subjected Isobel to a thorough scrutiny.

Isobel stood it well. Personally, he had always found his god-mama, a cousin of his mother's mother, a thoroughly alarming creature. She was wearing the latest fashions, all in black, and was fairly dripping diamonds. He had thought her ancient as a child—now he realised that she could not be more than seventy and used the appearance and mannerisms of old age to give herself licence to behave just as she pleased.

'Come here and let me look at you, gel.'

Isobel stepped forward until she was almost standing on the black silk skirts and looked back, calm and unsmiling.

'How do you stay in that garment?' Lady Grantly leaned forward and brandished her fan at Isobel's bosom.

'With the aid of very expensive couture and good boning, ma'am.'

'Ha! I like her, Halford. I shall leave her my emeralds. You can come to luncheon, child, without Leo, of course, and tell me all about yourself.'

'Thank you, ma'am. It will be a pleasure, although I cannot promise to reveal everything, you know.'

That made his godmother cackle so much that her

companion had to produce her smelling salts and a handkerchief. She waved them away. 'Go and flirt, my dear,' she said between coughs. 'Give him a run for his money. Ha!'

'She is a dreadful old creature,' Leo grumbled as they walked off.

'I thought she was splendid and I intend to be just like her when I am her age,' Isobel said firmly. 'There are the Eddingtons. I shall go and flirt with Sir Thomas, as instructed.'

'You will do no such thing,' Leo said, then realised that she was teasing him. He hoped.

'Why ever not?' she asked, giving him a mischievous look. 'You can, too. Not with Sir Thomas, obviously. Find a pretty young matron. It appears that harmless flirtation is quite the usual thing.'

Isobel was quite correct and he knew it. Gentlemen were expected to pay compliments and to make light-hearted remarks. Then the ladies pretended to be cast into confusion so they could make play with their fans and their blushes. In turn, they could discreetly admire a well-turned leg or a pair of broad shoulders and entice the gentlemen to come and talk to them with smiles and little gestures.

It was all perfectly harmless, part of a well-understood, highly stylised game. Harmless, that was, as long as it was played by those who knew the rules. Watchful mamas warned their daughters about the men who were inclined to presume too far, who would try to lure the innocents out on to the balcony or into a dark nook where they would snatch kisses, or worse. And, even if no physical harm was done, a reputation could be blighted if a young lady was considered to be fast and crossed that invisible line between modest and bold.

It was full of dangers for the gentlemen as well, especially the eligible and unmarried who might find themselves coaxed into the conservatory or the shrubbery and then surprised as they snatched a kiss by an apparently furious father and a delighted mama, both ready to hustle him to the altar with their daughter.

But he was married and so was Isobel and the worst that could happen was that she acquired the reputation for being somewhat dashing because, surely, she was far too awake to the dangers to risk being alone with another man.

Nor had he any reason to be jealous, Leo told himself, watching this rather alarming new Isobel dimpling a smile at Sir Thomas. He was not in love with Isobel, she was not in love with him. They had a perfectly... friendly—yes, that was the word, *friendly*—relationship with no messy emotions involved, which made it confusing to find himself resentful of his friend's offer to take Isobel for a drive in the park in his new phaeton, or of her enthusiasm for the promised treat.

Damn it, he thought, smiling through gritted teeth as he listened to Eddington's account of his search for the perfect pair of match bays to draw it, did she think he should have bought a phaeton, or found her a riding horse, on top of everything else he was having to deal with?

Then Isobel turned to look at him and smiled and tucked her hand into the crook of his arm. 'I have been running poor Leo ragged with all my domestic demands—you would not believe how tiresome it is choosing and buying mattresses for every bedchamber in the house, Miss Eddington!'

'I can well believe it. I can also believe that if we needed to do such a thing my dear brother would abandon me to the task,' Chloe Eddington said frankly.

'It would be practice for when you cease tormenting the unmarried men and allow one of the poor devils to marry you,' her brother retorted. 'Do, I implore you, Lady Halford, persuade Chloe how happy she would be married. I swear she enjoys leaving a trail of broken hearts behind her.'

'If I thought for a moment any of their hearts were in danger of so much as cracking, then I might yield,' Chloe said. 'But I will marry for love, like our friends here.' She beamed at them both, and Leo was very conscious of Isobel at his side. She must have once dreamed of finding a love match and instead had ended up with him.

'Do excuse us, I have just seen someone I must speak to.' Leo walked away towards a tall figure with copper-coloured hair he had just spotted at the far end of the room. 'I have been remiss in not buying you a carriage to drive out in,' he said as they wove their way through the throng. 'And a riding horse.'

'Not at all,' Isobel protested. 'You have had far too much to think about to worry about such things.'

'I should provide for you in the proper manner for a lady in your position,' he said, aware he was sounding thoroughly pompous.

'Oh, fiddlesticks, Leo. I did not marry you in order to drive about town showing off my smart new walking dresses and my husband's good taste in horse flesh.'

'I am well aware that you married me to escape an intolerable situation and because you wished to help me,' he said, somehow managing to keep his voice low.

'Are we having another row, Leo? Because I can think of better places to do so than the middle of Lady Archibald's reception.'

'Of course we are not,' he said, then thought about it. 'Yes, we are. I apologise. I have dragged you over here because the man with the red hair is Colonel Troughton and I hear he is reducing his stable. He's a very good judge of a horse and I hope to find a pair of carriage horses for a phaeton or a curricle and something for you.'

'Why is he selling up?' Isobel asked, keeping her voice low.

'His wife died last year and both his daughters have married. I hear he intends to spend more time in the country, so is selling up his town stable.'

Isobel took to the Colonel immediately. He had startlingly green eyes that she thought had once been full of amusement, judging by the laughter lines at their corners, but which now looked sad and thoughtful. Perhaps he was lonely now.

'You are after my stable, are you, Halford?' he asked when, after an exchange of greetings, Leo remarked that he intended to buy a phaeton or curricle.

'I was hoping you might have something suitable,' Leo confessed. 'And something for my wife: I would trust your judgement over anyone else I know.'

'Something quiet and steady, Lady Halford? Or something with more go to it? I have both—a handsome, very steady gelding my elder daughter preferred or a pretty, rather lively part-Arab mare that suited my late wife very well.'

'The mare sounds ideal, provided I am not overestimating my skill in the saddle,' Isobel said. 'It has been some time since I last rode.'

'You have an excellent seat and a light hand,' Leo said, 'but you should try both if the Colonel will permit.'

She glowed inwardly at his praise because it was so unexpected. She had ridden with Leo ever since she had first sat on a pony and he had never praised her riding before, although he had always seemed to expect that she could keep up wherever they went.

They agreed that Leo would call on the Colonel the next day to view the animals he had for sale and then made their way towards the supper room.

'Would you prefer I buy a phaeton or a curricle?' Leo asked as he found them a table in a corner.

'It will be your carriage. You must choose.'

'I thought you would like to drive, too. You have always driven a gig, haven't you?'

'I would love to learn to drive a pair,' Isobel admitted. 'But you buy whatever you think best. And now I am absolutely starving and hope you will bring me a positively indecent amount from the buffet.'

Leo chuckled and went off to join the men jostling for position in front of the choicest platters, and Isobel sat back to look at the crowded room and think about the evening so far.

She had certainly surprised Leo with her gown and she rather thought she had piqued his possessive streak by flirting. They had had a momentary argument, which hinted that he was more unsettled than he appeared, and now he was being very thoughtful and attentive. But then he usually was, so she could not build her hopes up on that score.

Her next step, she concluded with a definite sensation of butterflies in her stomach, was to start flirting with her husband. He would probably fall about laughing.

Leo was certainly amused by something when he returned, followed by a footman with a tray covered in little plates and another with a bottle and two glasses.

'This is wonderful,' she said admiringly as the footman left. 'None of the other ladies has anything like such an interesting spread in front of them.'

'I was informed by Jack Fielding over there that it was bad tactics to feed my lady so much, or all she would want to do was sleep,' he admitted. 'It was clear that he had never seen you at a party, making a clean sweep of the lobster patties and then being quite ready to dance the night away.'

'You make me sound so greedy, you wretch. But I suspect Mr Fielding was referring to the fact that we are newly married and that you might not want me sleepy for other reasons than the party we are at.'

It had always been fun to make Leo blush and she had certainly brought the colour up over his cheekbones now. 'Clearly he had not spotted that you have brought quite a few oysters,' she added in the hopes of fanning the flames. 'I am correct about the reputation that oysters have, aren't I?'

'You are, although I suspect it is complete nonsense. Have a lobster patty.'

'Thank you, I will take two. And an oyster, please.'

Leo added one to her plate and she promptly picked it up and held it to his lips. 'Open your mouth, Leo.'

He did, apparently to make a protest, and she tipped it neatly inside.

'Isobel!' he protested once he had swallowed and got his breath back. But there was something in the way he looked at her that made her think he was less annoyed than intrigued and the look in his dark eyes intensified as she made a lingering business of eating her own oyster.

Leo offered another little savoury pastry between thumb and forefinger and she took it, making no effort to avoid touching his fingertips with her lips. 'You have a crumb in the corner of your mouth,' he said, his voice husky as he reached out and brushed along her lips with his thumb. 'Another?'

'No.' She lowered her lashes. 'I am no longer hungry for...for food.'

She heard Leo's breath catch. 'You would like to go home?'

'Yes, please.'

They did not speak again except to thank their hostess and take their leave, not until the carriage had been summoned and they were seated side by side, swathed in their evening cloaks.

'We spoke of this,' Leo said abruptly. 'Of there being no need for haste.'

'You kissed me, Leo. And then… Then there were no more kisses. And we have been married for nine days.'

'I was not sure I trusted myself.'

Was that the truth? The kisses had ceased after their encounter with Lucinda and Isobel could not help suspecting that had more to do with it than Leo's inability to control his passions as far as the other woman was concerned.

But she was tired of being understanding and patient. They were man and wife in theory and it was time for it to be so in fact. Besides, she thought as Leo fell silent but took her hand in his, babies did not arise from wishful thinking.

She had accepted what she thought of as a misguided love for a young lady whose looks had blinded him to her character, but now she knew no marriage could survive on these terms. She was ready to fight for her husband with whatever weapons she could find.

'I would like to be married, Leo. Properly, fully, married.' She had intended seduction—now, it seemed, she was demanding. Ah well, best be entirely clear about what she meant or, knowing Leo's tender conscience, he would be imagining he had somehow pressured her into bed. 'I hope you feel that way, too,' she added when he was silent.

'Oh, yes,' he said and that husky rasp was back in his voice.

When they reached Mount Street they walked upstairs, speaking indifferently of items of gossip they had heard that evening. Leo went to his room and she heard him talking to Bertram, his new valet.

Nancy was running a warming pan through her sheets when she entered her own bedchamber.

'Oh, good evening, my lady. Are you retiring now?'

'Yes, I think so.' Isobel pretended to stifle a yawn, then stood still to allow her maid to unlace and unhook her and lift the gown over her head to be carried carefully away to the dressing room.

The nightgown Nancy produced was a soft primrose yellow with darker ribbons at the neck that matched the ties on the robe. Isobel sat at the dressing table, unhooking her earrings as Nancy unpinned and brushed out her hair, and put up her hand to stop her when she began to plait it.

'Leave it loose, please. I have a little headache.'

'It will tangle, my lady.'

'Never mind.' Leo had never seen her with her hair down since she had been a child and she rather thought the glossy fall of it was one of her best features. She unclasped her necklace, and Nancy carried the jewellery away to lock up in the strong box.

'Will you be retiring now, my lady?' Nancy had one hand on the covers, ready to turn them back.

'No, I will sit and read by the fire for a little. Thank you, Nancy. Goodnight.'

The door closed behind the maid and Isobel heard her say something. A male voice answered her—the valet, she guessed—then the outer door closed and all was silent.

Silent, except for the beating of her heart and the

soft sounds the fire made as burned wood settled into ash and, from the street below, the rhythmic sound of a horse's hooves on the cobbles.

What was the correct way to go about this? Presumably, Leo came to her. Was she supposed to be sitting up in bed? Or not? He was going to come to her, wasn't he? Perhaps he had changed his mind.

The clock on her dresser struck one, echoed by the deeper, distant, chime of the longcase in the hall below. She would give him half an hour and, if he had not appeared by then, she would go to him and to the devil with proper ladylike behaviour.

The thought was so energising that she jumped to her feet, heedless of the unread book that fell to the carpet. And the door opened to reveal Leo.

Chapter Thirteen

'May I come in, Isobel?'

'Yes. Yes, of course.'

Leo was holding a chamberstick in one hand and he placed it on the bedside table as he closed the door. Was it her imagination or did the flame waver as though his grip was not quite steady? More likely it was her own shaky knees.

He stood quite still beside the bed, looking at her. 'You look quite…exquisite.'

She almost told him that he did, too, in that gorgeous heavy silk robe and bare feet. Probably it was not only his feet that were bare.

'Are you quite certain about this, Isobel? I would rather you told me if not before I take another step into this room.'

She found her voice and her courage. 'Quite certain, Leo.' She took one step towards him, then another as he moved, too, and then she was in his arms and he was kissing her, one arm holding her close, one hand running through her hair.

'Your hair,' he said as he raised his head. 'It is glorious. And you... Isobel, all these years I have seen my friend, not the woman. I was blind.'

But I saw you, Leo. Oh, my darling, I saw you.

She told herself that she must remember all of this, their first time, that every detail must be stored away, kept for the bleak times that would surely come, the times that she must not think about now.

At first it was easy. Isobel found herself drawn against his naked form, enveloped in his silk-covered arms, marvelling at the sensation of his hard body, dusted with hair, against her own smooth softness. She knew what was happening as he unlaced her robe and sent it sliding to the floor, when his fingers, a little unsteady now, found the bows that secured her nightgown.

Even the shyness that swept over her when the last of the silk slithered to the floor and she was bare to him, still sheltered against his body, was welcome because it proved that this was real. It was not until Leo shrugged off his own robe and the only sensations were of the touch of skin on skin that her mind began to cloud, swept up in the strange, frightening magic of it.

Isobel was not so innocent that she did not know what it was that pressed so insistently against her. She wanted to touch, but dared not, so she spread her hands flat against Leo's back and clung to him as he kissed her.

'Let me look at you,' he said when he had reduced her to a quivering mass of barely understood desire. 'Or would you rather I blew out the candles?'

'No! I mean...' She lifted her head from her close

study of his collarbone. 'I want to look at you, too.' Now she was certain that she was scarlet.

Leo stepped back one pace, then stopped and looked, wordless.

Isobel stared, too. The last time she had seen Leo in the flesh he had been about eight, a skinny boy jumping in the horse pond at the nearby farm with his friends and being chased out by the farmer's wife brandishing a rake.

This was not a skinny boy. He had muscles and hair and he had grown into someone who might rival the Classical statues she had seen. Only they had fig leaves and she was fairly certain, after one rapid glance, that more than a fig leaf would be necessary to disguise quite that much masculinity.

'Well,' Leo said after a long pause. 'I think it is probably true to say we have both grown up.'

'Mmm…' was all she could manage and then, more clearly, 'Yes, we have', and smiled at him, into those dark eyes she knew so well, into that dear face she loved so much and Leo strode forward, lifted her and laid her on the bed.

It was then, she realised afterwards, that she had ceased to think rationally or even clearly, but only to feel. Feel the gentleness of Leo's hands with their rider's calluses stroking over her. Feel the touch of his lips on hers, on her face, her shoulders, her breasts. Feel the warmth of the long body lying against hers.

What he was doing made her gasp and quiver and move under his touch, turned her insides hot and liquid, made her feel hot and wet and increasingly desperate.

'Leo.'

'I am here,' he said, his voice coming from the region of her midriff, and she surfaced enough to realise that he was kissing his way down to her navel, teasing it with his tongue, then lower.

'Leo!'

'Shh. Let me…' Fingers were exploring, and she knew she ought to shriek in outrage, move away—but she could not. 'Open for me. There, just like that.'

This time she could not even say his name, only gasp. The rational part of her brain, the part that was hanging on to consciousness by a fingertip, told her that this could not be right, that this act meant he would put that part of his body into…into *there.* There where his fingers were exploring, gently probing, stretching, moving while something inside her was winding itself tighter and tighter until she was going to—

'Oh,' Isobel murmured as she realised that she was still lying on her bed and was not part of a celestial starburst.

Then Leo moved and his weight came down over her and she found her body knew what her mind did not. It shifted and wriggled and settled him between her thighs where he fitted as though she had been sculpted to receive him.

The warm glow still enveloped her, but her sigh of contentment turned into a cry of protest as he surged within her. 'Ow!' she exclaimed. Her eyes opened on to Leo's face, just inches from her own, his expression set.

'I'm sorry, sweetheart. I thought fast might be best.'

'There's rather a lot of you,' she grumbled and he gave a choked laugh.

'Oh, Izzy, darling. We will go slowly now.'

He began to move, just a little, and her body, despite the pinch of soreness, moved, too, rocking with his until there was no discomfort, only the miracle of being one with Leo, of feeling his strength captured by her softness, of a mounting pleasure, like the one before only this time fuller, deeper, better because he was with her.

She felt everything unravel and cried out and Leo surged within her, his own cry trapped between them as he found her mouth and then all she was aware of was pleasure like she had never known and the sheltering strength of Leo's body.

Leo came to himself to discover Isobel wrapped around him. They were sticky, hot, and he thought his right arm had gone to sleep. He also rather suspected that a gentleman should remove his sweaty body from his wife's bed, pour her water so that she could wash, inquire tenderly about her well being and then remove himself to his own bedchamber.

Be damned to that, he thought, carefully straightening his legs and then easing his numb arm out from under Isobel's limp form.

He sorted a sheet out from the rumpled bedclothes and drew it over them both, then propped himself up on one elbow to study her.

She was deeply asleep with a smile on her lips. That was encouraging, although for all he knew she always smiled in her sleep. Or perhaps she was thinking about lobster patties and oysters.

He turned carefully and sat up against the pillows. He had just made love to his dear friend. And his wife. He was not at all sure how he ought to feel, but he was fairly certain it was not this calm, bone-deep contentment.

He had resolved to banish Lucinda from his thoughts days ago. It took some effort, but he had largely succeeded. To pine after her felt almost adulterous and certainly disloyal. But there was no getting away from the fact that he had not expected to feel more than sexual satisfaction from lying with Isobel. But he had.

The sexual release had been wonderful, but there was more. Seeing her natural, sensual pleasure in his caresses had moved him. Experiencing her own untutored, shy touches in return had shaken him with a feeling that he could only describe as affection and…awe.

They had been rubbing along very well up to then, he thought. The twins were happy, the household was coming together in a way that had seemed impossible a short while ago and he and Isobel were developing a social circle that was interesting and entertaining. It had felt *domestic*, but had it felt *married*? No, it had not, he concluded, shifting to look down at Isobel who was beginning to stir and snuggle down against the pillows.

Now they were sleeping together, how would that change the dynamic of their lives, their relationship? There was a nagging worry at the back of his mind that Isobel might become…attached to him, might expect more than his cracked heart could offer her. She was not a woman to take a physical relationship lightly, he was certain of that.

She turned over, her arm outflung. It hit him squarely in the stomach, missing a more vulnerable part of his anatomy by an inch.

'Oof!'

That woke her. She lay there looking up at him through half-open eyes. '*Leo?* Oh, yes, of course, Leo. What happened? Goodness, I hit you, I am so sorry.' She fought with the bedclothes and eventually managed to sit up next to him, by which time the part that had experienced the narrow escape was showing unmistakable interest. 'Are you all right?'

Leo suppressed a strong inclination to roll over and demonstrate just how all right he was, but Isobel would not welcome his attentions, not so soon after her first time.

'I am perfectly fine, thank you. And you?'

Isobel did not pretend to misunderstand him. She wriggled experimentally and pulled a wry face. 'A little sore. I appear to have found some new muscles. And I feel strange, but in a good way.'

'I am delighted to hear it,' Leo said, meaning it, but she took it as a joking comment and dug him gently in the ribs.

'Stop fishing for compliments. But it was very… pleasurable. If improbable.'

'Improbable?' Of all the conversations he might have imagined having with his wife the morning after their first night together, this was not it.

'This is probably blasphemous, but if you were sitting down to invent a method for the human race to perpetuate itself, would you think of that?'

'I might,' Leo said. 'It is, as you say, very pleasurable.'

'Hmm. I think if a woman was involved in the process of design she would incorporate a few buttons. For later, you understand.'

That surprised a gasp of laughter out of him. 'You, Isobel, are a constant source of delight to me.'

'I am merely practical. That is probably my only talent,' she said prosaically.

'No, it is not,' Leo retorted. 'Yes, you are practical and sensible, but your finest characteristic is your warmth and understanding. Look how happy and content you are making us all, from the boot boy upwards.'

'Including you?'

'Most definitely including me.'

'You haven't kissed me this morning.'

'If I do, that will lead to other things and you have already said you are sore,' he pointed out.

The clock struck six before she could reply.

'I had best get up and retire to my own room to spare Nancy's blushes,' Leo said, sliding out from under the covers and finding his robe.

'I'm not sure she has any,' Isobel said. She held out her hand as he passed her. 'It is safe to kiss me now you are out of bed, isn't it?'

He was not at all certain it ever was exactly safe to kiss Isobel, it stirred such confusing feelings in him, but Leo stooped and pressed his lips to hers for a few seconds. 'Lie down and go back to sleep, Isobel.'

'You called me Izzy last night.'

'Did I? I am sorry, I forgot.' He smiled down at her. 'I had other things on my mind.'

'I don't mind. You can if you want. I rather miss it. I think I was feeling a trifle out of sorts that day when I asked you not to.'

He did not reply, but brushed the back of his hand lightly down her cheek and let himself out. She had not been feeling out of sorts, he thought. She had been struggling to find a balance in this strange new relationship of theirs. At least now she had realised that she did not have to abandon their old friendship to make this work.

Isobel slid over into the man-shaped dip in the bed that Leo had left and snuggled down. It was warm and it smelt of him. Plain soap, a hint of leather, the citrus cologne he used very sparingly and something faint and elusive that must be simply *Leo*.

I wish I could bottle it and carry it with me when he is not here, she thought, her eyelids drooping. *Darling Leo.*

Last night had been…incredible. She had felt all the things she had expected to—shyness, apprehension, a fear of doing the wrong thing—but she had not expected the pleasure, the closeness. Obviously it was, by its very nature, an intimate act, but this had seemed the intimacy of two souls and minds, not just two bodies.

I love you, Leo…

She slept.

The rattle of curtain rings and the scent of hot chocolate roused Isobel. The bedchamber was flooded with the cool sunlight of a wintery morning, but Nancy already had the fire crackling in the grate and from the dressing room came the sound of clanking and splashing that told her that the bath was being filled.

'What time is it, Nancy?'

'Nine o'clock, my lady. His Lordship said to leave you to sleep. He has gone out and the young misses are just leaving for a walk with Miss Pettigrew.'

She picked up Isobel's discarded nightgown and robe as she spoke, then put the fallen book on the table.

Isobel looked around the room. It must be very obvious what had taken place the night before and she felt her colour rising.

We are married, I have been pretending we have been sleeping together for over a week, so what on earth am I getting embarrassed about?

Isobel kept herself very busy all morning. There were letters to write, menus to approve and the morning's post to open.

There was nothing particularly interesting among the correspondence, except for one letter on heavy paper that had been hand-delivered. It looked legal and she broke the blue wax seal with a trepidation that she recognised as an innocent person's instinctive guilt at being confronted by the law.

It proved to be from Mr Parkin requesting the favour of an interview with Lady Halford at her earliest convenience so that he could report on his meeting with Lord Martyn. Would that afternoon be possible?

Isobel stared at the neat black copperplate script as

though it might speak. Now she felt the uneasiness return. Why not simply a report that her affairs were now in Mr Parkin's hands accompanied by a financial accounting? She wrote a note to say she would expect the lawyer at three o'clock, rang for a footman to deliver it and told herself that she was only feeling uneasy because of a residual sense of guilt for eloping.

If she had hoped for a cosy luncheon *à deux* with Leo, she was disappointed. Wilmore informed her that he had taken the liberty of ordering the table in the main dining room to be set. 'With yourself and Your Lordship, Lady Penelope and Lady Prudence, Miss Pettigrew *and* Mr Norcross, the smaller room seemed somewhat cramped, my lady.'

She rather suspected that the small dining room, which opened off the larger one through double doors, would be perfectly adequate even if there had been twelve of them and thought that Wilmore was flexing his muscles in his new post, but agreed without comment. There was no hope of any sort of intimacy, whatever the size of the room.

Isobel was not certain what she expected from Leo after the previous night, but when he entered the dining room he seemed just as he had on every day of their marriage: amiable, relaxed and conversable with everyone equally. Perhaps he was wary of embarrassing her with marked attentions, she thought, as she listened to his report on the morning's visit to a carriage warehouse.

'I have ordered a phaeton that both Isobel and I can drive—no, Penny, not a high-perch model—and a barouche that will take all four of us when we want to drive out in fine weather. Our existing carriage team can be used with that, but I must find a pair for the phaeton and riding horses for you three ladies. Colonel Troughton's mare will be coming on approval, but I need more for you to try out.'

'For us as well?' Prue was wide-eyed with excitement. 'But what about Daisy and Bluebell?'

'I rather think you have outgrown your childhood ponies, don't you? They can enjoy a comfortable retirement in the country.'

Having reduced his cousins to a state of blissful silence, Leo inquired how Giles Norcross was settling in and then smiled at Isobel. 'All well on the domestic front?'

Isobel restrained a sudden urge to upend the bread basket over his head. If he thought he was being tactful by not as much as hinting at their altered relationship, he was much mistaken. *Patronising* was the word she would have chosen.

'Certainly it is. The girls had a lesson on the harp this morning and Signora Bianchi is coming this afternoon for the first of their Italian lessons. Mr Parkin is calling on me at three.'

Leo raised an interrogative eyebrow, but merely observed, 'To report, I assume. Would you like me to attend your meeting with him?'

'I believe I can manage, thank you.' Rather belatedly, she remembered to smile.

Leo shot her a puzzled look, presumably for her snappish tone, but really, she thought resentfully, was it too much to hope for a touch of the hand, an intimate glance? 'Finding the right horses is much more important,' she added. 'But you will give us the final choice, I hope?'

'Of course. I will buy nothing without your approval.'

Perhaps Leo would linger after the meal… But, no, he asked Giles Norcross to join him in his study, made the twins giggle by bidding them farewell in Italian, and went out.

Not certain whether she was more upset than angry, Isobel had retreated to her desk and finished her correspondence in time for Mr Parkin to be announced.

When he was settled with a cup of tea and the pleasantries had been exchanged, he regarded her with a serious expression. 'You may have wondered why I have not reported to you before now, Lady Halford.'

'Why, no, I was not at all impatient. I confess I had no idea how long it might take you to settle the transfer of my affairs.'

'There were almost no affairs to settle,' he said grimly. 'I regret to say that your cousin has not been a faithful trustee.'

It took a moment to sink in. 'You mean he has *lost* my money?' The room seemed to spin a little, then she told herself it was not the disaster it might have been. As a married woman, her money was Leo's and he had enough now, more than enough, for both of them. But her inheritance represented her independence. And besides, there was the breach of trust and all the times Cousin Edward had assured her she did not have the funds to live independently. Of course she had not—he had spent them.

'I am afraid Lord Martyn has proved to have been most…misguided.'

Chapter Fourteen

'All my money has gone?' Isobel could say it more calmly now.

'I am glad to say, no. The books now balance, but what lengths Lord Martyn has been put to in order to achieve that, I cannot imagine. Yes, you have suffered losses, my lady, because your capital has not been put to work earning interest and, of course, you have had to manage on a small allowance ever since your father's death. But the capital is secured and we are now in a position to finalise the settlements made with Lord Halford.'

'My own cousin has been lying to me and cheating me ever since he inherited?'

'I fear so. You do, of course, have remedy in law should you choose to pursue it.'

'But that would create the most frightful scandal, would it not?'

'And would be, in itself, expensive and time-consuming. My advice would be to allow the matter to drop, unless you know of anyone else who is vulnerable to him.'

'No, I am the only person for whom he held monies in trust. Very well, I shall speak to him when I am next in Little Bitterns, but for the moment I am inclined to leave him to stew in the knowledge that I know what he has done.'

'Very well. Here is a summary of the financial position now.' Mr Parkin handed her a sheet of paper.

Isobel read it, blinked and read it again. 'This is a substantial sum of money.' Nothing like what Leo had inherited, of course, but far more than she had imagined. Added to Leo's fortune... Visions of restoring the Hall, the estate and this house to their full glory without having to cut corners, of giving the twins substantial dowries and perhaps of foreign travel flashed through her mind.

'My goodness, whatever is Cousin Amelia going to do when she discovers how much he has had to pay back? How ever did he raise it?'

'I did not enquire,' Mr Parkin said severely. 'I was not inclined to waste any sympathy on His Lordship's self-inflicted difficulties.'

'I shall tell my husband this evening and we will be in touch to finalise the settlements. I must thank you, Mr Parkin, for your energetic and efficient pursuit of my interests.'

'It was my pleasure, Lady Halford.'

Leo found Isobel quiet and strangely subdued when he returned from Tattersall's late that afternoon, but his immediate anxiety, that she was regretting what had occurred the previous night, was dispelled when she took his arm and steered him into the deserted drawing room.

'Come and sit with me on the sofa. Leo, I had the most disturbing interview with Mr Parkin this afternoon. Cousin Edward had been using my inheritance as his own. Mr Parkin has succeeded in getting all the capital repaid, somehow, and look—see how much it is.' She thrust a sheet of paper into his hands and he gave a soundless whistle when he saw the total.

'The absolute ba— That is, the swine. Not only was he stealing from you, but he lied to you as well—you could have lived an independent life of great comfort on this.'

'Yes,' she agreed, sounding very subdued. He was hardly surprised—to be betrayed by someone she should have been able to trust implicitly must be shattering. Then he realised something else—if she had known about the money she would have left Little Bitterns months ago. They would never have married. Was Isobel regretting that deeply now?

They would never have married.

He had trouble imagining that now. Lucinda might have been here in her place. Lucinda might have been the one to run his household, be a sister to the twins… It was suddenly very difficult to imagine that, to picture Lucinda in Isobel's place. He gave himself a mental shake. Lucinda was very young, immature. Of course it was difficult to envisage her as any man's wife. She would have learned, of course she would.

Leo pushed the thoughts away. This concerned Isobel and needed his full attention.

'This explains something I have been puzzling over ever since I received a letter from Harding, my estate manager, a few days ago. I know where he got some of the money to pay you back,' he told her. 'From me. He approached Harding to say he had decided to sell the old Farthingstone estate and did I still want to buy it. Your father purchased it years ago, if you recall, and apparently it was not part of the entail.

'I'd approached your cousin last year about it, hoping he might rent it at a reasonable sum, because it would make a considerable difference to how we use our land on that side of the estate, but he asked for a ridiculous amount of money. He still wanted a stiff price to sell, but I wrote back to Harding agreeing to it and organised a draft on my bank.'

'So he used you to dig himself out of this hole,' Isobel said angrily.

'Well, I have got the land I wanted and you have got the money back, so we have not lost by it,' Leo pointed out. 'But it would not clear all of this. I wonder what else he has sold.'

'Amelia's jewellery, I would guess,' Isobel said. 'She inherited some very beautiful pieces from her mother and grandmothers. With that and just about everything else he could scrape together it would repay the sum I was owed, I suppose. They must be feeling very angry indeed that I married and this came to light.'

'You know,' Leo said slowly, 'I am very glad indeed that we decided to elope. I do not like to think what might have happened if you had told them what you intended beforehand.'

'They could not stop me,' Isobel protested. 'I am of age.'

'You might have become physically sick. They might have called in doctors to certify that you were behaving irrationally—as a result of something they fed you in both cases, of course—and should be confined. It happens all too often to vulnerable women whose relatives find them inconvenient. There was a case in the newspapers only the other day.'

'What a horrible thought. And I suppose if I had insisted on leaving home, even if only to take up paid employment, they might have feared I would take legal or financial advice in the process. I do not want to think it of them, but I find that I am very glad indeed that we eloped.' She shivered and Leo put his arms around her and hugged her close.

'So am I. But they cannot harm you now, even if our worst suspicions about them are true.'

Isobel sat up straight and he let her go. She gave a decisive nod. 'And your man of law and Mr Parkin can finish the settlements now. And, I would have you know, I shall want a substantial quarterly allowance and generous housekeeping monies in light of this paper.'

Leo suppressed a grin. 'Just tell me what you want. You should take advantage of me discovering that I married a well-to-do wife.'

To his surprise, Isobel kicked off her pretty satin slippers and curled up on the sofa, leaning against his shoulder. It was an effort not to edge away. All day he had been resolving to somehow keep their relationship calm and friendly during the daytime and not to allow whatever passion they might experience at night to change things.

Women were romantic and sentimental, he believed. They were certainly not driven by the same bodily urges that men were. For Isobel to lie with him argued that she felt more than friendship, or was in danger of feeling more. And he could not return more than friendship and physical passion, however hard he tried to forget Lucinda and his feelings for her.

Those feelings had felt confused since his marriage, but he supposed that was inevitable. Certainly he had not fallen out of love, because, surely, that did not happen if the feeling was true in the first place?

He should have remembered that Isobel knew him very well indeed.

'What is wrong, Leo?' She twisted around a little so she could look up into his face.

'Just anger at Edward,' he said. Now he was lying to her. And this was Izzy, for goodness sake. His friend. His wife.

He wrapped one arm around her shoulders and pulled her closer. Immediately, she relaxed and, almost as quickly, he felt himself do, too. There was something very soothing about the warmth of another human body so close, so trusting. And so soft.

Isobel was tall and slender and, he supposed, quite active for a woman of her class. He had not expected the yielding, subtle curves, the supple femininity. Or, perhaps, he had been taking her for granted, hardly noticing that she was a woman at all before last night.

'This is nice,' she said and let her head rest on his shoulder. 'You are very comfortable to be with, Leo.'

'Comfortable?' He was not at all sure that was how he saw himself.

'Strong, reliable. A bit bony.' She wriggled into a more comfortable position, sending a frisson of arousal through him as she did so. 'That's better. I feel so safe with you, Leo.'

He digested that, then decided that he might as well make a complete fool of himself and ask, 'Safe as in dull, boring and tame?'

'No, you idiot.' Isobel gave him a playful jab in the ribs. 'As in, you would protect me from anything that threatened me and you would never hurt me.'

He began to protest and she added hastily, 'I do not mean physically. Of course you would never hurt any woman. I mean, hurt my feelings.'

That was the very thing he feared, hurting her loyal, affectionate heart. 'Oh, Izzy—'

She looked up at him again and he kissed her. She kissed him back, then wriggled so that she was against his chest, pushing him back towards the arm of the sofa. Leo went with it and Isobel laughed as she settled on top of him.

'I didn't know we would fit so well this way up.'

'Oh, yes,' he managed to say before she kissed him, then pulled away, her expression amused as she looked down at him.

'It feels different somehow, but I like it.'

Leo more than liked it. Isobel's full length on top of him and squirming was incredibly arousing and so were the mental images of what it would be like with them naked in bed and her on top. Riding him…

Then she lifted her head, listening. 'The girls have come down.'

Getting off him involved a near escape from a knee in his more delicate parts, an elbow in his stomach and an undignified scuffle as he attempted to disguise his state of rampant arousal and she found her shoes, smoothed her skirts and sat down with a bump in an armchair.

Penny and Prue erupted into the room, giggling. 'Oh, good, you are both here,' Prue said. 'We can count up to ten in Italian now and say good morning and good-bye and thank you and—'

'Eccellente,' Isobel said. *'Molto bene.'*

'That means excellent and very good,' Penny said. *'Mi chiamo* Penelope.'

'And have you any work to do between lessons?' Isobel said.

'We have vocabulary to learn. We can practise with you, can't we, Isobel? I expect your accent is very good.'

'It is very rusty,' Isobel said ruefully, 'but I expect we will improve together.'

'How were the harp lessons?' Leo asked from where he sat in the corner of the sofa, idly picking at the fringe of the cushion he had placed in his lap.

They were less enthusiastic about those. The strings made their fingers sore and Madame Zelinki was very strict, according to Prue. 'But it is very pretty when she plays, so I suppose we will get better in time.'

'I have found some horses and ponies that I think you

might like,' Leo told them. 'There were four ponies I
feel are promising and the owners will send them here
tomorrow morning so you all can choose. Riding horses
were more difficult and I have not yet found one that I
thought you would like to compare with the Colonel's
mare, Isobel. There are some perfectly decent hacks,
but none with that combination of good manners and
a certain spirit that I expect you would prefer to ride.'
As he said it the fantasy of Isobel riding, and not on a
horse, flashed into his mind.

Something in his expression must have reached her.
'That is always a good combination,' she said with a
twinkle in her eyes that was decidedly naughty. Leo decided to hang on to the cushion for a few more minutes.

It had been an interesting day of ups and downs,
Isobel decided as she sat at her dressing table, enjoying Nancy brushing out her hair.

At first Leo keeping so much at a distance had been
puzzling and a little upsetting, if she was to be truth-
ful, but his passionate response on the sofa in the afternoon convinced her that he had either been a trifle
embarrassed after the night before or had assumed that
she would be. Then there was the shocking news about
Cousin Edward, balanced by the discovery that she had
much more money than she had dreamed of.

Overall, she decided, things were going very well.
She was properly married, Leo appeared to find her
desirable, their financial future was even more assured
and the twins seemed very happy.

'How are you, Nancy?' she asked as the maid put

down the hairbrush and went to shake out the night-gown that had been warming by the fire. 'Are you settling into the household now?'

'Oh, yes, my lady. My room is lovely and I get on well with all the staff, although Mrs Druett is still rather starchy, but that's because Mr Wilmore is quite young, I think. I mean, we're all young except her and Cook now that Finkle's gone back to Little Bitterns, so perhaps we're a bit livelier than she is used to.'

'That must be it,' Isobel agreed, hiding a smile as she stood up so that Nancy could help her undress.

As she had the night before, she took a book and went to sit by the fire once Nancy had departed, although not before she had dabbed a little scent behind her ears. She could go and sit up in bed, she supposed, because she really was not concentrating on the book, but somehow sitting in bed waiting to see whether or not Leo would come to her felt uncomfortable.

Isobel probed the feeling. Passive, that was how it felt, and from the moment she had decided that she must leave Little Bitterns she had felt stronger, decisive, in charge of her own destiny. Now she was back to waiting on the desires of a man again, even if it was one she loved.

The clock on the mantel shelf chimed the half hour with a silvery tinkle. Half past eleven, she realised when she glanced up at it. Was Leo going to come or not? And wasn't sitting here by the fire waiting just as passive as sitting in bed?

Isobel stood up in a flurry of full skirts and started for the door, then hesitated. Perhaps he had gone out to one of his clubs. Or was downstairs in the library. Well, if he was in the house, she would find him and if he was not, then in the morning they would have a frank discussion about keeping each other informed.

The righteous indignation that she was working up in anticipation of that discussion—or, more likely, full-blown row—carried her across the little sitting room and through Leo's bedchamber door without knocking.

'Good evening.'

He was sitting up in bed, bare-chested under the silk robe that was draped around his shoulders, a book in his hand. He dropped it on the coverlet. 'Is something wrong, Isobel?'

'No,' she said, flustered and oddly short of breath at the sight of him, lounging there like some lord awaiting his... 'I mean, yes. I did not know whether you were going to come to my bed. Chamber, that is.'

Leo picked up the book, tossed it on to the bedside table and took hold of the covers as if to throw them off.

Even more flustered now, Isobel stammered. 'I didn't know what the usual thing would be. I mean, do we take it in turns going to each other's bedchambers? Or am I expected to wait, not knowing whether you are coming or not?'

Leo let go of the covers. 'I thought you might be sore after last night,' he said, the explicitness of it making her blush. 'I did not want to assume that you would be willing to receive me again.'

'Oh. You could just ask. I mean, I thought that this afternoon in the drawing room I...er...indicated, that I was perfectly willing.' She found she was studying the

ornate carving on the old-fashioned wooden bedstead as
though she had never seen it before. Probably she simply had not looked, just checked for dust and cobwebs.

'This is a splendid bed, isn't it? Mine is perfectly
good and very comfortable, but this must be an heir-
loom.' She went and ran both hands down the carved
upright supporting the nearest corner.

Leo made a low sound, rather like a large dog which
has seen someone approaching a particularly juicy bone.
'Isobel, if you want a good night's sleep, might I suggest that you stop fondling my bedposts.'

When she turned to look at him she realised that
something about bedposts spoke to the male erotic
imagination, because he had shrugged off the robe,
thrown aside the covers and was on his knees reaching
for her. And he was unmistakably eager to make love.

Isobel retreated around the post to the end of the
bed. Leo followed and she found she was becoming
very aroused herself. Goodness, this game of catch was
interesting...

The next bedpost appeared to be carved with muscular naked figures, although it was difficult to see in
the candlelight. She ran both hands down over what felt
like male buttocks and Leo pounced, missing her and
sprawling on the bed when she used the post to swing
clear and back to the other side of the bed.

'Oh, it is so hot in here.' She slipped off the robe, and
Leo dived for her, caught her in his arms and pinned
her against the bedpost.

'Isobel, have you come here to discuss seventeenth-
century furniture, the heating of bedchambers or—'

'Or,' she said. 'Most definitely or.'

The next thing she knew she had landed in the middle of the bed and Leo was on top of her. It was a big bed and, with the new mattresses, a soft one, too. 'Help, I am sinking!'

He rolled, taking her with him so that she lay full length of top, just as she had done on the sofa, only now there was only one layer of thin cotton batiste between their naked bodies.

'What do I do now?' she asked after a moment.

'Whatever occurs to you,' Leo said between gritted teeth. 'Only this time, be careful where you put your knees.'

It seemed to Isobel that she was wearing too much clothing, so she knelt up, straddled his thighs and wriggled until she could take hold of the hem of her nightgown and drag it over her head. When she emerged from its folds she found that Leo had closed his eyes.

'Leo! Have you gone to sleep?'

He opened them. 'I am attempting not to lose control completely and ravish you until we are both unconscious,' he said. He took her right hand and planted it firmly on his body. Instinctively, her fingers curled around him. 'Does this feel as if I have gone to sleep?'

'No,' she admitted, looking down. There were a number of things she was tempted to do. Stroke for one, taste for another. Both seemed too daring. Then she recalled the look in Leo's eyes when he had been talking about a spirited ride. His expression had made her feel warm and wicked without quite knowing why. Was this what he had meant?

Carefully, she moved forward until she was astride his hips and looked down to find that Leo's fingers were cramped in the rumpled bedding. From the expression on his face she was inflicting exquisite torture on him and she had learned enough already to know that this was a good thing. A very good thing.

Cautiously, she knelt up, then eased down, guiding him to where she needed him. Down, down… And then, with him fully within her, she simply froze, absorbing the sensation of exquisite fullness, the frisson of being in control.

'*Agh!* Could you…move?' he managed to gasp.

So she moved until they both cried out and she fell on to his chest and they clung together as the velvet darkness took her.

And, in her mind, she said, over and over, *I love you. I love you.*

Chapter Fifteen

It was all going to be all right, Isobel told herself as she surveyed the breakfast table the next morning. Everything would work out and she and Leo would be happy, their marriage would prosper, the twins would continue to grow into confident, talented young ladies, the household would run as smoothly as a fine French clock and—

'Why can't we have our dinner with you tonight?' Prue asked with something perilously close to a whine in her voice.

'Because, as you perfectly well know, you are not yet out and this is a dinner party for adults before we go together to Lady Notlett's masquerade ball,' Leo said with accuracy, but a distressing lack of tact in the use of 'adults'.

'But they are all friends,' Penny said. 'It isn't as though they are some stuffy people we do not know.'

Before Isobel could intervene, Leo put down *The Times*, which he had been attempting to read. 'It is not about what you want, Penelope. Our guests will wish to converse without having to consider which topics may or may not be suitable for your ears.'

The twins subsided and sat picking at their food with identical pouts.

To her horror, Isobel heard her own grandmother's words escaping her lips. 'If you pull faces the wind will change and you will be stuck like that for ever.'

'Yes, Isobel,' they chorused and replaced the pouts with artificial smirks which were twice as bad.

Leo picked up the newspaper again and vanished behind it with what sounded suspiciously like a growl.

Isobel sighed. At least if they had been her own children she would have had fifteen years to hone her skills at motherhood. She sent a silent apology to her dear mama for whatever horrors she had inflicted on her when she had been growing up.

But, sulking girls aside, her day went well. She and Leo had discussed their plans amiably over their diaries while Giles Norcross made careful notes, then Leo went off in pursuit of more riding horses for her, parting with a kiss that made her knees weak.

Isobel had floated happily through the rest of the morning, reviewing the dinner menu with Cook, writing letters, admiring the girls' piano practice and first tentative watercolour sketches and strolling out to the circulating library where she borrowed a small stack of entirely frivolous novels.

Leo had come back for luncheon, reported that he had identified another horse to be brought around for approval the next day, along with the ponies and Colonel Troughton's mare, and departed for a meeting at the House of Lords where he would take his seat in a few weeks.

Isobel had waved the girls off with Miss Pettigrew and their new drawing master to sketch in Green Park and settled down with the first of the novels she had borrowed, the notorious *Glenarvon* by Lady Caroline Lamb.

Their dinner guests were the Duke and Duchess of Northleigh—or, as they were now on first-name terms, Simon and Anthea. They also asked Giles Norcross to dine with them. He unbalanced the table, but as it was a small and informal gathering that hardly mattered.

'I have been attempting to read *Glenarvon*,' Isobel confessed as they gathered in the drawing room beforehand. 'But I suspect I am missing a great many allusions and sly jokes.'

'There is no doubt of that,' Anthea said. 'It is a true roman à clef and I am certain even those of us who have been out in society for years have not yet identified everyone in it. Glenarvon is Byron, of course, and Calantha is a self-portrait by Caro Lamb, but she has quite ruined herself with it, the silly creature. Almack's is closed to her and what hostess will invite her when most of them have been cruelly satirised in it?'

'I shall leave it until I am more familiar with all the notables then,' Isobel said with some relief. It had struck her as being entirely nonsensical.

'You look very happy, my dear Isobel,' Anthea remarked when they had retired to her bedchamber after dinner to prepare for the masquerade.

'I am,' Isobel admitted. 'At first I was not certain that I had done the right thing, eloping like that, but now everything is…wonderful.'

'Excellent. Now, what is your costume? Oh, a shepherdess, how charming. You look just like a Dresden china ornament.'

Isobel twirled in the full skirts that showed off her ankles and the criss-cross ribbons of her slippers. 'It feels a little strange having the waistline so low and I have no idea what I will do with my crook and my lamb if I am asked to dance, but I admit I like it.'

The bodice was cut with a square neckline and laced up the front, and the sleeves were puffed. Everything was trimmed with lace that would be highly unlikely on any real shepherdess and the little crook was decorated with pale blue ribbons that matched those around the neck of the toy lamb. Her hair was loose and twined with more ribbons and a blue and silver mask completed the costume.

'And what is Havelock disguised as?'

'Leo was undecided between a wolf and a shepherd until I pointed out that the wolfskin would be far too hot for comfort. Oh, I do like that.'

The Duchess's maid was helping her into a Turkish costume, with flowing silken skirts that parted as she moved to give daring glimpses of full trousers. There was a tight, heavily embroidered bodice and a turban constructed from more rich textiles.

'Simon is the Grand Turk himself, of course,' Anthea said, admiring her own slippers with their curling toes.

'Like you, he will have trouble with his accessories, only in his case it is a curving scimitar.'

'Wooden, presumably?'

'No, a real one, I fear. His father brought it back from the Grand Tour. I shall have to persuade him to send it to the cloakroom before the dancing begins or half the other dancers will be cut off at the knees by the end of the first set.'

They negotiated the receiving line and joined the crowds admiring each other's costumes without either putting out anyone's eye with Isobel's crook or inflicting any wounds with the scimitar. After a circuit of the room she tactfully persuaded the Duke to surrender his weapon to the footman she had found to take both crook and lamb from her.

Leo had interpreted a shepherd's costume as homespun breeches worn with stockings and sturdy shoes, a loose shirt open at the neck and a leather waistcoat, borrowed from one of the footmen. He had added a festive note with a red kerchief tied at his neck and coloured ribbons instead of laces at the knees of the breeches and confessed that the ensemble was considerably more comfortable than his normal evening wear. He certainly looked exceedingly attractive in it, Isobel thought, and the black silk mask added a dashing edge of danger.

Isobel had never been to a masquerade ball before and had heard them criticised as sad romps, with the anonymity of the masks encouraging both men and women to take more liberties than they normally would. So far, at least, this one appeared no more free and easy than any other ball and there was a great deal of amusement to be had trying to guess who everyone was behind their masks, especially as so many of the costumes involved elaborate wigs.

There was a portly Henry VIII who Anthea identified as an important member of the Whig party, a jester they all decided was Lord Titchfield, two versions of the goddess Diana who stalked about glaring at each other—Lady Fontley and Mrs Arbuthnott, Anthea whispered—and several gentlemen in ill-advised armour or chainmail who were already clanking stiffly and visibly sweating.

Some guests were making no attempt to disguise their identity while others, with curling powdered wigs and full-face masks, were impossible to guess.

The orchestra struck up for the first set and Leo, claiming husband's privilege, led her out on to the dance floor.

'How unfashionable of you, my lord, to partner your wife,' she teased as they took their place.

'Ah, but newlyweds are allowed some licence without being thought insufferably romantic,' he countered.

'Newlyweds? I suppose we are,' Isobel said, surprised. 'It seems as though we have been married for ever.'

'That is because we have been friends for ever.' Leo seemed somewhat struck by the idea. 'But you are right. We must be quite a novelty: married friends, although I suppose many couples do become friends over the years.'

They joined hands and began to make their way down

the set as the country dance began. 'It is working, isn't it, Izzy?' he said, looking down at her and smiling in the way that always made her heart flutter just a little.

'Admirably, I should say,' she replied, keeping her tone light, trusting that none of her hopes and feelings showed on her face.

They reached the end of their promenade, turned to form part of a circle and set to partners. Isobel was swung around by a dashing pirate complete with eye-patch and gold earring while Leo, she saw out of the corner of her eye, was hand in hand with a fairy queen with a pair of little gauzy wings and a mass of tumbling blonde curls.

The fairy laughed and immediately Isobel knew who she was.

Leo must have realised at the same time, but all he said was, 'Good evening, fair Titania.'

As Isobel guessed, Shakespeare was a closed book to Lucinda and what could be seen of her face was blank for a few seconds. When Leo released her and she went back to her partner, she laughed again. 'You have me wrong, sir,' she said and danced off.

Reclaimed by Leo, Isobel made no comment, but he said, 'You saw who that was?'

They were weaving in and out of the line now, which gave Isobel a moment to collect herself. 'Yes, Lucinda, in high spirits.' And looking very pretty, but she did not add that. He had eyes in his head, after all.

'Too high.' Leo glanced over her shoulder and, despite the mask, she could tell he was frowning. 'She does not have the town bronze yet to cope with the young bucks and smooth older rakes who will try to take advantage of the anonymity of a masquerade.'

'Her aunt and uncle will be here somewhere, I am sure,' Isobel said as another circle formed.

'Yes, of course.' Leo did not sound reassured as he stepped in to take the hands of the Elizabethan lady opposite him.

The Duke claimed the next dance from Isobel and she soon found her dance card filling, mostly with gentlemen whom she did not recognise, although Sir Thomas Eddington had not troubled himself with a costume and was wearing his dress uniform and the merest strip of silk as a mask.

As they waltzed she teased him for his lack of imagination and he snorted dismissively. 'Leave all that to my sister. The silly chit is all decked out as Cleopatra, Queen of the Nile, complete with asp—stuffed, you'll be glad to hear—and is probably even now flirting with some Roman emperor.'

'I am certain Miss Eddington would never overstep the mark.'

'Chloe might not, but half the young bucks here probably would, given one inch.'

'Never fear, if one of them took liberties I am certain Chloe would hit him with her asp.'

That made him laugh and he escorted her back to Leo with a smile on his face.

Leo was talking to a group, none of whom she was certain that she recognised, but when he saw her he broke away and came to take her hand. 'You did keep the supper dance for me, I hope?'

'Of course.'

The food was excellent and the wine flowed. Isobel was conscious that perhaps she had taken one glass too many and also that the atmosphere of the ball was becoming freer.

Leo looked across the crowded supper room and swore under his breath. When she followed his gaze she saw the fairy queen very close indeed to a tall figure dressed as Mephistopheles, all in scarlet with little horns showing among his shock of red hair.

'Who is the demon, do you know?' she asked.

'With that hair it can only be Lord Ludovic Carstares, Oldham's younger son. Not good company for any unmarried girl. In fact, not safe for any decent lady.' He had put down his fork and was staring fixedly across the room. His knife was still in his hand.

It was ridiculous to feel afraid, yet Isobel did. 'You are dripping cream sauce,' she said as prosaically as she could manage. They did not need any more drama.

'What? Oh, yes.' Leo put down the knife, but he still kept glancing across at Lucinda and her partner, who was feeding her little morsels of something from a spoon. Her laughter was audible even above the conversation and clatter of cutlery on china.

They finished their meal and Leo did not linger. 'Where the devil are her aunt and uncle? Lady Amberleigh ought to have more sense than to allow her to run wild at a masquerade.'

'Ah, my fair shepherdess. The next dance is mine, I believe.' A Harlequin, one of several present, bowed with a flourish. Isobel had recognised him as Mr Lisle, an acquaintance, and had earlier agreed happily to dance with him. Now she wanted to stay with Leo.

'I—'

But it was a waltz and Harlequin had already swept her into a hold and they were on the dance floor. She could not break away now without drawing attention to them and offending Mr Lisle, a perfectly decent young gentleman.

It was not easy dancing on a crowded floor, keeping up a polite flow of inconsequential chatter and looking out for Mephistopheles's red head. Leo's brown hair was less easy to find, but she would know his tall figure anywhere and, once she glimpsed him making his way along the left-hand side of the room, he was easy to follow.

Harlequin swung her around a corner and there was Mephistopheles, just disappearing through a door, which closed after him. Was Lucinda with him? She could not see her slight figure, but she could see Leo, shouldering past a group of laughing gentlemen.

'Oh!' Isobel stopped abruptly, almost throwing her partner off balance. 'I'm so sorry, I—' She almost said *stepped on my hem,* then remembered it was well clear of the floor.

'Something has broken,' she whispered in Mr Lisle's ear, clutching her chest in such a way that he hopefully would assume a major failure of her corset strings. 'I must—'

'Yes, of course.' He was blushing under Harlequin's mask and shepherded her to the edge of the dance floor. 'Will you be…? I mean, shall I…?'

'No, I will just go out and find the ladies' retiring room.' She gestured at the door where Mephistopheles had vanished. There was no sign of Leo.

Isobel slipped through the crowd, opened the door just wide enough to get through and closed it behind her. She was in a narrow, gloomy corridor, a service access, she supposed. There was light at the far end and she glimpsed a footman crossing with a tray of empty glasses.

Where had they gone? Then there was the sound of scuffling feet from behind a door a little way along, a faint shriek and a thud.

Isobel ran, wrenched the door open and found herself in a small room. Lord Ludovic Carstares was sprawled across a *chaise longue,* the blood running from his nose clashing nastily with his hair and costume. She hardly spared him a glance, except to note that, thankfully, he seemed semi-conscious. Certainly not dead, which was a relief.

In the centre of the room, Leo stood with Lucinda clinging to him and sobbing into his shirt front while he held her close with one arm and stroked her hair with his free hand, his head bent so that his mouth was in her hair, muffling whatever it was that he was saying.

The muddle of emotions that swept through her made Isobel feel queasy. She let the anger take control.

'Lucinda, come here,' she said sharply and, when the young woman looked up at her, snapped, 'Whatever did you think you were doing, coming into a room alone with a man? And stop blubbering, your face is not fit to be seen.' It was an untruth—Lucinda, along with many other unfair advantages, could shed tears quite charmingly.

Lucinda clung to Leo, who took one look at Isobel's tear-drenched blue eyes and put her gently away from him. 'Yes, Lucinda, go with Isobel. You cannot be seen like that.'

'Give me your handkerchief.' Isobel took the large white square that Leo produced and handed it to Lucinda. 'Cover your face with that and I will try to get you to the ladies' retiring room.'

Somehow she got Lucinda out into the corridor where she plucked off her wings and hid them behind a wooden chest, took off her own fichu and used it to wrap the betraying golden curls, then made sure that, with her hands to her face, the handkerchief hid the girl's identity.

She guided her down the corridor and out of the door into the ballroom, disconcerting two footmen who were just entering. It was slow work, getting around the edge of the room, but she kept saying, 'Something in her eye, I must get to the ladies' room and wash it out. No, we need no help, yes, thank you. Excuse me…'

After what seemed an age, but which was probably no more than a few minutes, they reached the sanctuary of the retiring room. One of the maids there took them behind a screen and provided a basin of warm water and Isobel handed the cloth to Lucinda.

'There. Wash your face and dry your eyes and do

not say a word,' she whispered. 'We do not know who else might come in.'

Lucinda sniffled, but obeyed. She took the cloth and dabbed daintily at her face, not troubling to acknowledge Isobel's help.

'There.' Isobel removed the fichu and tidied Lucinda's hair, then passed her the mask again. 'That will do.' She looked around the edge of the screen to find the room empty. 'Now, come with me and we will find your aunt and uncle and they will take you home.'

'I do not want to go home. I am—'

'Frankly, Lucinda,' Isobel said, getting to her feet, 'I do not care what you want. Come along.'

Thankfully, she found Lord and Lady Amberleigh not far from the retiring room door. Isobel told Lucinda's aunt who she was and what had happened in a whisper. Lady Amberleigh turned pale. 'Thank you, Lady Halford. We are very much obliged. Lucinda, we are going home immediately.'

As they turned to leave, Lucinda hung back. 'You are jealous,' she hissed. 'Because he loves me.'

It had been too much to expect gratitude, but the spite hurt. Swallowing hard against her own threatening tears, Isobel made her way back to the room where she had left the men.

Chapter Sixteen

Isobel found Ludovic Carstares on his feet, rather shakily blustering at Leo, 'I'll have satisfaction from you, my lord!'

'For what? Protecting an innocent young lady? I should be challenging you, Carstares, and you know it. And keep your mouth shut about this or I will deal with you as you deserve.'

The fuming young man stalked out, the effect somewhat spoilt by the fact that he tried to pull the door open instead of pushing it.

Leo turned and saw Isobel. 'Is she all right?'

And how are you? And thank you very much, dear Wife.

'She has gone home with her aunt and uncle,' Isobel said coolly. 'I do not believe that anyone saw anything untoward. What exactly was happening in here?'

'I followed them, as you know, but it took a few minutes to find the right door. When I opened it he had her on the *chaise*, kissing her. His hand was under her skirts.'

'No wonder she was so upset.' Isobel regretted her anger with Lucinda. She was spoiled and wilful, but, surely, she was too innocent to expect such an assault at a respectable ball. No wonder she had been in tears. Her unpleasant parting words had probably been the result of chagrin and shame.

'I hope it was that,' Leo said doubtfully. 'I cannot help but remember that Ludovic is the younger son of a marquess—and a rich one, too.'

'Which is no doubt why she flirted with him. Her mother or aunt should have a very frank talk with her and warn her what might easily happen,' Isobel said, wondering why she felt the need to defend Lucinda to him, then told herself that she was being unfair. If it had been any other young woman, she would have been just as determined to protect her.

Being a thoughtless flirt did not mean that Ludovic Carstares was justified in taking advantage of her lack of experience. 'Thank goodness that it was you and I who found them, or she would have been very seriously compromised.'

'We had better go back to the ball or we will be found here and, for a husband and wife to be caught, shall we say, frolicking, would be dreadfully unfashionable.' Leo appeared to have regained his sense of humour, which was something.

Isobel told herself that he had acted as any decent neighbour and gentleman would have done and that she had, herself, done her duty. It was unreasonable to expect Leo to be particularly grateful to her; in fact, he

could hardly do so without showing that he still har-
boured strong personal feelings for Lucinda.

She was back on the dance floor, executing an elaborate series of steps as the partner of one of the two
Roman emperors present, when she realised that she
was being foolishly optimistic.

'I do beg your pardon,' she apologised, untangling
herself from his toga. 'I lost my concentration for a
moment.'

He was a jovial Caesar and chuckled as he informed
her that he had no intention of throwing her to the lions.
'Ha-ha!'

Isobel chuckled, too, and made herself attend to her
footwork, but she found it difficult to keep a smile on
her face.

Of course Leo still felt strongly about Lucinda. He
would never have offered for her if he had not loved her
and he was no idle flirt: if he loved her a few weeks
ago, then he loved her still—the very tenderness with
which he had held her betrayed that.

Isobel was still wrestling with her miserable thoughts
when they finally left and were driving back through
the almost deserted streets, the darkness punctuated by
the lanterns over every door in the respectable areas,
the alleyways opening on to sinister darkness in others.

People remarried when their spouses died, even if
they had loved them deeply, she told herself. It did not
stop them being perfectly decent and faithful husbands
or wives to their next mate. Was it easier, or more dif-

ficult, not to resent someone who was a memory than it was to feel jealous of someone who was still very much alive? She could only wish that Lucinda was anywhere else but London, just at the moment. It felt as though her marriage was something fragile and precious and she wanted to hold it cupped in her hands to protect it from all the knocks that would bruise it.

Isobel was very quiet, Leo thought, watching her face in the sudden bursts of lights from the lamps that they passed. She had dealt with Lucinda in a way that was effective and calm, just as he would expect and, to his surprise, had defended the girl from his criticism.

He should have expressed his appreciation of her help, he thought, trying to read her expression. He had certainly felt as though a relieving force of cavalry had arrived in the room, which was strange, because he had the situation under control.

'I took you for granted,' he said abruptly. 'It must have been upsetting to walk in to a scene of violence and to deal with Lucinda so calmly and so kindly. I heard your voice and I thought, *Isobel is here...thank goodness for that.*'

He should have felt some guilt, Leo thought. After all, however good his motives, he had been found by his wife embracing another woman. But it had not felt like an embrace, not the kind that came from desire, more as though he had rescued one of the twins from some disaster and needed to comfort them. It would never have occurred to him that he could hold Lucinda

Paxton so closely and not feel the slightest tremor of desire, however guiltily.

'To say I was kind… I was quite sharp with her,' Isobel said, jerking him out of his thoughts.

'She was working herself up into hysterics and you stopped that. I was dealing with her in quite the wrong way.'

'It is good practice for when Penny and Prue are a little older, I expect.'

'How do you always stay so calm, Izzy?' Leo asked abruptly.

It took her a moment to answer and he wondered if she did not know herself, not consciously. Her reply told him that he had failed to understand her yet again.

'I have never found that being dramatic has any effect in a difficult situation. But then I am not an accredited beauty and beauties, like those of high rank, are always treated differently to those plainer and humbler.'

It was not said bitterly, more as if she was simply stating a fact. There seemed no answer to give, not a tactful one at any rate, but Isobel did not appear to expect one. Her eyes were closed and he saw there were shadows beneath them. Something inside him seemed to catch and he leaned forward, ran the ball of his thumb gently over the delicate skin where her lashes brushed.

'Are you very tired?'

'I have a little headache,' she confessed, her eyes still closed. He moved across to sit beside her and cupped her face in his hand. She leant into it with a sigh. 'It has been a long day.'

The carriage drew up and the groom jumped down

to open the door. Leo got out first, then, when Isobel was on the top step, caught her in his arms and carried her across the pavement.

'Leo?'

'You are weary and it occurs to me that I never carried my bride over the threshold on our wedding day, which is very remiss of me.'

'You can't carry me all the way up,' she protested when he put his foot on the bottom stair with no more than a nod to Wilmore.

'I most certainly can,' Leo said, silently thankful that it was only one flight. Isobel was slender, but tall, and he had no practice in carrying young ladies up steep inclines. Dropping her would be a disaster.

They arrived at the landing without mishap and, he was pleased to find, without him panting, although his heart rate did seem somewhat erratic when he looked down into Isobel's face, into the dark pools of her green eyes.

No, not an accredited beauty, but he found that no longer mattered. What he saw attracted him, strongly: her face, her supple form in his arms, the character of her.

It was an effort to set her on her feet at her bedchamber door. 'Have Nancy bring you something for that headache.' He brushed his fingers over the little groove between her brows. 'And then go to bed. I'll not disturb you.'

He bent and kissed her—quickly in case his willpower gave out and he joined her regardless of her weariness—and strode across to his own door where

Bertram, who had been snoozing in the chair by the fire, leapt to his feet and hurried to help him undress.

Ten minutes later he was in bed, all but one candle extinguished. He heard the soft murmur of voices as Bertram and Nancy met in the sitting room, then the faint click of the door closing. He closed his eyes, certain of sleep. It had been one hell of a day.

'Did you sleep well?' Isobel asked as Leo took his place at the breakfast table, although one glance told her that was extremely unlikely.

'I did not,' he confessed. Presumably he had looked in the mirror while shaving and knew a polite lie would not serve. 'Did you?'

'Yes, thank you. Nancy gave me some of the camomile tea that she makes to her mother's recipe. It is most effective.'

It had certainly sent her to sleep, but it had done nothing to calm the muddled and uneasy dreams that had haunted her slumber. Leo had, she guessed, been lying awake worrying about Lucinda.

She sent the twins a reproving look when they began chattering too loudly and they subsided with sideways glances at Leo who, she thought, resembled nothing more than a bear who had been awoken too early from his hibernation and was in half a mind to take a bite out of whoever was responsible.

'I believe the horses on approval will be arriving today,' she said when she calculated that two cups of coffee and a plateful of bacon and eggs might have improved Leo's thick head.

'Yes, at eleven. They are being brought around to the mews. Thank you,' he added as she refilled his cup.

Prue and Penny, reminded that this was a very good reason for exemplary behaviour, chorused, 'Thank you, Leo', and were answered with a smile as Wilmore brought in the post.

'There are a number of deliveries of flowers, my lady,' he added. 'I have placed them in the drawing room.'

'Flowers?' That was strange. Perhaps Lady Amberleigh had sent something. She turned to the pile of letters Wilmore laid beside her plate. There was a long screed from an old friend now married to a naval captain and living in Portsmouth. She set that aside for later. A few bills, some invitations—a reception, a musicale, a dinner—a note of thanks from the Duchess for last night's dinner and three notes from gentlemen.

Mr Lisle, with whom she had danced last night, would be honoured if she would drive out with him. Sir Thomas Eddington wondered if she might care to accompany him to an exhibition of water colours in Spring Gardens the following week and a Lord Carmichael also wished to offer to drive her on any fine day that took her fancy. Lord Carmichael? Oh, yes, at the unmasking she had asked who the pirate she had danced with had been and Leo had told her his name.

What on earth were they about, inviting a married woman? Surely she hadn't given any of them the impression that she might contemplate anything...irregular? She could hardly ask Leo about it and she did not wish to give offence, certainly not to Sir Thomas. She would ask Anthea, she decided. The Duchess knew her way around society and would advise her.

The flowers, when she inspected them, were equally as baffling, with the exception of a tasteful arrangement of hothouse blooms from Lady Amberleigh, with many thanks.

The others were from the three gentlemen who had issued invitations. No, she was most definitely not going to ask Leo about them, not with him in such a strange mood.

Breakfast had been late because of the ball the night before, so Isobel went up immediately to change into her riding habit and then to supervise the twins, who were so excited that they were proving a handful for the maid delegated to help them into their new habits.

'It is ages since we have been riding,' Prue said.

'I know. Your habits would hardly do up,' Isobel said. 'There now, you both look very smart.'

All their existing clothes had been matching, she found, so she had asked them whether they wished to be dressed identically or not.

'Miss Pettigrew said twins always were and that it was a saving to have two of everything made identically,' Penny explained. 'But I don't like it very much. We have different coloured hair and eyes and the same colours don't suit us both.'

Now Penny, the brunette, had a green habit and Prue, the blonde, a blue one, both with identical low-crowned hats with veils.

They went down to join Leo in the mews, all three

of them carefully lifting the long skirts of their habits. Four ponies of between twelve and fourteen hands high were already standing patiently, a groom at each head and all with side saddles.

The twins forgot their pose of being sophisticated young ladies, and their trailing skirts, and ran to pet them.

Isobel watched carefully to see how the animals reacted to two over-excited girls. 'The grey is rolling its eyes,' she observed to Leo.

'Yes, and it's the tallest of the four. Probably too much for either of them to handle. Yes, it has its ears back now. Mr Yates, take the grey away to the other end of the yard, please.'

That left three: a bay gelding, a chestnut mare and a black gelding. All were standing still, ears pricked, nuzzling politely at the apple slices the girls had begged from Cook.

'I like this one,' Penny announced, her hand possessively on the black's mane.

'And this is my favourite.' Prue fed the bay half a carrot. 'Although the chestnut is very pretty.'

'Let's put you up and see how they feel.' Leo gave them both a boost up into the saddles and watched while the grooms led the ponies up and down.

'They look sound and they seem calm. We'll take these two on trial, Mr Yates.' Leo lifted the girls down. 'No more now. We do not need distractions while Isobel tries the two horses. The ponies can get used to the stables here and we can take them out tomorrow,' he told them when they protested.

Isobel went to talk to the nearest of the two horses, a bay mare, who accepted the offered apple by lipping it up, then butted her gently on the shoulder when she was slow producing the next piece. 'Bossy, aren't you?' The mare pricked her ears and turned an intelligent brown eye on her.

'That's the mare from Colonel Troughton,' the groom told her. 'Part-Arab, my lady.'

Leo walked over from the twins, checked the girth, then boosted her up into the saddle, holding the rein just above the bit while she adjusted her skirts and slid her foot into the stirrup. The mare stood like a rock.

'Let her go, Leo.' Even then the horse waited for the pressure of Isobel's heel before she moved.

Isobel walked her along the mews and noticed that she passed the stable-yard cat, a big ginger tom, without a fuss and that she did not shy when one of the doors opened suddenly and a groom carrying a pitchfork walked out. At the end of the mews she turned and trotted back.

'She moves beautifully,' she told Leo. 'And she doesn't get distracted.'

He nodded. 'She's got excellent conformation. The gelding is a handsome beast. Do you want to try him now?'

The black gelding was certainly showy, with a long mane and beautiful tail. He fidgeted a little when she mounted, but responded when Isobel spoke to him, and walked on readily enough, turning his head to give the ginger tom a long look as they passed.

'There, not a tiger, after all,' Isobel told him and one ear flicked back to listen.

She turned and urged him into a trot, smooth as silk. There was a moment's warning, the feel of muscles bunching, tensing, as they passed the cat which stood up and stretched into what seemed an impossible length of tatty ginger fur, then the gelding shied sideways across the yard and took two bounding strides towards the open end of the mews.

Isobel sat down hard, used her hands and her voice, and he subsided, snorting and tossing his head. Leo, who had broken into a run, stopped, then walked slowly up to them.

'Are you all right, Izzy?' He was pale as he reached out and took the rein, his eyes never leaving her face.

'I am.' She kept her voice steady with an effort. It was well over a year since she had ridden and for a moment she had thought her old skills had deserted her. Those cobbles looked exceedingly hard. 'This beauty does not like cats, it seems.'

'And he can go straight back where he came from.'

'I like the mare, though. Can we keep her on approval?'

A groom hurried over to take the reins, and Leo held up his hands to lift her down. 'We can. Now come down before this animal decides it dislikes anything else.'

She kicked her foot free of the stirrup, lifted her leg over the pommel and slid down to be caught firmly around the waist and held, her feet several inches above the ground. 'Leo?'

He was still a little pale and his dark eyes were hooded, hiding his emotions, but she read them in the tightness of his grip and the way he held her so close.

'Leo?' she said again and he let her slide down to the ground.

'You may be out of practice, but you are still a very good horsewoman, Izzy,' he said at last. 'For which I am very grateful.' He stooped, there was a quick brush of his lips against hers, rough with the net of the veil between them, then he turned and went to talk to the men who had brought the animals.

Isobel watched him, the strength of his back, the expressive gestures of his hands as he made his feelings known about the black's behaviour, the respectful stance of the two men who listened to him.

He cared for her, there was no mistaking that. He had been frightened for her, moved that she was unharmed. But then, he had always looked after her, his little friend Izzy. It meant no more than that.

'Isobel, may we go and see the ponies in their stables? We want to think of names for them and—'

'No names, not yet. Wait until you have ridden in the park with Leo and he is happy for you to keep them.'

'Oh.' They were downcast, two disappointed girls. It was startling, the way they switched from schoolroom misses to young ladies and back again in moments.

'I am not going to name the bay mare either, not until I am certain I am keeping her,' she offered and they brightened. It had been a white lie. She fully intended keeping the name that had come to her as the mare had responded to her with such gentle manners.

Isobel left the twins behind with Miss Pettigrew who would escort them to their dance class that afternoon while she went to call on Anthea. It was not one of the Duchess's At Home days, so she had hopes of finding her friend alone and willing to be interrupted and she was in luck.

'Saved!' Anthea exclaimed. 'I was wrestling with a letter to my sister-in-law, Lady Bessington. Between us, my dear, she is the most intolerable bore and never ceases to bemoan her lot.'

'Is it so bad, then?' Isobel took a seat in the Duchess's pretty boudoir.

'It comprises an amiable husband who is an earl, a sizeable quarterly allowance, a houseful of servants and two charming children and still she can write four pages of complaint. I try to answer positively in the hope of supporting my poor brother, but it is a strain I am glad to postpone. So, tell me, what is amiss?'

'Men,' Isobel confessed. 'I am very confused.'

Chapter Seventeen

'Confused? Not about your delightful husband, surely?'

Yes, him, too. Not that she was going to confess that to anyone.

'This morning I received flowers from several gentlemen I danced with last night and invitations, too—to drive out with them, to attend art exhibitions. All couched in a perfectly normal social tone, as though I were not a married woman. None of them behaved at the masquerade in anything but a normal and proper manner and one of them is Sir Thomas. Why are they behaving like that?'

The Duchess laughed and reached for the bell pull. 'I will try to explain over tea.' The door opened to reveal a maid. 'Yes, Manning, a tea tray if you please. And some of Monsieur Gaston's macarons if they have been fresh baked.'

They made small talk until the tray was delivered. Anthea was interested in the trial of the horses and ponies and laughed about the account of how their new butler and their established housekeeper were gradually coming to terms with each other. She poured tea and sat back. 'Now, your worrisome gentlemen. What does Halford say?'

'He doesn't know. I didn't say anything. I didn't want him rushing out challenging anyone.'

'I doubt he would. You have heard of a cicisbeo?'

Isobel frowned in recollection. 'I think so. Were they not the escorts of ladies in the last century?'

'Exactly. A fashionable accessory, one might say. Sometimes they were lovers, but chiefly they were gentlemen who enjoyed the company of married ladies of fashion. And many ladies in society today still have them, although with today's fashions they are far less flamboyant. They are usually gentlemen who want to be out and about in society without having to worry about attracting young ladies and who enjoy the company of an intelligent married woman. They can be gallant without commitment and they can make female friends without comment. Some of them, of course, are gentlemen who are not, shall we say, the marrying kind, if you understand me. A married lady is safe.'

'Oh. I see. And husbands do not mind this?'

'It depends on the gentlemen involved, on both sides. But most husbands are perfectly capable of assessing the intentions of other gentlemen and are quite content for their wives to have safe escort where they cannot, or do not wish, to accompany them. I am rather fond of concerts of ancient music myself, but Northleigh would have to be driven at knife point to attend, so I always have the escort of one of my male friends. So, who are these gentlemen?'

'Mr Lisle, Sir Thomas Eddington and Lord Carmichael.'

'Now those three I can decipher for you. Sir Thomas, I am certain, likes you and hopes you will be friendly with his sister, who is proving rather skittish as far as the Marriage Mart is concerned. Mr Lisle is a poet and a romantic and will very much enjoy a hopeless and perfectly respectable passion for you while you will inspire his verse and, possibly, a novel or blank verse play.'

'Goodness. And Lord Carmichael?'

'Is, I suspect, a gentleman who would not wish to marry, but who enjoys the company of intelligent ladies. Being seen with you will counterbalance the occasions when he is seen with rather attractive young men. But I would not call his attentions cynical. As I say, he seems to be attracted to women of character as friends and companions.'

'And how would Leo see this?'

'As I do, I imagine. You might mention that you were talking to me and I suggested Sir Thomas's motive. I am certain he is already aware of Mr Lisle's verse and Lord Carmichael's, er, preferences.'

'I can see that is good advice. Certainly I can hardly expect him to appreciate my keeping rendezvous with other men in apparent secrecy.'

'Quite so. Even with a man in love it is always best never to give them an excuse for getting hold of the wrong end of the stick!'

'Oh, no, he doesn't lo—' Isobel broke off, appalled.

'Not love you? Surely you do not believe that? Why, the way he looks at you—'

'We are old friends.' Suddenly it was a great relief to tell someone the truth. 'Very good friends. Leo loves another lady and she refused his offer of marriage. Then we discovered that to inherit his great-aunt's fortune, which he needed desperately, he must marry. I was extremely unhappy at home. I suppose we proposed to each other. A marriage of convenience.'

'But you love him,' Anthea said gently.

Isobel nodded, afraid that if she spoke she would give way to tears. 'He doesn't know, of course.'

'No, of course. Men can be quite amazingly dense about emotional matters,' Anthea said with a sigh. 'Um, things are all right in—that is, you are fully married?'

'Yes. That is very much all right. But then men do not need to be in love with a woman to…to go to bed with them.'

'No,' the Duchess said and nibbled thoughtfully on a macaron. 'Do try these, Isobel, they really are excellent. No, the male animal is primed like a shotgun. Squeeze the trigger—' She broke off when Isobel gave way to giggles.

'Oh, dear, perhaps that was rather too apt a simile. Yes, their emotions do not have to be engaged, but what I mean to say is that a considerate lover will find himself drawn more and more to the lady with whom he lies. Do not dismiss what the two of you have together in the bedchamber.'

'Thank you. That seems very good advice.' Isobel

took a deep breath. 'And now, do you think your chef will give me the recipe for those macarons for my cook?'

'Giles is dining out with friends and the girls are a trifle over-excited by a combination of ponies and dance class, so they are eating with Miss Pettigrew upstairs, which means that we are dining *à deux* tonight,' Isobel informed Leo as he joined her in the drawing room.

'Excellent.' And it was. One part of him enjoyed having their extended 'family' around them, but tonight he wanted Isobel to himself. That incident in the mews when for one hideous moment he had imagined her broken and bleeding on those cobbles under the hooves of the horse had shaken him badly. He was not certain she would enjoy him fussing over her, though.

'We have a fine display of flower arrangements,' he remarked, searching for a neutral, unemotional subject. 'One in the hall and three in here.'

'The one outside in the hall is from Lady Amberleigh, as a thank you. These three are from my new admirers.'

Leo almost dropped the stopper of the decanter. He put it down with care and filled the second glass of Madeira. 'Admirers.'

'Yes, isn't it amusing? Thank you.' She took the glass he offered. 'I had no idea I was so fashionable. The Duchess explained all about it. Apparently, Sir Thomas is hoping I will be a good influence on Chloe, Mr Lisle is looking for poetical inspiration and Lord Carmichael finds feminine company pleasant and rather, um, useful. So, I have one invitation to an art exhibition and two for drives in the park. Aren't I dashing?'

'Very,' he said drily, trying to look amused and un-concerned. Definitely not in the slightest jealous, possessive or critical. The Duchess was quite correct and ladies of fashion could be escorted to anywhere respectable by gentlemen other than their husbands without an eyebrow being raised. The general opinion appeared to be that none of them would risk being seen with a lover in such a way and in any case, the sensitive antennae of the ladies of the *ton* would soon twitch if it were not a perfectly acceptable arrangement.

Of course he could trust Eddington, he told himself. Carmichael was, indeed, a gentleman whose tastes lay elsewhere and Lisle was known to be tolerated by a number of ladies who found him amusing company and were not averse to finding themselves the inspiration for his verse, which was considered quite accomplished.

Even so, it gave him a jolt to think of Isobel jauntering around town with other men and so soon after the wedding, too. He should take her around more himself, but somehow there hadn't seemed to be time, what with shopping for the house, dealing with the staff, buying horses, having discussions at Westminster, re-establishing himself in his clubs.

He hadn't really been treating her as a wife at all, except in the bedchamber, he thought guiltily. Isobel was still Izzy, his friend, helping him with the house, the twins, his plans for the estate.

That no longer felt right, Leo realised, although he could not quite put his finger on what exactly had changed.

'So you have no objection?' she persisted.

'Goodness, no. All perfectly decent fellows and, in any case, I trust your judgement absolutely.'

'Oh,' she said, rather blankly. Then, 'Thank you.'

Wilmore entered and announced that dinner was served and they went in, arm in arm.

Leo felt uneasy, as though Isobel had expected something more from him. Surely she hadn't expected him to be jealous? Hadn't *wanted* him to react possessively?

They ate their dinner, which was excellent, exchanging news and gossip, ideas about what should be priorities when they returned to Little Bitterns and discussing Leo's thoughts about his political affiliations once he took his seat in the Lords.

'I think I am more of a Whig than a Tory,' he said. 'I certainly support reform in all fields, although as a country landowner I have some Tory sympathies.'

'Do not commit yourself,' Isobel suggested. 'Vote with your conscience on each issue. That will not win you a place in the administration, though!'

He shook his head. 'I've no political aspirations, but it is my duty to take an interest. I think you are right. You have no ambition to be a political hostess, then? Entertaining the great and the good, and having the ear of cabinet ministers?'

'Absolutely not,' Isobel said with a shudder. 'But I am interested.'

They continued to discuss political issues when Isobel persuaded him to bring his port into the drawing room and keep her company. Not that any persuasion was necessary—he was enjoying their debate too much.

The fire had been built up and Isobel curled up comfortably on the sofa, leaning against his shoulder as they exchanged ideas. They both agreed on the abolition of slavery and the extension of the vote, which put them firmly in the Whig camp, but Leo earned himself a sharp jab in the ribs for laughing at the idea of female suffrage.

'Wives will simply vote as their husbands tell them,' he said.

'Not if the ballot was secret.'

'A secret ballot? Whoever heard of such a thing? I cannot imagine any politician voting for that.'

'No, I suppose not,' she said with a sigh.

'Men are very unsatisfactory, are we not?' Leo said, teasing.

'Exceedingly, although you are good for some things.' Isobel twisted around so she could reach up and kiss him and one thing led to another with an early night spent in her bed and, most definitely, no discussion of politics.

The next morning they all set out early to try their new mounts in Green Park before it became too busy. Giles Norcross was stabling his horse with them, so he came, too, along with a groom to help keep an eye on Penny and Prue.

Isobel was very conscious of Leo watching her, however carefully he tried to hide his anxiety, but the bay mare coped with brewers' drays, a coal cart and a crocodile of charity school children with perfect equanimity and, once they were within the bounds of the park, did no more than stare at a group of young men thundering past at the gallop.

A gallop was very tempting, but Isobel kept her to a walk while they all watched the twins, who rode very well, she thought.

After half an hour of walking, trotting and a canter, Leo pronounced himself satisfied with the ponies. 'Now, stay with Yates,' he told them. 'We will try out the mare's paces.'

'I'll race you both to that grove of trees,' Isobel said, pointing, and clicked her tongue. The mare needed little encouragement and, when she heard the sound of the two larger horses behind her, settled down into a beautifully smooth gallop.

They caught her, of course. Leo's chestnut stallion, Saturn, the one valuable thing he had managed to hold on to through all the difficult months, simply ate up the ground and Giles's Roman-nosed grey gelding had a fair turn of speed, too. They beat her by two lengths and a head respectively.

'She is lovely and I am keeping her,' she announced as she straightened her hat. 'I shall call her Dora.'

'Dora?' Leo looked at her quizzically.

'Because she is a*dora*ble, of course,' Isobel said and sent the mare curvetting across the grass to where Penny and Prue were trotting to meet them with Yates bringing up the rear.

'May we keep them? Please, Leo,' the girls chorused and Yates nodded his approval.

'You may. We have three new horses, it seems. This

is Dora.' He gestured to the mare. 'Have you thought of names?'

They shook their heads. 'We didn't dare in case you said we may not keep them,' Penny explained. 'If we had named them, then it would have been a *tragedy*.'

The ride back to Mount Street was enlivened by endless suggestions for names. Isobel did not expect a decision in the near future.

Leo watched from the drawing room window as Isobel was driven off in Carmichael's dashing curricle, all glossy black paint with yellow trim and a pair of equally dashing blacks to pull it. At least he had no need to worry about that young man's intentions—to show off his new rig with a lovely lady up beside him. No more, no less.

Even so, he felt restless and ill at ease. Perhaps the stack of estate papers waiting for him in the study made too great a contrast to the morning and the pleasure of watching Isobel on horseback, seeing the flush of pleasure on her face, her sparkling eyes, her laugh. Prue and Penny had pleased him, too. He was proud of their horsemanship, amused by their enthusiasm.

Now... *Work*, he told himself and strode out into the hall. In front of him were the flowers that Lady Amberleigh had sent Isobel.

Damn. Leo stopped in front of the side table. He should have called and made certain that all was well with Lucinda, perhaps have a quiet word in her aunt's ear about the character of Lord Ludovic Carstares. Lucinda must be upset and shocked still, because, of course, she would never have expected the man to take such liberties. He recalled the soft curves pressed to him, her sobs—and his own feeling of relief when Isobel had entered the room. It had felt like a rescue.

When he arrived on the doorstep of the Amberleigh town house, just the other side of Berkeley Square, he discovered that it was one of Her Ladyship's At Home days, with two ladies he did not know leaving and another, Mrs Spencer, her daughter beside her, just behind him.

He bowed and stood aside for all four and then followed Mrs Spencer in. 'Good afternoon, ma'am. Miss Spencer.'

Olive Spencer, the possessor of mouse-brown hair, a rather large nose and a warm and lovely smile, bestowed the smile on him shyly and made polite small talk while their various items of outdoor clothing were taken by the footmen and the butler went upstairs to announce them.

One glance around the room told Leo that he was not going to be able to have any words aside with Lady Amberleigh, who was presiding over the silver urn and dispensing tea to two young gentlemen, two matrons and two young ladies, one of whom was Lucinda.

She flashed him a brilliant smile when he came in, greeted Mrs Spencer politely and completely ignored Miss Spencer, turning back to talk to the two men. Neither of them was known to Leo until the introductions revealed them to be Lord Henry Gascoigne and Sir Matthew Breem.

One second son of a marquess and one baronet, Leo thought, as the two rose, bowed and were immediately recaptured by Lucinda. He collected teacups for Mrs Spencer and Olive, then settled with his own between them and began to chat to Olive, who had been sitting quietly, hands folded in her lap.

Not that she had much option, he thought. Lucinda had her shoulder turned and was monopolising the bachelors instead of including Miss Spencer in the conversation. Occasionally, she would glance at him as though assessing the amount of attention he was paying to her.

Leo felt a growing irritation at the treatment and set himself to draw out Miss Spencer. After a few moments he coaxed a ripple of laughter from her. It was as delightful as her smile, and Sir Matthew glanced over at them.

Immediately, Lucinda turned. 'How is dear Lady Halford?' she asked sweetly. 'I thought she looked a trifle... That is, she was rather brittle at the masquerade. London must be so tiring if one is a little older.'

'Isobel is in the best of health and I am sure will be grateful for your concern. She has a great deal to concern her at the moment—some people can be very inconsiderate and foolish and she does try to help them—but we are greatly enjoying ourselves.'

Lucinda coloured. Even with her normal self-regard she could not help but realise that comment was directed at her. She turned back to the two men, but, with a murmured apology, Sir Matthew got up and came to take the seat on Miss Spencer's other side.

And that is just what you deserved, Leo thought, and then realised just how angry he was with Lucinda.

He had heard the people talk of scales falling from their eyes and it had always seemed an exaggerated expression. Now he realised it had happened to him.

He had been dazzled by her beauty, mesmerised by all her pretty tricks and had fallen feet first into the trap of believing outward beauty must be reflected in the soul.

He was not in love with Lucinda Paxton and he never had been.

Chapter Eighteen

It isn't her fault, Leo thought, watching Lucinda's lovely profile turned haughtily away from him.

She had been raised to believe that absolutely nothing mattered but catching herself the most eligible husband and, because she had beauty, she had been spoiled and indulged. With time perhaps she would mature, become wiser and kinder, but he very much feared that nothing but a loveless and empty marriage lay before her.

What if he had not proposed when he did, but after he had heard the news of his great-aunt's legacy? Lucinda might well have accepted him and then how long would it have taken for him to realise what lay behind those wide blue eyes? It was a mercy that her laughing refusal and frank acknowledgement that she intended to marry for status and money had prevented him making a second attempt.

Beside him there was another ripple of laughter from Miss Spencer and he turned a little to see Sir Matthew was intent on her plain, friendly, unaffected face, his own alight with interest. Olive had not the remotest idea how to flirt, she had no little tricks to catch and hold a man's attention and she had absolutely no need of them, just as Isobel had not.

Isobel. What did he do now? Go home and tell his wife that he was no longer in love with another woman and had never been? Admit to being a fool, along with most of the men between the ages of fourteen and sixty in the neighbourhood?

Izzy understood Lucinda's character perfectly, he was sure of that, and yet she had never once spoken unkindly of her, or recounted stories that he was certain she would know that showed Lucinda in a poor light. She had been loyal to the other woman and she had been loyal to him, her friend. He recalled how shocked she had been when he told her that he had proposed. She must have thought him too sensible to do such a thing.

She had always agreed with him when he had said how hopeless his feelings for Lucinda were, but that was as far as she had gone. Wise, kind Izzy.

The two other gentlemen were rising and taking their leave, as were the two ladies who had been there when he had arrived. Sir Matthew was taking a very warm farewell of Olive Spencer—he would be paying calls on her soon, Leo was sure—and Lucinda was making a great fuss over Lord Henry. He had no problem interpreting the look she gave him as he turned to go.

There are plenty of other fish in the sea, that look said. *How right I was to turn you down.*

Lucinda's eyes went wide when he smiled at her in

return. Smiled warmly and with real gratitude for allowing him to see her clearly at last.

How foolish to think that what he had felt for her was love, he thought as he began to walk slowly down the stairs. What he felt for Isobel was—

No. Leo stopped dead halfway down. No, he was not going to try to analyse what he felt for Isobel, not with his mind still half occupied with Lucinda. Isobel deserved his undivided attention, not the dazed state he feared he was in.

Below him in the hall, someone cleared his throat and Leo realised that he was still standing on the stairs and a footman was waiting with well-concealed impatience, holding his top coat, hat, gloves and cane.

Leo found a coin in his pocket as he descended to the hall and passed it to the man in exchange for his hat. 'Wool-gathering,' he explained.

The man blinked, clearly unused to one of the toffs actually apologising for something. 'Thank you, my lord.' The coin slid smoothly out of sight.

The sun was shining as the footman opened the door. Leo clapped his hat on his head at a jaunty angle and felt a wave of happiness sweep over him, a lightness of the heart. Perhaps even of his soul. He had a wife, now it was time to woo her as she deserved and surely then he would understand his feelings for her and could tell her of them honestly.

He found he was grinning as he ran down the steps to the pavement. So what? He did not care if passers-by thought him half-seas under at three in the afternoon. A curricle rattled past with a flash of glossy paint and yellow wheels and Leo took a step back from the kerb. Light-hearted rapture was all very well, but he was not going to be able to do much courting if he ended up under the busy traffic.

Still smiling, he negotiated the road more carefully, tossing a sixpence to a startled crossing sweeper.

'Gawd bless yer, guvnor,' the lad called after him.

Leo went on his way, whistling.

'Are you all right, Isobel?' James Carmichael asked, glancing towards her as he slowed the blacks. They had easily reached first-name terms after one circuit of Green Park and cemented their friendship by the time they were halfway through St James's Park.

'I am fine,' she assured him and he turned his attention back to the busy road just in time to avoid a mongrel that darted out from a side turning.

No, I am not all right, she thought grimly.

That had been the Amberleighs' house and that had been Leo, bounding down the front steps with a grin on his face and so far in alt that he had almost stepped out under their horses' hooves. He certainly had not noticed his wife.

Presumably, he had been to see how Lucinda was and, no doubt, she had cried prettily on his chest again and he had dried her tears and perhaps dropped a kiss on those rosebud lips. In a purely neighbourly spirit, of course.

Isobel found she was grinding her teeth together and made herself relax her jaw. It was her own fault that she felt so angry and betrayed. She had allowed herself to believe that Leo could somehow allow his feelings for Lucinda to subside into a kind of nostalgic, regretful ache.

How could she have let herself think that when she knew her own love for him would never fade and grow cool? Her fault—but his, too. She had trusted him to behave with discretion, not to carry on in public in a way that could only humiliate her, yet there he was, flaunting his attachment to Lucinda.

The anger was hot and curiously strengthening. She was not going to turn the other cheek and be 'good old Izzy' any longer. Leo was her husband and she was going to fight for him, even if all she won was the right to be treated with respect.

When they reached Mount Street, James Carmichael refused an invitation to come in and take a glass of wine on the grounds that he did not want to keep his pair standing. 'Thank you for your company, Isobel,' he said as a footmen came to help her down from the carriage. 'May I hope you will join me again if the weather holds?'

'With great pleasure.' She reached up to shake hands. 'It was a very enjoyable drive.' Up to a point. And a very informative one, too.

Once inside, Isobel changed from her walking dress into a simple gown and let Nancy set her hair to rights, but she resisted the temptation to have her style it elaborately, or to wear her prettiest new gown or add lamp black to her lashes or rouge to her cheeks. She was not going to enter into some kind of competition with Lucinda, one she could never win.

The battle for Leo's heart was not one she was going

to win either, she told herself, selecting simple pearl studs to fix in her earlobes, but she was going to go down fighting, and with dignity.

Prue and Penny joined her in the drawing room, bringing their embroidery. It was Miss Pettigrew's day off so they had spent the afternoon bickering over names for their new ponies while pretending to study their French grammar books.

Isobel glanced at the clock. An hour before they needed to go up and change for dinner. She picked up her own embroidery and proceeded to make a tangle of it while asking about the progress on names.

'Toffee,' Prue said. 'Because he is just the colour of that wonderful toffee that Cook makes.'

'Merlin,' Penny announced. 'I was going to call him Merle, because that's the French for blackbird, but it wasn't quite right, so I decided on the wizard instead.'

'Those are both very good names,' Isobel agreed. 'I was very impressed with your riding.'

That released a flood of chatter about how they had learned to ride with Mama and how worrying it had been after she died and Papa was so strange and money was so tight and their beloved old ponies really should have been retired to grass.

Half an hour... Was he not even going to come in for dinner?

There was the sound of the front door closing, a murmur of voices from the hall and Leo came in, his arms full of yellow roses.

Isobel simply stared at him, but Penny piped up, 'Oh, what have you been up to, Leo? Mama always used to say that when Papa brought her flowers it was because he had a guilty conscience.'

'I saw them and thought it wrong that everyone sends my wife flowers but me,' Leo said. 'Do you want to arrange them, Isobel?'

'Give them to Wilmore and ask him to see to it,' she said coolly, suppressing the urge to throw the lovely things into the fire. 'There is no time before dinner.'

She must have spoken more frigidly than she intended because Penny faltered, 'I was only joking.'

'Of course you were, dear,' Isobel said, smiling at her. 'I cannot imagine what Leo would have to feel guilty about, and they are very beautiful.'

Everyone, including Leo, seemed to relax. Isobel stood up. 'Time to change for dinner. Are you joining us, girls?'

They nodded. Miss Pettigrew had gone to have supper with her widowed sister-in-law, it seemed. 'Giles is in, though,' Prue said. 'He is working in the study. Shall I ask if he is coming?'

'Thank you, Prue. That would balance the table a little. We cannot have Leo overwhelmed with ladies, can we?'

She said it lightly, but she noticed the shadow that passed across Leo's face. He had picked up something in her tone and she told herself to be careful. The last thing that she wanted was to descend to Lucinda's spiteful remarks.

The meal was…normal. The food was excellent, the twins were cheerful and Giles Norcross kept up his end of the conversation with good humour and some interesting comments.

Isobel was determined that this was how things should be. She could not challenge Lucinda in looks, in feminine wiles or sheer lack of conscience, but she could build a home for them all and perhaps one day Leo would see that was the place where he could be truly happy.

But she was dreading the time when they retired to bed. Would she be able to keep her emotions hidden when they were such a miserable mess of love and anger, determination and resentment?

For once she did not encourage the gentlemen to bring their glasses of port through to the drawing room. Instead, she let Penny and Prue sit up with her and look through an album of Italian views that she had borrowed from the circulating library while she attempted to restore some order to her embroidery. It seemed a metaphor for her feelings, she thought. Clashing colours, missed stitches and a lumpy knot or two. She set herself to unpicking it with great care. If she could set this to rights without it bearing the scars of her miseries, then perhaps it would be an omen for her marriage.

Leo and Giles came through as the tea tray was brought in and she let Prue and Penny practise their social skills by serving it. Giles was really very good about almost getting a lapful of hot tea, but his leaving to remove his soaked shirt was a signal to send the girls to bed.

Isobel went up with them, kissed them goodnight, then went to her own bedchamber to find Nancy laying out a choice of nightgowns.

'That one,' she said, pointing to the plainest. It might be lacking in frills and lace, but it was also the finest fabric, a pale ivory lawn that draped her body, hinting at what lay beneath. There was no point in attempting to seduce Leo with lush curves she did not possess, or masses of feminine frippery that made her look ridiculous. She would counter the obvious with subtlety.

The chair by the fire would be perfect, she thought, going to it with a book. She made certain it was the right way up because she knew she would not read a word and an upside-down book was a somewhat embarrassing giveaway, then settled down to wait.

Leo joined her almost immediately. There was a tap on the door, he came in, and Isobel promptly forgot to be angry or upset and simply looked at him.

His looks were not why Isobel had fallen in love with him, but that did not mean that she did not enjoy the sight of him. He was dressed in that gorgeous, decadent robe. His feet were bare, a deep vee of skin was exposed at his throat and she was certain that he was naked under that heavy silk.

When he did not move, but simply put a hand behind him to push the door closed, she put down the book with deliberate care on the side table and stood up, then moved slightly so that the firelight was behind her.

Leo's lips parted and she saw the sweep of his tongue over his upper lip.

Yes, Leo. When you first lay with me you said that now you saw me. See me again. Your wife, your friend. Your lover.

'Isobel.'

Well, that was a start, she thought ruefully. *He remembers which woman he's with, at least—*

The thought went unfinished because Leo took three strides across the room, swept her up in his arms and carried her to the bed. He sat her on the edge, her legs dangling, and went down on his knees in front of her.

Puzzled, she reached out one hand and touched his head, bent as though he studied her feet. Then he began to lift the edge of her nightgown, his big hands rolling the delicate fabric up past her knees, along her thighs. It was under her as she sat, but the skirt was full enough for him to be able to lift it to her waist, exposing her to his gaze.

She had stood before him naked before, lain beside him, but she had never felt so exposed, so vulnerable. Leo stroked his hands over her thighs, his horseman's calluses erotically rough on her pale flesh.

'Your skin smells of roses,' he said. 'It is not your soap, it is not the creams you use and it isn't a perfume. It must just be you.'

'How do you know—that it is none of those things?' She had to steady her voice.

Leo looked up, laughter in his eyes. 'Because I have been in here, trying to solve the riddle of you, Isobel. Smelling your soap—plain Castile; your creams and lotions—lavender and orange blossom—and the perfume that you hardly ever wear. That is complex and spicy.'

'You—' He thought *she* was a riddle to be solved? She didn't understand him, just couldn't. This was a man who still hungered after a heedless ringleted chit;

a man who smiled with pleasure as he left her company; who brought a guilt gift of flowers to his wife and coloured when challenged about it—yet he knelt at her feet, desire evident in every tense muscle of his body, and talked of the scent of her skin.

Leo's hands slid up over her hips until they reached her waist and then he pushed gently until she flopped back on the bed, too confused by her own feelings, let alone his, to resist as he parted her thighs.

She could feel his breath on the sensitive inner flesh and felt the heat of her blush sweep over her breasts, up her neck to her face. Leo was looking at her *there*. Yes, he had touched her, stroked her, penetrated her there, but never stared in silence like this. She was wet with longing for him, hot with embarrassment, and the suspense was killing her. Was this all he was going to do? Look?

At the moment when she plucked up courage to lift her head she felt a touch, then a kiss, right there on the folds. Then what could only be his tongue parting them, touching the nub of her pleasure, stroking heat and flames of sensation through her.

Isobel gasped, arched up, not to escape but to press closer. So wanton, so shameful—and then Leo began to alternate his kisses with little sucks and she quite simply lost herself. Lost her shame, her shyness, her anger with him. Everything was abandoned in the whirlpool of sensation.

Too intense, too new. It seemed to take seconds before her climax took her, possessed her, transported her. *Where am I?*

Isobel blinked up at the ceiling, its moulded shapes highlighted by flickering firelight. Where was Leo?

'I am here,' he said as though she had spoken his name aloud. Perhaps she had, perhaps she had been screaming it.

He lifted himself over her and her body instinctively moved to hold him. 'You are so beautiful in your pleasure, Isobel.'

Beautiful? But she was in no state to argue with him, and he slid easily into her body, so open and eager for him. She curled her legs around his hips as her muscles tightened to hold him and he lowered his head to kiss her.

Leo tasted strange, salty and musky, and she realised that this must be her own essence. It should have thrown her into a confusion of embarrassment, but instead it felt powerful. He wanted her this much, he wanted to immerse himself in her, the scent of her skin, the taste of her body. And yet… And yet he did not love her.

But even as that thought filled her mind her body was responding to his and she arched up, crying out as her climax took her and she heard his voice as he joined her.

Chapter Nineteen

'I love you.' Leo whispered it into the tangle of hair his mouth was buried in. Isobel's body was relaxed in his arms, her breathing steady, so he risked it again, a little louder. 'I love you, Izzy.'

'Mmm…?' She stirred and wriggled and her face, rosy with sleep, looked up at him at an odd angle.

'Good morning,' he said. 'And a fine one if I can judge by the sunlight leaking in around the edges of the curtains.'

'It must be late,' Isobel said, yawning and sitting up. 'The weather has been so good that I keep forgetting it is almost November.'

'One day to go,' Leo agreed. 'It is almost nine and I had wanted to ride out this morning.' He sat up, too, and swung his legs out of bed.

At home in Kent, he had exercised hard daily because there had been so few staff to help in the stables, on the estate. He had been in the saddle for hours, had groomed his own horses, had helped repair fences and roofs. Now town life offered few opportunities for exertion and one had to make them. He must join one of the boxing salons and learn single-stick and get involved in some bouts of boxing. He must certainly ride every day.

'Wait for me, I'll come, too.' Isobel leaned out of bed and jerked the bell pull as he found his robe.

'There's no time for breakfast first if we are to enjoy a good gallop,' he protested. 'The parks will be filling up soon. We can go out again this afternoon. Good morning, Nancy.'

The maid bobbed a curtsy as he walked through to the sitting room. Bertram was already in his bedchamber, laying out his riding clothes.

Nancy called from the sitting room, 'Mr Bertram, have you brought enough coffee for my lady as well? She will be riding this morning.'

'Yes, Miss Farne. You just need another cup.'

Well, his wife and their servants had decided he would have company that morning, it seemed. Not that he would not enjoy riding with Isobel, but he had this instinct to shelter her, make her rest more. Ridiculous, because she was bursting with health, but something, some instinct, was making him uneasy.

Their horses were fresh and eager and Leo could not help but smile at the sight of Isobel on the adorable Dora in her green habit that matched her eyes.

'What are you smiling about, Leo?'

'I was thinking how well you look on Dora.'

'Thank you so much for her, she is perfect.'

'You do not have to thank me. You must have what

you want, what you need, without having to feel it is given as my largesse. What we have is ours equally.'

Isobel flashed one of her enigmatic smiles. 'But you found her and for that I do thank you.'

They crossed Park Lane and entered Hyde Park. 'It is not too crowded yet,' she said. 'Shall we gallop?'

Galloping was frowned upon once the park became busier because of concerns over the safety of children and nervous riders, but first thing it was common for riders, usually gentlemen, to give their horses a good workout.

Isobel did not wait for his agreement, but gave Dora her head and the mare went from a walk into full stretch in a few paces.

Leo sent Saturn after her, but kept him from racing because he was enjoying the view of his wife, so poised in the saddle, so fearlessly enjoying the speed. Yes, he must teach her to drive a pair because she would enjoy cutting a dash from the driving seat of a high-perch phaeton. And he would enjoy watching her.

She reined in short of the track circling the Serpentine where there were already a few groups of riders and turned her flushed, laughing face to watch him ride up. 'Slowcoach!'

'I was admiring the view,' he said blandly and grinned as she ducked her head, shy at the praise. 'Shall we hack around the water to the West Carriage Drive and then cross into Kensington Gardens?'

He was already turning Saturn's head when she said, 'Or we could go the other way, down towards Hyde

Park Corner and then we can have another gallop up Rotten Row.'

There were more riders that way and he started to argue, but Dora was already trotting away from him so Leo shrugged and followed.

They rounded the end of the Serpentine at a walk, watching the birds on the water and discussing whether more planting might improve the park which led to what might be done to the gardens at the Hall.

Rotten Row stretched in either direction in front of them and Leo glanced up it towards Kensington Palace. 'It is quite clear,' he said. 'We can— Isobel?'

Dora had stopped and Isobel was staring at a group of riders clustered close to the gate leading out to the Hyde Park turnpike gate.

Leo narrowed his eyes and studied them, puzzled by Isobel's interest. All were men except, in the middle of the riders, was one lady in a sweeping pale blue habit. She was mounted on a pretty pale grey horse and, as Leo watched, she laughed, the unmistakable tones reaching them quite clearly. Lucinda.

'She has clearly worked out that early morning in the Park is an excellent time to meet gentlemen,' Isobel said coolly. She turned to look at him. 'Are you not going over there to extricate her and send her home safely?'

'No,' Leo said. 'She has a groom with her and she is such a nervous rider that I do not think for a moment that she is going to venture far.'

There was a quality about Isobel's silence as she turned Dora's head away from the gate that had him urging Saturn up alongside the mare. 'You thought I had come here to meet her? You thought that was why I tried to persuade you not to come with me?'

'You did not appear surprised that she was here.' Isobel had her gaze fixed on the distance.

'Nothing that Lucinda does would surprise me,' he said, but Isobel had given Dora her head and Saturn was sidling and mouthing the bit, eager to give chase. Leo swore, then let the stallion go.

He caught up with Isobel just as she reached the end of the Row. However furious she was, she would not career on into the parkland in front of Kensington Palace. It might be open to respectable members of the public, but not to horses ridden at anything but a walk.

Leo guided Saturn towards one of the rides radiating out from the Round Pond in front of the Palace. 'This way,' he said. It was a statement, if not quite an order, and for a moment he thought Isobel would turn and ride off.

'I did not come here expecting, or wanting, to see Lucinda,' he said flatly. 'I do not know what I can say to convince you of that.'

Silence. Then Isobel said, 'I have never known you to lie to me, Leo.'

'I never have and I am not starting now.'

'I accept that,' she said. 'I accept that you did not expect to see Lucinda here. I apologise for assuming that you had.'

So why did that feel as though she had just accused him of infidelity and had slapped his face? To say anything else would sound defensive and that was the last thing he felt. Hurt, yes, and confused about why Isobel was behaving as though she mistrusted him. He had been honest with her about his feelings for Lucinda in the first place. When he had found her with Carstares, Isobel had helped him. Why now was she prickly with unspoken suspicions?

It felt particularly unjust now, given that a week ago she might have had grounds for thinking that he still thought of the other woman with a lingering regret. But now…

But now he was not going to descend into self-pity, muttering to himself that this was unfair. Somehow he had to convince Isobel that his feelings for Lucinda had been shallow, superficial, compared to what he felt for her now. He loved his wife, he could see that now. It was as if the shock of her mistrust had jolted everything into focus.

So how *did* he convince her? To tell her now would seem like an insincere attempt to mend this breach that had opened like a crevasse between them. And he had his pride—pleading was not in his vocabulary.

Leo felt as though he was standing on thin ice. To move in any direction would make it crack and the only safe thing was to stay still. This was the same and he could not think of the words to carry him safely over it, because to get it wrong now, he sensed, would be fatal.

'It is all right, Izzy,' he said. 'We are bound to have misunderstandings and rows. We might know each other very well as friends, but perhaps we took it too much for granted that it would take no more effort to live together in harmony.'

'Yes,' she agreed and Dora, who had been fidgeting

as they walked along, stepped out more calmly, clearly mirroring her rider's mood. 'You are quite right. I allowed Lucinda to aggravate me and that is foolish.'

After a moment she added, 'It does not help that I feel sorry for her. If she had been brought up with less concern for her own looks and taught how to develop her mind and her character, she would be much happier in the future.'

'That is generous of you.'

Isobel shrugged. 'I am trying not to descend to spite as she does.' She glanced across at him. 'I am sorry, Leo. I do try not to let her upset me.'

'You have no need to apologise to me for that,' he said warmly. 'I know she has never been kind to other women and I think it will not be long before she wishes she had true friends.'

Isobel reined in and he had to circle Saturn around to come back to her. 'Leo, are you telling me that you are no longer in love with Lucinda?'

'Yes,' he said bluntly.

I never lie to you, Izzy.

'But she is so beautiful.'

'Outside, yes. And like virtually every male in the district, that was all I could see.'

'Men can be idiots sometimes,' Isobel observed.

He couldn't tell whether she was pleased by his admission or not.

'We can and I fear that just as a magpie is inflamed by shiny objects and has to steal them, men seem unable to see beyond a lovely face sometimes.'

'And bountiful...er...' Isobel made a gesture towards her own rather less than bountiful bust.

'That, too. We are led by our—' Now it was his turn to grope for the right word.

'Breeding organs,' Isobel said and, praise be, the corners of her mouth were turning up into a definite smile. 'And I suppose that the true gentlemen among you cannot admit that you are harbouring disgracefully lustful feelings towards an innocent young lady, so you all tell yourselves it is love.' She pronounced it *lurve*, with a simper.

'You know, that is a very perceptive remark,' he said, much struck.

In unspoken agreement they began to walk on again. It was time to let the subject drop, Leo thought. Let the realisation that he no longer thought himself in love with Lucinda sink in until Isobel truly believed it. To announce now that he loved her instead would sound too much as though he bounced from one infatuation to another.

But this was no infatuation. He looked across at her profile, at the face that was becoming so very dear to him, and prayed for the instinct to know when the right time was.

Isobel was not certain what she expected after that morning in Hyde Park. It had been full of revelations—most vitally that Leo no longer loved Lucinda and seemed to recognise that it had never been a true love.

Balancing this good news was the realisation that she must have appeared not only jealous of Lucinda, but lacking in trust in Leo. She should have explained that she had seen him leaving Lucinda's house looking so happy that she had believed him even deeper in love, but doing that on horseback in the middle of a public park had seemed impossible.

Leo had not set out that morning to meet Lucinda in the park and he did not love her. So why had he been so distracted by his happy thoughts that day that he had almost walked under Lord Carmichael's carriage wheels?

There was no accounting for it and there was no mistaking the fact that the realisation did not appear to have affected Leo's feelings for his wife. He was still affectionate during the day and passionate at night and seemed perfectly happy with that state of affairs. He certainly gave no hint that her jealousy and suspicion might have betrayed her love for him.

Their daily life resumed its pattern. Penny and Prue attended their classes, made new friends and happily frittered their pin money. Miss Pettigrew purchased a new bonnet and spencer and a smart new evening dress. Nancy and Bertram bickered in a way that made Isobel suspect that they were becoming attracted to each other and wished them well of it and Mrs Druett and Wilmore settled down to a state of exceedingly polite armed truce. As for Giles Norcross, he was still his pleasant and efficient self, but she had surprised him daydreaming more than once. She suspected that he was in love.

Isobel went for drives with Lord Carmichael and Mr Lisle and did her best to appreciate the great romantic verse play that Mr Lisle was wrestling with. Lord Carmichael, who accompanied her to a musicale when

Leo had another engagement, made no such demands, but she was concerned because he seemed to be hiding some sadness beneath his amiable manner. Perhaps his own love life was not going well. Not that she could ask him about it.

As for Sir Thomas Eddington, his motive in seeking her out was, indeed, to involve her with his sister about whose future he was fretting.

'She shows no interest in any of the young men she meets,' he lamented as they strolled around an exhibition at the Society of Painters in Watercolour's rooms. 'I know for a fact that she has turned down three proposals from highly eligible gentlemen because they asked my permission first. Goodness knows how many others she has spurned.'

Isobel turned from a rather attractive landscape she had been enjoying and summoned up a sympathetic smile. 'Chloe has the sense to wait until she finds the man she feels she will be happy with,' she said. 'After all, she is going to have to live with the consequences of that choice for the rest of her life.'

And, believe me, I know what I am talking about.

'I have decided to hold a small, informal dinner party for friends, one that the twins can attend,' she announced the next Monday morning as they sat with Giles and the diaries organising the next few weeks.

Giles produced a fresh sheet of paper and waited, pen poised, to note the guest list. 'Lord Carmichael, Mr Lisle, Miss Turlington—she enjoys poetry, perhaps she and Mr Lisle will get on well. Let me see, I don't have to worry too much about balancing ladies and gentlemen as it will be informal and the twins will be there. You, of course, Giles.'

'Sir Matthew Breem and Miss Olive Spencer,' Leo said. 'I met them the other day and I suspect they would enjoy furthering their acquaintance.'

'Matchmaking, Leo?'

'Guilty,' he said with a grin.

'And Sir Thomas Eddington and Chloe,' Isobel concluded.

Giles dropped his pen, ink spattering across the neat list. She looked at him and he blushed.

How very interesting. Unless Giles was hiding an unrequited passion for Sir Thomas, of course... Isobel smiled at him and the blush deepened, but before Leo noticed anything, Wilmore came in with the second postal delivery.

Giles gathered up his papers, but Leo held up his hand. 'Just a moment, Giles, in case there is anything here. Good God.' He was staring blankly at the letter he had just opened, then passed it to Isobel.

'Cousin Edward wants to sell you Long Mead? But why?'

'Because he is now very short of funds, I imagine,' Leo said drily. 'They have another house and small estate in Northumbria, do they not?'

'Yes, left to Cousin Amelia by her maternal grandfather. They are running away, aren't they?'

Giles, who knew all about Isobel's inheritance, cleared his throat. 'Might I suggest, sir, that the price,

should you decide to buy, should reflect the interest
Lord Martyn owes Her Ladyship?'

'Oh, yes.' Leo's smile was one of deep satisfaction.
'I am not surprised—it would be extraordinarily embarrassing for them living so close whenever we are
down at the Hall. What do you say, Isobel? It is your
family home, after all.'

'I would like it back,' Isobel said. 'I do not even have
to think about it. And I am so thankful we will not have
to be civil to my cousins.'

Giles took himself off, promising to calculate interest owing on the embezzled funds and research current land prices.

'What will we do with the house, though?'

'The dower house at the hall is beyond repair,' Leo
said. 'It would be an ideal replacement. And it will
make an excellent estate for a son to manage, don't
you think?'

'A… Yes, of course.' She swallowed. 'In the mean-
time?'

'We can rent it out, if you have no objection to that?'

'No, none at all. Tenants that we can choose will be
a vast improvement on my cousins,' Isobel said with
some feeling.

When Leo left the room she sat for a while. *A son.*
Oh, goodness. Leo was thinking about children and that
was something they had hardly discussed. Although…
No, it was too soon to be certain. She couldn't think
about it, let alone speak to Leo about it. Not yet.

Chapter Twenty

'This is a very perfectly splendid party,' Penny whispered in Isobel's ear as the guests milled about, reorganising themselves as the men came in from their port.

It was rather, she thought with some satisfaction. A group of pleasant people enjoying each other's company, an atmosphere that was not at all formal, simply comfortable, and the satisfaction of seeing the twins having the time of their lives, albeit while behaving with a shy determination to obey all Miss Pettigrew's long list of instructions for young ladies.

There was also the interest of watching Giles Norcross and Chloe Eddington trying to pretend that they didn't want to find a quiet corner and sit gazing into each other's eyes all evening. How on earth had they become so close? They must have met here at Mount Street and Giles had a good social life of his own, so perhaps they had encountered each other at parties. From there it was not too far a leap to arranging meetings in the park or at the library.

How was Giles going to support a wife? She must have a word with Leo…

And, thinking about young lovers, there was a free seat beside Miss Spencer, Leo's protégée. She strolled over and sat down.

'We have hardly had the opportunity to exchange a word since you arrived,' she said. 'Are you very familiar with London?'

'This will be my second Season,' Olive said. 'Mama and I have come up from Dorset to prepare. Papa will join us later.'

'Are you looking forward to it?'

'I wasn't,' she confided. 'I'm rather shy and not at all pretty.' She bit her lip and glanced across the room. 'But this time… Lord Halford was so kind and now I have met Matthew… I mean, other people.' She blushed.

'I thought Sir Matthew Breem to be a very pleasant gentleman,' Isobel said. 'But tell me, what has my husband to do with this? You said he was very kind to you.'

'Oh, I was at Lady Amberleigh's house, visiting with Mama, you know. And… Well, Miss Paxton was not very…welcoming. But Lord Halford talked to me and was so nice and he made me laugh and Sir Matthew left Miss Paxton and came over to sit with me and I think she was angry. Lord Halford was…was not pleased with her, I think. And she said something catty about you—'

She broke off, looking aghast. 'I am *so* sorry. I must sound a complete cat myself.' She fanned her flushed face with her hand. 'So indiscreet. What must you think of me?'

'Nothing bad, I assure you, Miss Spencer. But when was this?'

Olive's first meeting with Sir Matthew was clearly never to be forgotten. She knew the day, the date, even the time.

The day I went driving with Lord Carmichael. The afternoon I saw Leo leaving the Amberleighs' house.

That must have been when he realised that he did not love Lucinda, the occasion that had finally revealed to him what her true character was behind the beautiful face. He had been happy because he was freed from her. There was no mystery about that day, no ambiguity about his feelings for Lucinda.

She felt so joyful that she could have stood up and told the entire room. Instead, Isobel took Miss Spencer's hands in hers. 'I hope you and Sir Matthew will be very happy together, and if there is ever anything I can do to assist you, you have only to ask.'

'What are we going to do about Giles and Chloe?' Isobel asked. She had been awake since before six, trying to think sensibly about her own marriage and had finally given up and decided to worry about someone else's for a change.

'Mpph?' Leo lifted his head from where it had been resting between her breasts and blinked himself awake. 'What?' he managed to say more coherently.

'I am worrying about Giles and Miss Eddington.'

'Then don't.' Leo applied himself to doing distracting things with his tongue around her left nipple.

'But we must.' Isobel slid down the bed until they were

nose to nose. 'He cannot afford a wife on a secretary's salary.'

'Wife? Giles is not getting married.'

'No, he isn't, not unless we do something to help.'

'After breakfast,' Leo said firmly. 'After this.' He moved, sliding over her, and began doing things that banished any thought of other people's marriages completely from her mind.

'What were you saying about Giles when I woke up this morning?' Leo asked. They had the breakfast table to themselves. The girls were still asleep after the exciting party the night before and Giles had, according to Wilmore, gone for a walk.

'He and Chloe are in love. We have to think about promoting his career so he can afford a wife. Has he ever said what he wants to do, other than be a secretary?'

'Farm, I think. But he has no capital and his father cannot afford to buy land.' Leo poured himself more coffee. 'He is an excellent secretary and I do not want to lose him. Besides, Eddington would never agree.'

'Nor do I want to lose him, but we must not be selfish and if he had prospects, then Sir Thomas would be more inclined to give his assent. If only you were more interested in politics, then there might be openings for him there.'

Leo disappeared behind his newspaper with what sounded suspiciously like a grunt and stayed in hiding until the arrival of the first post.

'Would you like a driving lesson?' he asked abruptly as they began turning over their respective letters.

'With a pair? Very much.'

'Then we will go as soon as you can be ready. There is nothing here that will not wait and as Giles is presumably drooping about, composing odes to Chloe's eyebrows, that can only be a good thing.'

'Don't be unkind and she has very pretty eyebrows.' Isobel pushed back her chair and stood up.

'So have you.' Leo reached out as she passed him, caught her around the waist and pulled her on to his lap. 'I feel the need to kiss them.'

'Idiot.' But she stayed perched on his knee, exchanging kisses, until a rattle of the door handle had her jumping up. 'Half an hour?'

A plain walking dress, some sensible leather gloves and a small hat with a veil, firmly secured, seemed the most practical outfit for driving Leo's new phaeton which, to her disappointment, he had ordered without a high perch on the grounds that such vehicles were not for beginners.

Leo was standing on the front step when she came down. 'I think it is going to rain.'

'Perhaps later.' She stepped out beside him and looked up. 'It might blow over, it is certainly quite windy, but not enough to unsettle the horses, do you think?'

'No, they are a steady pair. I bought them expecting you would drive them and I did not want to take any risks.'

As he spoke the groom brought the phaeton around from the mews. It was black with red detailing and the pair drawing it were well-matched bays.

'Very elegant,' she approved. 'I can only hope I do not prove to be hopelessly ham-handed and will do the rig credit.'

'You will always do me credit,' Leo said gallantly, handing her up before going around to take the driver's seat. 'Let them go, Yates.'

'Which park?' Isobel asked as they proceeded at a brisk trot across South Audley Street towards Park Lane.

'Green Park, I thought. It should be the quietest.'

They emerged into Piccadilly, turned right and then left on to Constitution Hill where Leo drew up.

'There, a nice long smooth track past the end of the little reservoir and well clear of all the children with their nannies and dogs around the northern part.'

The rain had held off, although the wind had become gusty now. Leo handed her the reins, jumped down and, when she had slid across to the driver's side, climbed up beside her. To her relief the bays stood quite still, although their ears were flicking back and forth as they tried to work out what the humans behind them were doing.

'Now, whip in your right hand, reins like this.' Leo helped her sort out the double set of reins. 'Give them verbal commands as well, just as you would a single horse in the gig.'

'Walk on,' Isobel said, relaxing her hands and trying to sound calm and in control. They were larger animals than she was used to and there seemed to be three times more leather in her hands.

But the bays obediently stepped out and walked placidly along the track.

'Trot!' she called and eased up with her hands—and, miracle of miracle, they obeyed that, too. 'Botheration, it has started to rain.'

'We'll cut back up to Piccadilly when we are past the end of the small reservoir,' Leo said. 'That's right, nice and steady. I've had a thought about Giles, by the way.'

'You have?' She turned her head to look at him and felt the bays swerve slightly.

'Look where you are going. There are people walking just ahead by the waterside.'

'I see them.' Out of the corner of her eye Isobel saw it was a pair of ladies walking together. They both stopped and raised their umbrellas, one blue, one crimson, but the pair trotted on steadily, ignoring the flash of colour, so she relaxed again.

The gust of wind came without warning, whipping at her veil, sending wavelets across the reservoir and catching one of the umbrellas, spinning it across the grass like an unwieldy hoop until it became airborne, right in front of the horses.

It was too close to steer them around it. Isobel reined in hard, Leo's hands coming down over hers, but the crimson umbrella was under the pair now, tangling in their feet, the metal struts jabbing at their legs.

The pair bolted

Leo's right arm came across her, holding her back in the seat, his left tightening on the reins, dragging the horses' heads round to the right, forcing them off the tracks into the longer grass, making them circle.

For a moment Isobel thought he had done it, that the

bays would tire and stop. Then, as they began to slow, the offside wheel hit something and the phaeton jerked, lurched and tipped. Isobel clung to the side rail, felt something in her sleeve rip, then she was falling, the world upside down. Leo was shouting, but the ground was coming up too fast. Too fast—

'Nothing is broken, my lord.' Sir Lorrimer Fewkes straightened up from the bed and gestured to Nancy to pull the sheets back over Isobel's still form. 'As far as one can tell while she is unconscious, that is.'

'How long?' Leo found he had to make a conscious effort to get the words out. 'It is two hours since the accident.'

'Impossible to say in these cases. She suffered a blow to the head, you say?'

'I cannot be certain that she did not hit her head on the wheel as she fell. She certainly hit her head on the ground.'

'Hmm. There may be bleeding on the brain, of course, although her pupils appear normal.' He bent over and lifted Isobel's eyelids again. 'Her reflexes are normal, so the risk of a paralysis is small.'

Small? Leo, who had assumed from the doctor's satisfied mutterings when he had tapped knees and elbows and drawn a finger down Isobel's bare instep that there was no risk, felt a cold chill in his guts. And bleeding on the brain?

'Her breathing is normal, so I doubt a lung has been punctured.'

You doubt? You don't know for certain?

He told himself that ranting at the doctor would not help.

'What can we do?'

'Nothing, my lord. Nothing but keep watch over her. Nature is a great healer.' He produced the platitude as though it were a great original thought. 'If she shows signs of regaining consciousness, try to get her to drink a little water. If she becomes feverish, send for me, otherwise I will return at the same time tomorrow. Good day, my lord.'

'Thank you,' Leo said vaguely as he sat down beside the bed. From the moment that gust of wind had hit them everything had seemed to move at great speed and, at the same time, at a crawl. Now he took a deep, steadying breath and took Isobel's hand in his.

Under his fingers her pulse beat with reassuring steadiness. He looked up and saw Nancy on the other side of the bed.

'She's a fighter, is my lady,' she said, meeting his gaze. 'And she doesn't give up. Not on you, my lord. Not on anything. I'll go and get some fresh water and something for a compress for her poor head.'

'What did she mean by that, Izzy?' he asked out loud as the door closed behind the maid. 'You won't give up on me? I wouldn't blame you if you did, your poor fool of a husband who doesn't know how to tell you he loves you.'

Nancy came back with a jug, followed by one of the housemaids with a basin and cloths and another with a bowl of broth.

'You eat that, my lord. You've had a shock and it don't—*doesn't*—do to ignore that.' She went on talking as he took a spoonful, then another, realising that he was ravenous and cold. 'I reckon we shouldn't leave her and we ought to keep talking to her so she knows to come back,' she said. 'And we must take it in turns tonight because otherwise we won't be fit for anything if she needs us.'

The broth had gone. Leo looked in surprise at the empty bowl. 'Yes, you are right, Nancy, thank you. You carry on with bathing her head.'

He sat holding Isobel's hand and talking to her until he was hoarse. Giles came in to tell him that the bays were back in their stable and had only minor injuries. There were many inquiries from their friends and acquaintances, but he was dealing with those by saying that Lady Halford was very much shaken by the accident and was resting. Miss Pettigrew was doing her best to reassure the girls and he would stay with them as much as possible.

Leo, fortified by a dinner tray, passed all that on to Isobel as she lay there unmoving. When Nancy went to lie down so that she could relieve him during the night he swallowed a glass of brandy for his throat and searched for something to talk about.

'I have a plan for Giles and Chloe,' he said. 'I will suggest to Eddington that he pays the first five years' rent on Long Mead as a wedding present for them. Giles should be able to make a go of it in that time and I'll give him work to do for me as well. What do you think, Izzy? Will that answer? It all depends on Eddington, of course.

I'll give Giles a first-rate recommendation, naturally. Otherwise they'll just have to wait until she is of age.'

No response.

Doggedly, he kept on until, at midnight, Nancy came out from the dressing room. Between them they shifted Isobel on the bed, so that she did not get sore from lying in one position, and moistened her lips.

'Sleep, now, my lord.'

Leo kicked off his shoes, took off his coat, waistcoat and neckcloth and lay down on the bed on the far side of Isobel as Nancy took his chair. 'Wake me at four unless she stirs,' he said. He wouldn't sleep, of course.

'My lord?'

Leo sat bolt upright. 'What has happened?' Beside him, Isobel still lay quite still.

'Nothing, my lord. But you said to wake you at four and it has just struck the hour.'

Four o'clock. The dead time of night, the time when the sick so often gave up their hold on life and slipped away.

He must have made a sound because Nancy turned back, her hand shielding the candle flame. 'She hasn't stirred.'

As the door to the dressing room shut, Leo moved across the bed. Isobel might have been in a natural sleep, he thought as he positioned himself close beside her, his arm across her so that his fingertips rested against the pulse in the angle of her neck and collarbone. Any change, any movement, and he would be aware. Against his skin her pulse beat steadily.

'I love you, Izzy.' Leo closed his eyes and focused every nerve, every sense, on that pulse of life.

I love you, Izzy.

It was a good dream, she thought. A perfect dream if only she did not hurt so much. Her head, her shoulder, her back...

Isobel's eyes snapped open on to candlelight and the familiar sight of her bedchamber ceiling. Not a dream now, although the pain persisted. She closed her eyes again and then opened them at the confused image of the ground rushing up to meet her, of a spinning wheel, a splash of crimson.

A carriage accident. She had fallen from the phaeton in Hyde Park.

No, please, no.

She made herself think. Where did she hurt? Everywhere, it seemed, but not her stomach. She wiggled her toes and they worked, so she was not paralysed, she had feeling everywhere. She had fallen on her shoulders, hit her head. Her fingers trailing across her belly encountered bare skin.

'Are you safe?' she whispered.

Beside her something moved and she was aware of the weight across her breast, the touch of fingers in the angle of her neck.

'Izzy?'

'Leo.' She turned her head towards him, ignoring the pain. 'I'm all right.' He sat up and she saw that he looked dreadful. Pale, unshaven, with dark shadows under his eyes. 'You...hurt?'

'Only my heart,' he said. 'I thought I had lost you. God, Izzy, I love you so much and I thought I would never be able to tell you.'

She knew that a blow to the head caused something…caused concussion, which made the sufferer confused. Was that what was wrong with her?

'Isobel, say something.' Leo got out of bed and came around to her side as she tried to make her cracked lips form words. 'Here, you must be parched, drink some barley water.'

He gathered her gently up against his shoulder and held the glass to her lips and she swallowed gratefully.

'Better. Leo… What did you say?'

'I love you. I didn't know how to tell you, when to tell you. I think I must have loved you for years.'

The room was spinning. 'Oh,' she said weakly. 'Oh, Leo. I love you, too. For so long.' The darkness closed in again, but not before she saw his face in the candlelight transformed into joy.

Chapter Twenty-One

When Isobel woke again there was daylight bright around the screen that had been set between the window and her bed and beside her, on top of the covers, was Leo, deeply asleep, his hand possessively curled around hers.

As she stirred, careful not to wake him, Nancy came around the screen, beaming when she saw Isobel was awake.

'Oh, my lady,' she whispered and reached for the glass beside the bed.

'Nancy, have I— Did I—?'

'It is all right, my lady. I had a word with the doctor, quiet-like, not to worry His Lordship, and he says everything is just as it should be, so very early. Here, drink this, I put a headache powder in it.'

Isobel was too relieved to even speak. She had wondered, but then she always was a little irregular and so much had happened it was enough to upset anyone's natural rhythm. Nancy had clearly drawn her own conclusions.

'Will you tell him?' she whispered now.

'Yes.' Leo would want to know. Leo, who loved her. 'He wasn't hurt, was he?' How could she not have asked? But then she had hardly been capable of believing what he had been telling her.

'Lots of bruises and a few cuts, Bertram says. Nothing to worry about. Would you like a cup of tea, my lady?'

'Yes. Yes, I would. Thank you, Nancy.'

As the maid tiptoed out, Isobel turned her aching head to look at Leo and, as though he had felt the weight of that look, he opened his eyes.

'Izzy.' He was up on his knees in moments, leaning over her, one hand on either side of her head, his gaze searching her face. 'My poor darling. Does it hurt a great deal?'

She grimaced, but she did not lie to Leo any more than he lied to her. 'It feels as though I fell out of a carriage on to my head,' she said, managing a smile. 'Nothing that will not get better soon.'

'I saw you lying there and I thought you were dead,' Leo said. 'The horses were panicking and thrashing around, those women were screaming, people came running—but all I could hear was this voice in my head saying, *You never told her you loved her.*'

'When?' she managed to ask, unable to look away from the heat and pain in those dark eyes.

'For ever, I think. I just never realised. You were Izzy, my friend. I just took the way I felt about you for granted, never saw how much deeper and complicated those feelings were than the superficial attraction I felt for Lucinda. And then that day at her aunt's I suddenly saw her for what she was and understood that what I felt for you was the real thing, true love. I walked out of that house on air and almost ended up under a carriage for my pains.'

'I know, I saw you. I was in that carriage with Lord Carmichael and you looked so happy, coming away from Lucinda, and I thought... I was so angry.'

'No wonder you were suspicious of me in the park.'

'I should have trusted you. I am sorry.'

'I deserved it. I thought I needed to woo you, find a way to convince you of my feelings before I actually said anything. And all the time you loved me, too?'

'I was sixteen,' she said. 'And watching you play cricket. You hit the ball a mighty blow and I realised I was admiring your muscles and then it was caught, so you were out, and you laughed and called out to congratulate the fielder and I realised that I loved you.'

'Cricket?' He laughed and her heart gave that familiar flutter. 'Oh, Izzy, my darling. At least we are married: we do not have to waste any more time.'

Tell him. Tell him now.

Dare she? What if the doctor was wrong?

Courage, Izzy.

'I do not think we have been wasting time, exactly,' she said and took Leo's hand, pulled it under the covers and down to rest on her stomach. 'Apparently the doctor thinks he is all right, despite the fall.'

'He?'

'Or she.'

It was a while before they emerged from the intense

and very gentle kiss. Leo cupped her face in careful hands. 'I thought when we married that we were saving an estate. But we were not. We were making a family, making a future, making a home. I did not think I could love you more than I did yesterday, Isobel, but it seems I can, that love grows every day.'

'Every hour, every minute. Oh, Leo, we are going to be so happy.'

'I thought that we would be aunts,' Penny said in a whisper so as not to disturb the shawl-wrapped bundle in her arms.

'Leo is your cousin, not your brother, so you are cousins, too,' Isobel explained. The *chaise* in the shade of the big beech tree on the lawn at Havelock Hall was very comfortable and she was enjoying the rest. It was incredible how much work a baby could make, let alone—

'She has woken up.' On her other side, Prue smoothed back the shawl from a tiny face screwed up in a definite expression of displeasure and handed Lady Laura Amanda Havelock over to Isobel.

Her Ladyship uttered a squawk of protest, echoed by Lord Jonathan Andrew Havelock, Viscount Carsington.

Isobel found herself with both arms full. 'Call for Nanny,' she said. 'I think the two youngest members of the family require some attention before their luncheon.'

Nanny Tolliver, young, cheerful and exceedingly capable, swooped on the twins and carried them off. Leo passed them as he came down the lawn and paused to tickle both of them, earning himself a mild reproof from Nanny.

He collapsed elegantly in the shade next to Isobel and took her hand in his. 'Well?'

'Very well,' she said, reaching out to smooth his tumbled hair. 'Have you been up on the roof again?'

'Just surveying progress,' he admitted. 'And Giles and Chloe are home at Long Mead. I saw their carriage drive past.'

Penny and Prue got up and went off towards the house. 'Let's go in,' they heard Prue say in what she clearly thought was a whisper. 'They are going to start kissing again.'

'Are we?' Isobel asked Leo.

'Oh, I hope so, my love. Shall I come up or will you come down?'

Isobel tumbled off the *chaise* into Leo's arms. He promptly began to attack the fastenings on her gown. 'Behave yourself, my lord! You are the staid and respectable head of a household now.'

'Nonsense. I am a man in love with his wife and if I want to make love to her on my own back lawn, I will do so.' He freed the last hook and smiled down at her. 'No one can see us. Do you want me to stop, my darling?'

'No,' she confessed. 'Not now, not ever.'

* * * * *

*If you enjoyed this story, be sure to read
Louise Allen's other great reads.*

A Proposal to Risk Their Friendship
The Duke's Counterfeit Wife
The Earl's Mysterious Lady
His Convenient Duchess
A Rogue for the Dutiful Duchess

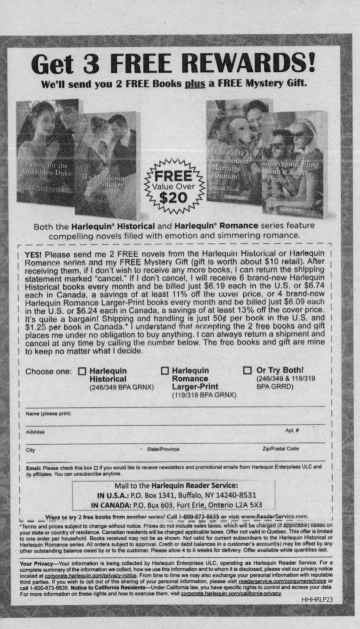